*Readers of Amish fiction love*
*Jerry Eicher's Little Valley series...*

Ella Yoder, a young, independent Amish woman, suffered a terrible loss. But now she must pick up the pieces of her shattered life and move forward. Will her faith in God and in her community survive?

Ella and Aden's wedding and their move to their dream house is set for June. The beautiful wedding quilt is almost finished when tragedy strikes and the life they'd planned together is demolished. *Why would God take my true love home?* Ella wonders.

With Aden gone, Ella's future is uncertain. Daniel, Aden's brother, decides to finish Aden and Ella's dream house. Should Ella sell the home and land? Or will she go against tradition and move into the home alone?

When a very eligible bachelor calls, Ella faces family and community pressure to accept his courting. Torn between her heart and Amish expectations, Ella must choose...

Ella Yoder has moved into her dream house. Living alone for the first time, she ponders her options. *How will I make a living? How will I live without Aden? What will become of me?*

Two would-be suitors soon make their intentions known. Ella agrees to take care of Preacher Stutzman's three motherless girls. Her heart is touched by their love for her. Is their affection the answer for Ella's shattered heart? Does God want her to marry Ivan so she can be the mother his three children need? But there's the bishop's offer of marriage to consider...and the unusual option to consider of staying single and living in the home Aden designed.

Ella loves the widower Ivan Stutzman's children. She is genuinely devoted to Ivan and keenly aware of his desire to propose, but her feelings stop just short of romance. Is her love for Ivan's children enough to make a marriage work?

When a handsome *Englisha* man seeks Ella out to ask about the Amish faith, Ella is wary but intrigued. She agrees to meet with him—but only with the bishop's approval. Soon Ella is torn between her devotion to Ivan and his children and her growing feelings for the *Englisha*. With dire consequences at stake, Ella must decide what her heart really wants, what God's will is for her, and whether she will stay true to her Amish heritage.

Jerry Eicher's **Hannah's Heart series** follows Hannah Byler's quest for true love within the traditions of the Amish faith. Although life in rural Montana is unfamiliar and at times dangerous, Hannah learns to thrive as she shoulders new responsibilities, deals with sudden hardships, and embraces her place in this small community of believers.

Hannah Miller's Amish faith is solid, and her devotion to family and the Amish community unquestionable. Yet her young spirit longs for adventure and romance. Troubling circumstances arise that provide a good excuse to spend the summer in Montana at a relative's ranch.

Her heart awhirl with emotion, Hannah dreams about her future. Sam, the boy Hannah has known all her life, is comfortable and predictable. Peter is a wild card. And Jake is unpredictable and mysterious. Hoping for a dream come true, Hannah leaves the life she's known and sets out for the wilds of Montana.

Hannah and her husband live near a small Amish community in a rough log cabin that is far from everything Hannah holds dear. Anxious about her new role as wife and soon-to-be mother, Hannah understands she must learn to control her anxious heart if her marriage is to survive.

When her husband loses his job and answers the call to ministry, they discover hardships will either drive them apart or draw them closer together. With winter pressing in and money scarce, Hannah is determined to find hope despite the fearful conditions.

Hannah is adjusting to married life. While her husband works long days as a furniture maker and minister, she stays busy keeping their home in order. Both anticipate their baby's birth with joy.

When word of a Mennonite tent revival spreads and worry about losing church members mounts, Hannah's sister arrives and quickly catches the eye of a bachelor whose brother left the church during the last revival. And when an *Englisha* neighbor announces his interest in one of the Amish widows, Hannah's husband is caught in the middle of the controversy.

Will Hannah and her husband's determination to stay faithful to God and the traditions of their church survive the turmoil?

# FOLLOWING YOUR HEART

Jerry S.
Eicher

HARVEST HOUSE PUBLISHERS

EUGENE, OREGON

Scripture quotations are taken from the King James Version of the Bible.

*Cover by Garborg Design Works, Savage, Minnesota*

**FOLLOWING YOUR HEART**

Copyright © 2012 by Jerry S. Eicher
Published by Harvest House Publishers
Eugene, Oregon 97402
www.harvesthousepublishers.com

Library of Congress Cataloging-in-Publication Data
Eicher, Jerry S.
Following your heart / Jerry S. Eicher.
    p. cm. — (Fields of home ; bk. 2)
ISBN 978-0-7369-4478-6 (pbk.)
ISBN 978-0-7369-4479-3 (eBook)
1. Amish—Fiction. I. Title.
PS3605.I34F65 2012
813'.6—dc23
                                                        2011032582

**Printed in the United States of America**

12 13 14 15 16 17 18 19 20 / LB-CD / 10 9 8 7 6 5 4 3 2 1

# CHAPTER ONE

The early morning light streamed through the kitchen window, sending sunbeams bouncing across the plain white walls. Susan Hostetler closed her eyes as she listened to the sound of her *daett's* deep voice leading out in morning prayer. It was so *gut* to be home again, she decided, feeling the warmth of the stove on her back, noticing the soft touch of the hanging tablecloth on her arms, and taking in the delicious smell of *Mamm's* breakfast filling the room. Already Asbury Park seemed thousands of miles away, another world lost in the distant past. Yet it had only been a few days since she'd returned home, bringing Teresa and baby Samuel with her.

Beside her Teresa sniffled as she pulled a white handkerchief from the pocket in her new Amish cape dress. Her hand hit the side of her head covering and knocked it askew as she dabbed her eyes. Teresa wasn't quite used to Amish clothing, Susan thought. She smiled. Teresa had insisted on wearing the dress *Mamm* had made for her the moment she saw it.

Menno's deep voice was wrapping up the prayer. "And now, may the God of all peace comfort our hearts with His holy grace. And be with us this day, oh Lord. Lead us in the path of Your righteousness. In the name of the Father, the Son, and the Holy Spirit. Amen."

Teresa stuffed the handkerchief back into her dress pocket. Susan gave her friend's arm a quick squeeze under the table while she reached with the other to pass the plate of eggs.

Susan's *mamm*, Anna, glanced at both girls. "I have things I need at the Dutch Barn this morning. Do you girls want to drive down for me? The weather isn't too bad, and it would give Teresa a chance to see more of the community."

"I don't know why not," Susan replied. "Teresa, do you want to go?"

"What about Samuel?" Teresa asked, glancing toward the upstairs doorway.

"I'll watch him," *Mamm* offered, smiling. "You've fed him already, haven't you? And I already love the little fellow."

A quick smile spread across Teresa's face as she nodded.

"Then he'll be okay for a few hours," *Mamm* said.

"I don't know much about babies," Teresa replied, her smile fading. "I'm so thankful you took me in. You don't know how much it means to me."

"You're very welcome here," *Mamm* said. "And you can stay as long as you wish."

Susan's *daett*, who had been listening to the conversation, spoke up. "*Da Hah* gives His grace to all of us, does He not?" He helped himself to some eggs. "We are more than glad to help out."

Susan thought Teresa was going to pull her handkerchief out again.

Teresa gathered herself together instead and, barely speaking loud enough for them to hear, said, "I have wanted this for so long. You have no idea how much I have wanted this. At first I was thinking only of my son, but now I want this life for me too. It's an answer to my prayers."

"*Da Hah* is a very gracious God," Menno said. "And you're welcome here, Teresa. Just remember, we are all human, even here in the community. But I suppose you'll be finding that out as time goes on."

"That's for sure," *Mamm* said. "And none of us should ever be forgetting we are not perfect."

"But I think you are all wonderful," Teresa protested. "I haven't seen anything but saintliness so far. You are such sweet people. I know I can never be a true Amish person—like from birth—but Samuel can. He is almost the same as being born Amish since Susan was right there with me the whole time."

"As Menno said, you really shouldn't think too highly of us," *Mamm* corrected gently. "Even if you feel very good about us right now. No doubt you will be seeing our faults before long."

Teresa didn't look convinced, but she let the subject drop.

Menno frowned, deepening the weather-drawn lines on his face. Apparently he was not going to allow the matter to end here. "*Mamm* and I are very glad Susan is back with us, Teresa," he said. "And that you could come with her. You must remember, though, that *Da Hah* wishes no one to consider themselves perfect. Our life here may be different from what you are used to—and hopefully better. But only *Da Hah* is perfect, and He is a very jealous God."

"Yes," Teresa said, raising her eyes to meet his face. "I'm going to try to live the way I ought. It's just that I've never been taught a lot of things about God like you people have been."

Susan breathed a sigh of relief. Thankfully the discussion this morning at the breakfast table was going quite well—better than she had dared hope. Teresa was joining in freely, and *Mamm* and *Daett* were being very gentle and kind with this touchy subject.

"There will be plenty of time to learn," *Mamm* said, getting up from the table. "*Da Hah* makes sure of that."

"I hope there is," Teresa agreed. "But I have a very long way back from where I've been. And I want to say again that I'm sorry about the baby…being I'm not married. Do you think God will forgive me?"

"*Da Hah* already has," *Mamm* said, coming back with freshly baked bread that had been sliced.

"He has?" Teresa looked up at *Mamm's* face.

"One only has to look into that baby's face to see the hand of *Da Hah* already working," *Mamm* said. "*Da Hah* makes the walk of obedience as easy as possible."

"But Samuel—he didn't sin. I did."

"We have all sinned, Teresa," Menno said. "As even my own Susan has. Just not in the same way. And *Da Hah* has forgiven her."

"*Daett*!" *Mamm* gasped. "You don't know what Susan has been doing while she was gone."

"Perhaps not, but she was away," Menno said. "That is serious enough. And the world calls to our weak flesh at every turn. Even Susan's."

Teresa looked up and spoke slowly. "I hope you're not thinking bad thoughts of Susan because of me. I know I've made awful choices in my life, but Susan hasn't done anything like I have. She's a holy woman. She dated only Christian people, like Duane Moran. He was a nice man."

Menno dropped his fork on the table. It bounced once before clanging on the floor. "Susan spent time with an *Englisha* man? She spoke to him of love?" he asked.

*Oh no!* Susan thought. *Here it comes. Now what am I going to do? Oh, why did I ever confide to Teresa about Mr. Moran?* She had known it was only a matter of time before her *mamm* and *daett* started asking questions about her time spent with the *Englisha*.

"*Daett*," *Mamm* said, reaching over to stroke his arm, "we knew Susan had to be doing some things like that."

"But she is my *dochtah*," Menno said.

Susan got to her feet and walked over to her father. She wrapped her arms around his shoulders. "I'm home, *Daett*," she said. "Can't you just leave it at that? And I haven't done anything wrong. Really."

"But you spoke of love with an *Englisha* man?" Menno raised his eyes to Susan's face.

"No, I didn't. He was a very nice person, *Daett*," Susan said. "I went out to eat with him in a restaurant. I did not agree to marry him. Okay?"

Menno thought for a long moment before he sighed. "I had hoped to never hear of such things happening to my youngest daughter."

"You have lots of other daughters, *Daett*," Susan said. "They've all turned out okay."

Menno sighed again and then bent down to pick up his fork. "So what have we done wrong with you?" he asked. "What have we not taught you that we taught the others? How could one of my girls just up and leave so suddenly like you did?"

"But she's back!" *Mamm* said before Susan could answer. "So let's be thankful for that. Perhaps *Da Hah* will give us grace to continue from here."

That was the answer they'd be the most satisfied with, Susan figured, taking her seat again.

"I'm sorry," Teresa told Susan quietly. She pushed her food around with her fork.

"You helped me get back home!" Susan whispered back, leaning over to give Teresa a hug. "Let's not forget that."

"*Da Hah* moves in mysterious ways," *Mamm* said. "I'm glad to see how much you two girls love each other. It helps make my heart feel better about your time away from us, Susan. If *Da Hah* can bring about this love, then your time among the *Englisha* was not completely lost."

Menno nodded in agreement. "*Da Hah* also forgave sinners while He walked on this earth. Perhaps I should not have spoken so harshly."

"I understand, *Daett*," Susan said, mustering up a smile. "And if I didn't know that you and *Mamm* loved me, I never would have come home."

"I am glad you are home," Menno said. "But surely you won't be having those *Englisha* boyfriends coming to visit the farm, will you?"

Susan laughed. "I think Robby did mention something about coming. But he's not my boyfriend. We're just friends. His mother owned the bakery where I worked."

"Susan!" Anna gasped. "How could you do such a thing? Inviting an *Englisha* boy here?"

"He's only a friend, *Mamm*," Susan repeated. "And I doubt he'll come anyway."

Menno nodded with a hint of a smile on his face. "That Thomas of yours came by looking for you over Christmas. Has *Mamm* told you about this?"

"No, she hasn't." Susan glanced over at her *mamm*, who was staring at her plate.

Menno smiled. "Perhaps this thing can be patched up between the two of you?"

Susan took a deep breath before answering. "I may not want to patch things up with Thomas, *Daett*, so please be understanding. What I want is a man who will love me. Someone who will not fall in love with my best friend the first time I turn my back."

"We all have made mistakes," *Daett* said. "We all have our faults."

"Did you fall in love with *Mamm*'s best friend while you were seeing her?" Susan asked him.

"No," Menno said. "That one I did not do."

"That proves my point," Susan said.

Menno fell silent, but *Mamm* didn't look ready to drop the subject. Moments later she spoke up. "You always were the fiery one of the girls, Susan," she said. "Don't you think you're overplaying this a little? Thomas does seem like a nice man, and he did go all the way to Asbury Park to visit you over Christmas, not knowing you'd left already. It shows you he is serious now."

"I didn't know about that," Menno said, leaning forward over the table. "That does sound serious—and quite *gut* to me."

"I think it counts for a lot," *Mamm* said. "It clearly shows that whatever affection he had for Eunice, it was very short-lived."

Susan glared at the wall at the thought of Thomas and Eunice. "It was long enough for me to see what kind of man he is," she said. "And I will have nothing to do with him. Thomas was kissing Eunice!"

"Well…" Menno said, "remember, we need a younger man on the farm soon. And I think Thomas would be more than willing. Perhaps you need to find forgiveness in your heart for the boy."

"This has nothing to do with forgiveness, *Daett*," Susan said. "It has to do with trust, and I don't trust Thomas."

Menno sighed. "Then *Da Hah* will have to do His work in His own slow way, I suppose. But I wish He would hurry because I'm getting old and my body isn't going to hold out much longer."

"You're much tougher than you think," Susan said. "And I'm willing to help out as much as I can on the farm. You know that."

"Okay, enough of this," *Mamm* interrupted. "This is getting us nowhere. If everyone is done eating, let's pray. The sun is climbing quickly into the sky, and I need those supplies from the Dutch Barn."

"There will be more time to discuss this later," Menno said. He bowed his head, praying silently this time.

Susan caught Teresa's eye moments later and smiled.

The girl looked perfectly terrorized. She must not be used to such frank discussions. But it had been only a few days since they had arrived on the Greyhound, and this was indeed another world to Teresa. A *gut* world, but why did the discussion of Thomas have to come up so quickly? Her parents meant no harm. They just hadn't seen Thomas like she had, all starry-eyed and flat-footed while Eunice beamed on him with her sweet smiles. How Susan's heart had been torn at the sight of the two outside the washhouse that Sunday night after the hymn singing. What a betrayer of friendship Thomas was. Well, let Thomas marry Eunice if he thought she was so wonderful.

Susan jerked herself out of her thoughts when her *daett* stood to his feet and pushed his chair back under the table.

"Can I help with the dishes?" Teresa asked.

"We'll both help," Susan said, getting up. "Then it's off to the barn to get the horse."

"I'll work on my list now," *Mamm* said, disappearing into the living room.

Susan went to the sink to turn on the hot water, while Teresa moved the dishes from the table and used a plastic scraper Susan gave her to remove the food particles.

"Are they clean enough to wash now?" Teresa asked moments later, setting two plates on the counter.

Susan nodded. "You're doing really well."

"I guess it helps that we never had a dishwasher in that dump of an apartment," Teresa said. "Perhaps God was preparing me for this life, though I never scraped dishes clean before I washed them. Mom was different, you know."

"Yes, I remember," Susan said with a smile. "Have you written your *mamm* to let her know you and Samuel arrived safely?"

"Yesterday," Teresa replied. "I mailed the letter to Laura's address. I'm sure she'll be kind enough to take it down to Mom."

The two girls worked together, moving between the sink and the kitchen table. Moments later Susan saw a frown flit across Teresa's face. She stopped what she was doing and asked, "Is something wrong?"

Teresa didn't answer right away. Susan was ready to ask again when Teresa said, "Do your parents hate me? After all, I haven't lived like they believe a person should. I have a son and I'm not married."

"Of course they don't, Teresa!" Susan said. "Don't even think such thoughts."

"I hope my being here doesn't make trouble for them," Teresa worried.

"They like you and little Samuel," Susan said. "I know they'll love you when they get to know you better. They're wonderful people, and they don't hate anyone, especially you."

"But you talk about things…" Teresa's voice drifted off.

"Things that seem private to you? That's one of the many things to get used to," Susan said. "We keep few secrets—from each other or from the community."

"Really?"

"*Yah,*" Susan replied. "Are you sure you want that?"

Teresa took a deep breath before speaking. "With all my heart I want it. Even more than you can imagine. I so want to get away from my old life. I want to find the peace I feel around here. I want to raise little Samuel to be a godly man and see him marry a wonderful Amish woman someday."

"Those are good things to want," Susan said. "Just be aware that it's going to be a long, hard road. That's all I can say."

"You keep saying that," Teresa said. "But look where I've already come from. Was that easy?"

"I guess not," Susan admitted.

"Then why should I expect this to be easy?" Teresa asked. "No, even if it's hard, I'm going to live and die Amish from here on out."

## Chapter Two

Susan drove south on the graveled road with Teresa beside her. Their shawls were wrapped tight over their shoulders, with their *kapps* pulled forward on their heads. Like *Mamm* had said, the southern Indiana weather had given them a balmy winter day, but there was still a nip in the air. Susan offered more of the buggy blanket to Teresa, who smiled but didn't pull the blanket any higher over her knees.

Already Teresa looked like an Amish woman with her white *kapp* and apron dress *Mamm* had given her, her cheeks rosy from the wind.

"I'm fine," Teresa said when Susan continued looking at her. "I really am."

"Well, wrap yourself up if you get cold," Susan said. "You're not used to riding in a buggy in this kind of weather."

Teresa took a deep breath and pushed her *kapp* back. A moment later she gave Susan a quick glance, a question in her eyes. "Is this okay?" Teresa asked. "I don't want to be inappropriate. But I do want to look around on my first real buggy ride since I've been here."

Susan laughed. "That's fine, but don't push the *kapp* back too far or it will blow off. And you will have to learn to look by turning your head instead of just moving your eyes."

Teresa looked astonished. "But then people will know when I'm looking at them," she said.

"It's called being Amish," Susan said. "Didn't I tell you it would be hard?"

"That's not hard," Teresa said, her voice resolute. "In fact, it might keep people more honest if everyone knows what we're looking at. Now isn't that a good thing?"

Susan tightened her grip on the reins as her horse threw his head back, neighing as it flicked its ears toward the bend in the road ahead of them.

"What is that all about?" Teresa asked.

"Toby must smell another horse coming around the corner," Susan said.

"I don't hear anyone coming," Teresa said, leaning forward on the seat.

"*Yah*, there is someone coming."

Ahead of them a horse appeared from behind the trees along the curve in the road, its head erect, its ears thrown forward. It was followed by an open buggy driven by a man.

"It's one of our ministers—Deacon Ray," Susan commented to Teresa. "Be sure to smile when we go past."

"But he doesn't even know me."

"You're planning to stay around, aren't you?" Susan asked as the buggy fast approached.

Susan took one hand off the reins to wave as they passed the man, and Teresa did likewise. Deacon Ray's hat was pulled firmly down over his head, his lengthy beard spread over one shoulder. He gave a little wave as he passed, although he did stare at them.

"I smiled," Teresa confirmed when the rattle of wheels behind them had died away.

"*Gut*," Susan said. "Now his head is spinning like a top as he tries to figure out who you are."

"Did he know you were back?" Teresa asked.

"He likely did," Susan said. "Things have a way of getting around in the community. For that matter, he may have figured out who you are too."

"How?"

"Like I said, word gets around. Most people, including Deacon

Ray, probably know where I've been, when I got back, and who I brought with me. He probably knows better than I do if I'll stay or if this is just a visit."

"You mean you don't know?" Teresa asked.

"I can hardly believe I was living in Asbury Park only last week," Susan said. "Or has it even been that long? It feels like two years since we were there. How silly I was to ever think I could get away from all this."

"Why did you want to?" Teresa asked, pushing her bonnet back again.

"You haven't been here as long as I have," Susan said.

"But, Susan, you were happy to come home, weren't you?" Teresa asked. "Or did you come home just because of me? Please say you didn't, Susan, or I won't be able to stand it."

"Now, now," Susan consoled. "I came home because I wanted to. But I do miss Laura and Robby. Did you know he took me out on the ocean before I left? As a goodbye gift. It was really wonderful, and now I'll probably never see the ocean again."

"Are you in love with him? Is that why you sent that Mr. Moran packing?" Teresa asked. "But you did tell your parents this morning you weren't."

Susan laughed. "Of course I wasn't. Robby's not the kind of man I'd fall in love with. He's more of a brother—but a *gut* one. And I will always remember him for the wonderful times we had together."

"You'll go back, Susan," Teresa said. "Your voice is full of longing."

Susan reached over to touch Teresa's hand. "You're imagining things," she said. "I'm staying here with you and Samuel."

"No, you sound like you came home just because of me," Teresa said. "That's awful. It makes me sick in my soul."

Susan turned to face Teresa. "Look," she said, "I needed to come home, okay? So don't worry about it. Perhaps you were part of the reason I came home, but you've seen *Mamm* and *Daett*. They also need me. They're getting older, and I can decide what to do with my life from here as well as I can in Asbury Park. Perhaps a little better. It's quieter here, and a person can think without all the noise and busyness of the city."

"I know *I'm* staying, Susan," Teresa said. "If I have to sleep in a barn, I'm staying."

"No one's going to make you sleep in a barn!" Susan chuckled. "So stop talking like that."

"But what about your minister back there?" Teresa asked, looking over her shoulder. "Will I be able to gain his approval?"

"Well," Susan said, thinking a moment, "you'll have to obey the *Ordnung,* of course. That is, if you plan to stay very long. Beyond that, he has little to do with you."

"I guess he looked friendly enough," Teresa said with a sigh. "But what if he finds out I'm a girl from the world and have a baby without a husband?"

"He might already know. If not, that's bound to happen sometime soon," Susan admitted. "Right now, I think the only thing people need to know is that an *Englisha* girl with a child has come home with me. That's really *all* they need to know."

Teresa's eyes grew wide. "So now you tell me," she said. "I thought you said I would be accepted in the community."

"I'm not saying you won't be. It just might be hard at first. You're liked by *Mamm* and *Daett,* so that's a *gut* start. It just might take a little longer with some people. But you can prove yourself, and then everything will be fine."

"I don't think the not married and having a child thing will be such a small matter," Teresa muttered.

"That's true," Susan agreed. "We could tell them you're widowed. That might work and be better received."

"I hope you're not serious!" Teresa turned her head so fast her bonnet bounced against Susan's shoulder.

"Of course I'm not serious," Susan said with a laugh. "Lies get a person nowhere. Eventually everything will come out. But let people get to know you first. When they know you, they'll like you. You're a nice person and very tenderhearted. People will see that. Then you can share more of your situation."

"You're going to have me crying all over the place," Teresa said. "With such compliments," she added.

"Well, you *are* nice and tenderhearted, so there!" Susan affirmed.

"I'm not worried about me," Teresa said. "If Samuel can have a wonderful life, that's all I ask for."

"See, that's what I mean," Susan said, turning to face her again. "You should care about yourself—at least a little."

"No, I shouldn't. I don't deserve it. I've been with a man, Susan. And that makes me a bad woman."

"Oh, Teresa!" Susan scolded, switching the lines to one hand and hugging her friend with the other.

"Well, doesn't it?" Teresa asked.

"No, it doesn't," Susan said, her voice firm. "We *all* make mistakes. Everybody does."

"Have you ever been with a man?" Teresa asked.

"No, but…"

"See what I mean?"

"But you can always start over. *Da Hah* will help you do that," Susan encouraged, giving Teresa another hug. "I think you're giving yourself too hard a time. You weren't raised like I was."

"People will always look at me and see how much I've failed," Teresa said. "Especially your people. To them I'll always be the *Englisha* woman who has sinned horribly."

"W-e-l-l-l-l…" Susan said while looking up at the sky, "let's see. We could marry you off to old Yost Byler. He has a small farm, a dirty house, and two horses nearly at death's door although they manage to get him around. They say he lives on beans and corn every day…and maybe an egg on Saturday morning. The only thing he doesn't have is a wife because no Amish woman will marry him."

"That sounds like what I deserve," Teresa said in a low voice. "If that."

Susan peered around the edge of Teresa's bonnet.

"Will I see this man on Sunday?" Teresa asked.

Susan looked even closer at Teresa's face. "You don't think I'm serious?" she asked. "Surely, Teresa…"

"Well, this fellow sounds about right to me," Teresa interrupted.

Susan sat back in the seat with a sigh. "Listen. There will be no Yost Byler in your life, Teresa. You have too good a heart for him. And I wouldn't marry you off to a person like him anyway. I was teasing you."

Teresa looked determined. "Well, don't make jokes about it," she said. "Right now any husband would look good to me as long as he's Amish."

"I said I wasn't serious, Teresa."

Teresa shivered. "I think I would marry *any* Amish man who would have me. I would close my eyes and think only of Samuel and what's best for him."

"Do you know what I think lies ahead for you?" Susan asked as they turned onto the blacktop road.

"No," Teresa said.

"Smooth sailing, that's what. Just like the road we're on now."

Teresa laughed. "You do have great flights of fancy, Susan. I'll be happy if I'm just allowed to stay here."

"Okay then," Susan agreed with a sigh. "If your sights are that low…"

"I'm prepared to eat corn and beans, sleep in haymows, and dress in rags," Teresa said. "Whatever it takes."

"Teresa—come on and cheer up," Susan said. "It won't be that bad. But let me give you a little advice, just to be safe. For starters, don't talk about your past with anyone. And I mean *anyone*. Remember that anything you say to someone other than to *Mamm* or me, and perhaps some close friend you develop in the future, will get passed around the community. It's not that our people are gossips. It's just the way people are. So the less said the better. What needs to be said, *Mamm* and I will say at the proper moments and in the proper amounts. As for you, you will be with us. You will live at our house, safe and secure. Make sure you don't blurt out things, okay?

No matter how you feel or what you think. Talk to us first so we can explain the ways of the community."

"I feel scared already," Teresa said, watching the fields go by.

"That was supposed to make you feel better," Susan said.

"I know," Teresa said. "And I will try because I know this will be worth it in the end. For me and Samuel. And I can't wait for my first Sunday and the church services. I'm sure I'll feel much better being in the company of so many holy people."

"I don't know about that," Susan said. "Do you know anything about what happens at an Amish church service?"

"Only what I've seen on the movies and TV," Teresa admitted.

"Well, it won't be exactly like that, believe me," Susan said.

"But the peace, the happiness, the contentment—surely they will be there?"

"*Yah*," Susan said, turning to Teresa. "I guess there's some of that. But you do need to be careful. It's best that you stay in the background at first. You will be with us, so you will be accepted as a guest of ours. Join in, but don't say much. And let's see, maybe I could teach you some German words quickly. People will warm up to you faster if they hear you trying to speak our language."

"I'll speak German all day long," Teresa said. "Anything to help Samuel get accepted into the community. For his sake, you know."

"And for your own," Susan added. "Now, try saying *ich swiecht net Deutsch*."

Teresa tried the strange-sounding words, rolling them on her tongue.

"Try again," Susan said. "That was close."

"What does it mean?" Teresa asked. "Perhaps that will help."

"It means 'I don't speak German.'"

"Oh, that's really cute," Teresa said. "I'm speaking German and saying I don't speak it."

Susan chuckled. "Don't worry," she said. "Your accent isn't even close, so people will know. Besides, it's intended as an icebreaker."

"I'll never get this down," Teresa groaned. "How am I supposed to get a German accent?"

"You probably won't for a while, but that's fine. No one will expect you to have the right pronunciation right away."

"So what else will happen on Sunday?" Teresa asked.

"Well, let's see. Lots and lots of people will be there, and they will all wonder who you are, so stick close to me or *Mamm*. Especially after church when we eat together."

"Are the services kind of long? What if I have to feed Samuel?" Teresa asked.

"About three hours. If you have to feed Samuel, what you do is watch where the other mothers go with their babies and follow them. I'd help you out there, but you'll have to sit with *Mamm* since you're a mother. We sit segregated according to gender, marriage status, and age."

"What if I can't get my dress pinned up correctly afterward?" Teresa asked. "I'm not quite used to pins yet."

"Maybe you should wear your *Englisha* dress for a few Sundays. No one will think ill of you."

Teresa shook her head. "No, it's sink or swim," she declared. "No *Englisha* dresses."

"Then you'd better practice a lot before Sunday, that's all I can say," Susan said. "And you can always ask one of the women to help you. They will be glad to give you a hand."

A long silence followed. Susan finally looked over at Teresa and saw tears running down her face. "Now, now," Susan said. "What are the tears for? It won't be that hard, I'm sure. Our people are very accepting. They'll like you when they get to know you."

"I hope so," Teresa said as she sniffled. "Your family has been so wonderful. I'm getting to experience all this while Mom is living in that rundown place. I wish she could be here with me."

"You poor thing." Susan wrapped her arm around Teresa's shoulder. "I'm so sorry your mom isn't here. I'm sure you miss her."

"Maybe more miracles will happen in the future," Teresa said. "Like Mom coming to join me."

"I hope that happens, Teresa," Susan agreed. "That would be quite wonderful."

"I don't really believe Mom will ever come," Teresa said. "If she did, she might not be happy here like I am."

Susan tightened the reins, slowing Toby down as they approached the small town of Livonia.

"That's where we came off the bus," Teresa said, pointing out the spot.

"*Yah*, it is," Susan confirmed.

"That will always be holy ground for me," Teresa said. "It's where I first set foot in the promised land."

# CHAPTER THREE

Carrying bags of groceries, Susan and Teresa came out of the Dutch Barn and made their way to where the buggy was parked.

"No one's staring at me," Teresa noted.

"The owners are Mennonites," Susan said. "And you look Amish. Around here seeing the Amish isn't considered unusual."

Teresa laughed. "I really am an Amish woman! I can hardly believe it."

"Well, becoming Amish will take more than dressing the part," Susan said, stacking her bags into the back of the buggy. "But it's a *gut* start."

Teresa handed her bags to Susan. "Well, I'm thankful for any little sign of progress. Even if it is just wearing the right clothes."

"I agree," Susan said, filling the last space behind the buggy seat. "Do you want to drive Toby on the way home?"

"Me? Drive the horse?" Teresa gaped. "I've never driven a horse in my life!"

Susan shrugged, a teasing smile on her face. "You have to start sometime. You just hold the lines and pull right or left, depending on where you want to go."

"Like it's that simple," Teresa said, climbing into the buggy while Susan untied Toby.

Throwing the tie strap under the front seat, Susan pulled herself into the buggy. She held the lines toward Teresa. "It's easy," she said. "I'll help you."

Teresa looked at the buggy lines with big eyes. "You're really going to make me do this?"

"Not if you don't want to, but I learned how to drive a car when I was in Asbury Park."

"I remember," Teresa said, still looking at the leather lines in Susan's hands.

"Just don't tell *Mamm* or *Daett* I can drive a car," Susan reminded. "So how about it? Do you want to drive home?"

"No," Teresa said, looking away. "Someday soon, but not now."

"Okay." Susan guided Toby out to the main road and turned toward home.

Teresa leaned back against the buggy seat as the steady clip-clop of the horse's hooves on the blacktop filled the air.

"Little brave me," she muttered. "I'm so scared of some things— like driving buggies—but the big things I take in stride. What do you think is wrong with me?"

"There's nothing wrong with you," Susan said, abruptly handing the reins to Teresa. "Drive for a little bit on the main road and you'll feel better."

Teresa took a deep breath, sat up straight, and clutched the lines.

"Just tighten them up a bit," Susan said, keeping an eye on the road, "so Toby feels like you're in charge. But don't pull back too much or he'll stop."

Teresa took in the lines a little.

"That's better," Susan assured her. "Just keep going. Nothing bad will happen."

"What if he makes a dash for his freedom?" Teresa asked. "I'll be known forever as the *Englisha* woman who wrecked an Amish buggy."

Susan chuckled. "Old Toby has never made a dash for anything, let alone freedom. After all these years he thinks he belongs in front of a buggy."

"There's a car coming," Teresa groaned.

"Toby won't mind," Susan assured her. "Be careful not to jerk the lines."

"Oh, God, please," Teresa prayed aloud, "I don't want to have a wreck."

"Here." Susan leaned over and placed her hands on top of Teresa's. "Is that better?"

"Yes, much better!" Teresa said.

The car passed them with a whoosh and then the sound faded into the distance. Susan took her hands off the lines and glanced at Teresa's face.

"I'm sorry I'm so scared," Teresa said.

"Don't worry about it," Susan said. "Someday you'll be driving your very own buggy like a regular Amish woman, and little Samuel will be seated right beside you."

"Yes, I think that day will come," Teresa agreed. "But *later*. I think this is enough horse driving for one day."

Susan took the reins Teresa handed her, pulling back on them as they approached the outskirts of Livonia. "Would you mind if we stopped in to speak with Laura's sister Bonnie for a few minutes?" Susan asked. "I'd like to thank her for the good recommendation she gave me so I could get a job when I left for Asbury Park. I used to take care of Bonnie's children. If they're home I'd love to see them again."

"You don't have to ask me," Teresa told her. "I'm not driving the buggy."

"Okay. We won't stay long," Susan promised as she pulled onto a side street. "I'll tie Toby to a tree so we can both go in. I'm sure Bonnie will enjoy meeting you."

"I think I'll wait out here," Teresa said. "I've had enough excitement for the moment."

"If you're sure," Susan said, waiting a minute or two. When Teresa nodded, Susan said, "Then I'll be right back." She pulled to a stop in front of a nice house. Getting out of the buggy, she took the tie strap from under the front seat and secured Toby to a tree. She went up the front walk and rang the doorbell. After a few moments when no one came to the door, she rang it again. She rang a third time and then heard soft footsteps approaching inside the house. It had been a while since she'd seen Bonnie, so she hoped the woman would be pleased to see her.

"Good morning!" Susan said when the door opened.

"Susan!" Bonnie exclaimed, a smile spreading across her face. "Why, do come in!"

"I can't stay long," Susan said, motioning toward the buggy. "I have a friend along. She came home with me from Asbury Park."

"Well, she's welcome to come in too," Bonnie said.

"She's tired so she said she'd like to wait," Susan replied. "We've been to the store for *Mamm,* so we really have to get back home soon. I wanted to stop by for a few minutes to say hello."

"Well, I'm a bit surprised to see you. I hadn't heard you were coming back. Laura hasn't emailed since before Christmas. What brings you back to Indiana?" Bonnie asked. "Didn't you like New Jersey?"

"Oh, I loved my time there with Laura and her family," Susan said. "Your sister went out of her way to make me feel comfortable. I'm sure I did so many things wrong those first few weeks I worked at the bakery. But she was always supportive."

"Well, that's good to hear," Bonnie said. "Laura's a good person, and she's got a good husband. Her son, Robby, is very nice too. How did you get along with him?"

"Like a brother! We had such great times together. He even taught me how to drive and took me out on the ocean. But I've got to get home, so maybe I can come by another time to find out how your family is doing and share more about my time in Asbury Park. I just wanted to stop today to thank you for putting in a good word for me with Laura."

"I'd do that anytime for you," Bonnie said, patting Susan on her arm. "I hope your folks weren't too upset with me."

"Well, I didn't tell them," Susan admitted. "They would have understood—I think. Anyway, my leaving was my own doing. I needed to get away for a while."

"So now you're back!" Bonnie beamed. "Are you looking for work again? I've not replaced you with anyone else yet, and the house sure could use your cleaning hand. And the children miss you a lot. I'd invite you in to see them, but they aren't home right now."

"That's so nice of you to offer," Susan said. "I'd better stay around home for a while at least, what with my being gone and then bringing Teresa and her baby boy back with me. *Mamm* is pretty excited… and a bit overwhelmed."

"Teresa is the girl in the buggy?" Bonnie asked. "Is she from the outside?"

Susan nodded.

Bonnie raised her eyebrows. "Isn't that going to be quite a change for her? What did your ministers say?"

"Nothing yet. We haven't been home for a Sunday. Teresa wants to join the community. She says she's willing to do whatever it takes."

"Well, I hope for the best," Bonnie said. "I'm so glad you stopped. It's great to see you again. And please come by again."

"It's *wunderbar* to see you too," Susan said. "And thanks so much for your recommendation to Laura."

"Anytime, dear," Bonnie said. "You have a good day now. And behave yourself."

Susan laughed as she turned and walked down the steps. Untying Toby, she climbed into the buggy and waved again to Bonnie just before turning Toby around.

Bonnie, still standing in the doorway, returned the wave.

After stopping at the corner to check traffic, Susan turned Toby onto the main road.

"She seems like a nice lady," Teresa commented as they drove out of town.

"Very nice," Susan said. "Bonnie is much like Laura."

"I sure can't complain about how Laura helped me out," Teresa said. "But then I can't complain about much of anything right now. So many people are helping me out, trying to make life easier for me. Your mom and dad are just jewels. I can never thank you enough, Susan."

"You might want to hold on to your thanks. There's still a hard row ahead to hoe," Susan warned.

They rode in companionable silence, listening to the beat of

hooves against the pavement. Eventually Susan guided Toby down
a gravel road.

"Even if it is hard, it will be worth it," Teresa asserted. "Every minute will be worth it. Samuel will grow up in this wonderful place, and
someday he will find a beautiful young woman to be his bride."

"You do have an imagination!" Susan said.

"I know." Teresa sighed. "I even wonder what Samuel's wife is like
now as a little girl. I think I'm going to walk around on Sunday and
look at the baby girls and try to imagine which one it will be. She'll
probably be lying on her mother's lap, a sweet little smile on her face,
dreaming thoughts of heaven on earth."

Susan laughed again. "Just don't mention such things to our people. They're going to be more concerned about whether you will keep
the *Ordnung* than who your son will marry."

"I'll not breathe a word," Teresa promised, leaning back against
the buggy seat, a smile on her face as they moved along at a steady clip.

Rattling into the driveway at home, Susan pulled to a stop by the
back door of the house. She stepped out of the buggy, leaving the lines
dangling on the storm front.

The door whipped open and *Mamm* greeted them. "So you're
back! How did everything go?"

"*Gut,*" Susan answered. "Teresa even held the reins for a while."

*Mamm* laughed at the news and took two sacks into her arms.
Teresa picked up what she could carry and followed Susan and her
*mamm* to the house.

"Deacon Ray stopped in while you were gone," *Mamm* said, holding the door open for them.

"We went by him on the road on our way out," Susan said, passing through the doorway sideways, her arms full of groceries. "I suppose he was too curious about Teresa to wait until Sunday."

"He talked to your *daett* in the barn," *Mamm* said. "I've been too
busy to go ask what he wanted."

"I made sure Teresa was smiling when we passed him," Susan said.
"I sure hope that helped."

"Now how was that a proper thing to do?" *Mamm* asked. "You know we're supposed to be respectful to our elders. Have the *Englisha* people spoiled all your *gut* training?"

Standing beside them Teresa groaned. "I just knew it was me he was going to ask after," she said. "Dear God, please let him like me."

Anna stared at Teresa.

Susan noticed and shook her head. "*Mamm*, it's just the *Englisha* way. They kind of talk like they're praying out loud sometimes."

"Oh?" Anna responded, still puzzled at the explanation.

"What did I do?" Teresa asked on the way back to the buggy.

"We don't say such things out loud," Susan said. "It would be better to wait until you're in your room before addressing the Almighty. Or speak to Him in your heart only."

"But your dad was praying out loud this morning," Teresa said. "It sounded to me like he was addressing God."

"That's official prayer time, and he's a man," Susan said. "Still, even men don't pray out loud much between prayer times, especially when others are around."

"Dear Lord in heaven, there are more rules here than I thought there would be," Teresa said.

Susan glanced at Teresa but didn't say anything.

"Sorry," Teresa said, clapping her hands over her mouth. "I'll try to remember. I promise."

"Here comes *Daett* now, so learn fast," Susan said. "And smile."

"Hi!" Teresa said, trying on her best smile.

Susan burst out laughing.

"I'm glad to see my approach so amuses my youngest," Menno said with a grin. Then his face turned sober. "Did *Mamm* tell you Deacon Ray stopped in?"

"*Yah,*" Susan said.

"Dear God," Teresa whispered. She suddenly turned away and clamped her hands over her mouth.

"What did she just say?" Menno asked.

"*Daett,*" Susan said, taking his arm and turning him away from

the white-faced Teresa, "I've been expecting Deacon Ray to be interested in why I'm back, and we did pass him on the road." Anticipating
her *daett's* concern, she continued. "So I'm sure that's how he knew
I'm here. It probably wasn't because of any talk going around, okay?"

Menno took a deep breath and rubbed his hands together. "That
does sound better than what I imagined. I couldn't figure out how he
knew to stop in."

"He saw us on the road, and he was curious, that's all," Susan said.
"I will speak to him whenever he wishes about my time away from
home. Perhaps this Saturday evening he will be back for a visit—now
that he knows I'm here."

"You will not tell him about the *Englisha* loves you had," *Daett*
admonished. "He will never let such things go by without discipline."

"You forget I'm not a church member, *Daett*," Susan said. "And I
told you this morning they were just friends."

Menno sighed. "*Nee,* I have not forgotten," he said. "It is ever
before my mind and conscience, Susan. But I'm sure Deacon Ray
will find some punishment for you if he hears of time spent with *Englisha* boys, member or no member. But really, Susan, did your excur-
sion into the world at last free you to join the church? Surely you have
seen all there is to see and are ready to settle down. How can you even
think of going back out there again?"

"But, *Daett*!" Susan protested. "I haven't said anything about
going back."

"It's in your eyes, my *dochtah,* and in your heart," Menno told her.
"You do not hide such things well from me."

"I will always love you and *Mamm*," Susan assured him. "You
know that. I wouldn't break your hearts on purpose for anything."

A look of joy crossed her *daett's* face. "You have decided then?
That your stay at home will be a permanent one?"

"*Nee, Daett*," Susan said. "I haven't decided anything. Please don't
put words in my mouth or think them. I'm home and we're together
again. Is that not enough for now?"

Menno sighed and nodded in resignation.

"Thomas will be over soon to speak with you," he said. "If you could find it in your heart to give him a good word, then this would gladden my heart greatly."

"So other buggy wheels have been in the lane since we left?" Susan asked.

"*Nee*," Menno said, turning to go. "But I know Thomas will come soon. He still loves you."

Menno walked toward the barn without another word.

Susan watched him go before going back to where Teresa was standing beside the buggy.

"This deacon didn't say anything about me, did he?" Teresa asked, grasping Susan's arm when she arrived.

"I'm sure Deacon Ray asked about you," Susan said. "And knowing *Daett*, he told him everything."

"Everything? Did he have to?" Teresa moaned. "And this soon?"

"I'm afraid he did," Susan said. "It's the way of our people, and I guess it's best if we get things out in the open. I think you'll be okay."

"Dear God in heaven, please spare my soul," Teresa whispered.

## Chapter Four

S usan stood in the stillness of the winter evening, watching the last of the quick snow shower passing by outside her bedroom window. Already the wind gusts were quieting down. The bare tree limbs were outlined against the scurrying clouds. In the yard below, *Daett* walked toward the barn, his black coat collar turned up, his hat pulled low on his head. He stopped to open the barnyard gate before disappearing from sight around the side of the barn.

Winter was far from over, that was for sure, Susan thought, pushing the drapes back to look further down the road. Dim buggy lights could be seen approaching the house, but at this early evening hour it could be anyone. Would this be Thomas coming, as *Daett* had predicted? It was possible, but tonight would be a little early even for him. She strained her eyes down the road, but the buggy was still too far away to recognize.

Obviously Thomas still felt he was in love with her. Susan laughed out loud at the thought. What did the boy know about love? He was an Amish cabinetmaker's son, still wet behind the ears. Thinking he could kiss Eunice and get away with it.

Not that Susan had always thought so negatively about the boy. There had been a time when she thought the sun rose and set on Thomas. How things had changed. She'd never dated anyone else from the community. That was the way things had turned out. Since their school days, Susan and Thomas had made eyes at each other, and from there things had simply happened. Just as they had happened for others who had grown up and married in the colony. It was like the sun rising in the sky. Like the wind blowing across the fields. Like the clouds racing across the sky. Susan sighed, thinking about the past. Well, that might all be *gut* enough for Thomas to go back to, but it was no longer *gut* enough for her.

Thomas would no doubt come to say he was sorry, and that he didn't mean what had happened to happen. Well, it *had* happened. Thomas had kissed Eunice right outside the washroom door that Sunday night. Thomas couldn't explain that away—not in a hundred years.

So then why wasn't Thomas seeing Eunice now? *Mamm* hadn't even mentioned Eunice since Susan had come back. It was as if Eunice didn't exist. Well, let *Mamm* and *Daett* ignore Eunice. She might be forgotten and unnoticed by all of them, but she was still there. *Very* there.

Eunice would no doubt be at the service on Sunday, casting her brown eyes dutifully to the floor at the sight of Susan. Well, the girl ought to be ashamed of herself. And what had Eunice been doing with those eyes the past few months? Likely they had been fixed on Thomas. Probably trying to lure Thomas into more kisses or at least into taking her home Sunday nights.

Susan pinched the drapes hard with both hands. Why did this still bother her? Most of her time in Asbury Park had been spent trying to get rid of Thomas's memory. So why was she even thinking about him now that she had come home? And why was she back at all? The answer was, of course, Teresa. But, given enough time, Susan knew she would likely have come back on her own.

She looked again for the buggy on the road, but it was gone now.

With a sigh, her thoughts continued. Was it even possible that one could get up and just walk away from so much that had been taken for granted? She had tried, but the pull had still been there. It had been there while she studied above the bakery for her driver's license and GED exam. It had been there during the nights alone in bed. It had been there while Robby was giving her driving lessons, and the longing had even been there in the midst of their laughter together.

Home had always been in the back of her mind, and it would

likely remain no matter where she walked the earth. It was frustrating, but it was nevertheless true. She would either have to figure out how to finally leave for good or stay for good. But which? To stay would require making peace with Thomas.

Susan slapped the drapes at the thought. No doubt Thomas would say love was the answer to all the *gut* things in life. This love Thomas talked about was the kind of love the community expressed to each other whenever one of them was in need. It was the kind of love the Amish farmer had for his land. It was the kind of love they passed down from generation to generation through the traditions of the fathers. And above all, it was that *gut* kind of love a man had for his wife.

This love was enough to satisfy any hurting soul, Thomas would say. And he, of course, was the best man to give her this love. Well, Thomas was in for a surprise. She was not ready to mend fences with him. If he was so eager to be in love, let him love Eunice.

Susan heard footsteps below and the sound of *Mamm*'s voice carried up the stairwell. "*Daett* is coming in, and it's time for evening prayers."

Susan glanced out to the backyard at the figure of *Daett* walking toward the house in the dim light. He looked old, bowed with care, as if the weight of the whole world was on his shoulders. Tears sprang to her eyes, and the thought raced through her mind. *Was she to blame for this sorrow in* Daett*'s old age?* Was she adding to the weight which bore down on him? Likely. Yet how else could things be? She wasn't like her sisters, compliant and meek, agreeing to marry off regardless what capers their boyfriend had pulled off.

Miriam's Joe had dropped her for two months and started to see a girl from Holmes County he had met at a wedding. "Men are like that," one of the girls had whispered at the hymn singing in the weeks after Miriam's jilting. "They're shifty and always looking for a better bargain." But Susan had asked, and Miriam said this wasn't true. She said Joe would come back. And she had been right. Miriam had taken Joe back the Sunday after the girl from Holmes changed her mind.

"Be like Miriam," Susan remembered her *mamm* saying after she'd finally shared Thomas's betrayal with Eunice. "It happens all the time. Boys have their moments before they are married. But once the vows are said, it seals their hearts forever." Yes, that was what *Mamm* had said. And it was also the way of the community. Susan wondered if it was really true. Perhaps many of them did seal their hearts with vows of faithfulness, but did the wildness of all that had gone on before just lie down and die?

"Susan!" *Mamm* called again.

Susan forced herself to move. She made her way downstairs. Teresa was already seated on the couch with little Samuel in her arms. Faking a smile, Susan sat down beside her. Shuffling noises came from the washroom and then silence. A few moments later the door swung open and *Daett* came in.

"We're waiting," *Mamm* told him. "I knew you wanted an early bedtime tonight."

"*Yah,*" Menno said, his face sober. "The visit from the deacon has wearied me greatly. And I fear what is yet to come."

"*Ach,*" *Mamm* said. "You shouldn't speak of such things in front of the girls."

"I know," Menno said. "And I'm sorry. I know it's my responsibility to bear the burden before *Da Hah*."

"Who was the buggy that just went by?" *Mamm* asked.

Menno took his seat on the rocker.

"I think it was one of Ada's children," he said. "They must have been out on some errand."

*Well,* Susan thought, *at least it wasn't Thomas. I'm spared for another night.*

"Let us pray," *Daett* said. Menno knelt in front of his rocker as he opened the prayer book. Susan got to her knees, and Teresa followed suit, laying baby Samuel on the couch in front of her.

"Almighty God and heavenly Father," Menno prayed, "we ask of You, the One who sees and knows all our weakness and failures, that You would help us. You know that we can of ourselves see nothing or find our way in the world of weakness and sin. You alone, oh holy God, are the light and the lamp that falls on our path. Give us, oh heavenly Father, grace, that we might give to each other that same grace. Give us courage to follow Your ways. We ask in Spirit and in truth, oh great God. We ask that we might live lives that bring You praise and glory. We ask that we might serve You, and together walk in hope, in obedience, and onward to eternal life. Amen."

Susan stood and picked up Samuel before Teresa got to her feet.

Teresa pushed herself up, her face tense. She followed Susan silently upstairs. When they got to her room, Teresa asked, "Does your dad always pray like that?"

"*Yah*, we have prayers every night, just like we've had since you've been here," Susan replied.

"I mean…well, it seemed like your dad prayed extra hard tonight."

Susan shrugged. "He's probably worried about the deacon's visit."

"I hope I pray like that someday," Teresa said. "I want real faith burning in my heart."

"I'd say you've already come a long way," Susan said. "You're here, aren't you?"

Outside the faint sound of buggy wheels clattered in the drive-way. Susan held still. Behind her Teresa collapsed on the bed, and lit-tle Samuel, in her arms, started crying.

"It's the deacon coming for me!" Teresa wailed.

"*Shhh…*" Susan whispered. "That makes no sense at all. And we don't make loud fusses like that regardless of what is happening."

"I'm sorry," Teresa said, choking back further sobs and words.

"I'll go see who it is," Susan said, disappearing into her room.

*Don't let it be Thomas,* she prayed silently. A quick look from her window would tell. Surely Deacon Ray would have enough sense to come during the daytime, but a person could never be sure. Her words to Teresa were brave, but news of Teresa's unwed state while she was staying at the Hostetler place might already be run-ning through the whole community and creating unrest. She had faith it would all turn out okay, but having Deacon Ray downstairs would be enough to shake her hope. Why did she ever think Teresa could come here and fit in? Everything had looked so different from Asbury Park.

Pushing back the drapes, Susan groaned at the sight of Thomas tying his horse to the hitching rack. His back was toward her, and his hat was tilted sideways on his head. Obviously the boy hadn't changed a bit. Perhaps she should send *Mamm* to the door again. She could tell Thomas to drive his horse right back out to the road and be gone. But that would only delay the inevitable. Plus *Mamm's* pained look would be written all over her face. Clearly Thomas would have to be faced by her tonight.

"It's that old lover boy of mine," Susan said once she was back in Teresa's room.

"Thomas!" Teresa said with relief.

"I'm afraid so," Susan said. "I'll have to go out and speak with him."

"So how do you feel about him?" Teresa asked. "Do you love him?"

"I used to," Susan admitted. "But I don't now. I guess I'll have to go down and renew his acquaintance with the word 'no.'"

"Don't be too hard on him now," Teresa said. "Even though I've never seen him, he probably likes you. It's wonderful to have someone feel that way about you."

Susan tried to smile for Teresa's sake. She walked into the hall and shut the door behind her. As she came through the bottom stairway door, *Mamm* was waiting for her in the living room. She was wringing her hands.

"He's come back, Susan," *Mamm* said. "Oh, he's come back. Do make things right with Thomas, Susan. *Please.* Will you? Will you at least try?"

"I'll speak with him," Susan said. "That's all I can promise."

"Speak with great care, Susan," Menno said from the rocker as a knock sounded on the front door. "The boy loves you."

Susan didn't answer. She grabbed her coat from the washroom and then walked to the front door. She opened it, stepped outside, and closed the door behind her.

"Well, good evening. I see I was expected," Thomas said, stepping back.

"Don't give yourself airs!" Susan snapped, making her way down the steps.

"Where are you going?" Thomas called after her.

"Out to the barn where this conversation is appropriate," she said.

"What are you talking about, Susan?" Thomas asked, running to catch up with her. "I've been trying to speak with you for the longest time. I even traveled to Asbury Park to visit you, but you'd left already."

"That's all well and good," Susan said over her shoulder. "But it doesn't solve your Eunice problem. Remember? You were kissing her the last time I was with you."

"Come on now," Thomas said. "That was a long time ago. And you're not without your faults, from what I hear. That woman in Asbury Park spoke of a Mr. Moran—or something like that. And a Robby too. Sounds like you were quite busy after you left here."

"We can talk out here!" Susan jerked open the barn door and stepped into the darkness.

"You have a lantern, don't you?" Thomas asked as he followed her inside. He looked around, the dim light coming though the barn windows just revealing Susan's face.

"*Yah, Daett* keeps one on the shelf," Susan said, putting action to her words. She grabbed the lantern, pumped it up, struck a match, and held it under the mantle. The lantern was still warm under her hands from when her *daett* had been in the barn earlier. The light came on with a soft *poof* when she turned the gas knob. Shielding her face with one hand from the sudden light, Susan left the lantern sitting where it was and turned to face Thomas.

He was as good-looking as always. He had a face that could send shivers around any woman's heart. Confident and poised, Thomas was. He'd always plucked her heartstrings with ease. But that had been until another girl plucked his.

"Well, aren't you going to wish me welcome home again?" she asked when he didn't say anything.

"Welcome home, Susan," he said, a smile spreading across his face. "I really am glad to see you. And I'm glad I finally have a chance to tell you how really sorry I am."

"Are you? And how is little Miss Eunice doing? Have you been giving her any buggy rides?"

"Now, Susan, really." Thomas stepped closer. "You know I don't love the girl. And I don't know what happened to me that night at the hymn singing. It's just that I began noticing her, and it was like I couldn't help myself. But she's not the girl I want to marry, Susan. You know that. And look at us. We've known each other since our school days. What could ever come between such a relationship?"

"Apparently a girl." Susan met his gaze. "And it wasn't just suddenly, Thomas. You had been noticing Eunice for a long time. I know that now, and I knew it then. I guess I was ignoring your wandering eyes, hoping they would tame down. But that's not what happened. They acted on what they saw. And so now, as far as I'm concerned, you can see all of Eunice you wish to see."

"Is that why you took off?" he asked. "Without even giving me a chance to explain myself? Susan...really...that wasn't necessary at all. I love you! We can make a go of things. We really can."

"Are you afraid I found out there are other men in the world?" she asked. "Is that what's bothering you, Thomas?"

A pained look crossed his face. "Please, Susan. I've always known how wonderful you are. I've known that since we were children. We shouldn't just throw all that away. And now that you're back and we've had a chance to talk, please let's make things right between us. Because it would be so *gut* to have you by my side in the buggy on Sunday nights again."

"Thomas, it just wouldn't work. I'd still be seeing you kissing Eunice that night after the hymn singing."

He swallowed hard. "Then I will wait until you're willing," he finally said. "I will wait for whatever time it takes."

"That is *if* I even decide to stay, Thomas," she said. "I don't know yet that I will. I've been out in the world now, and I've seen things. You may have a mighty long wait."

A frown played on his handsome features. "I've seen your city, Susan. And it's not a place for people like us. We belong close to the earth, and to *Da Hah,* and to each other."

"Well..." She paused. "We will have to see about that, but in the meantime my answer to you is no. Please let that sink deep into your thick head. And don't come around anymore. We have lots of work to do and things to deal with since Teresa came home with me."

"That's another thing," he said, trying to take both of her hands in his. But she pulled away. "Why did you bring a girl from the world home, Susan? It can bring nothing but trouble for our people. I know you and your parents can't be blamed because you have soft hearts in such matters. But send her away, Susan. Please, before it's too late."

"I will do no such thing," Susan said. "Teresa has her heart set on joining our people, and I'll help her if that's what she wants."

"Your folks are getting old," he insisted. "Think about them, Susan. The farm needs better keeping than what your father can give it. We could be marrying this year. Think about that. You don't really want to go messing that all up over an *Englisha* girl you hardly know."

"It's a *no,* Thomas," Susan repeated. "That's *no,* spelled n-o. And the farm will be taken care of. Don't you be worrying about that."

"Okay," he said, hanging his head. "But remember, I'm not giving up. We have too much going for us, Susan, to throw it away."

"Goodnight, Thomas," Susan said, turning her back to him.

"Goodnight." He turned and walked slowly out of the barn.

Susan waited until the buggy wheels had died away before turning out the lantern. In the darkness she found the barn door and opened it. She stepped into the night air. Pulling her coat around herself, she walked toward the house.

## Chapter Five

✦

Snow lashed against the windows of her *mamm* and *daett*'s bedroom, piling little drifts on the ledges before blowing them away again. Susan heard faint bumps and bangs sounding from the basement as heat poured out of the floor register and rose toward the tall ceilings of the old farmhouse. She ran a damp cloth over the top of the dresser and glanced over to the corner of the room where Teresa was sweeping in earnest.

"The room doesn't have to be really, really, clean," Susan said.

"But Amish houses are spotless," Teresa said. "They aren't like Mom's apartment, where we seldom cleaned. I want to learn how to be a good Amish woman."

"We'll do all the deep cleaning during spring cleaning in a few months," Susan said. "Then even the walls are scrubbed down thoroughly. For now, Saturday cleanings are more general. You just sweep the floor of visible things."

"Oh," Teresa said, moving out of the corner. "But you'll be sure to tell me when I'm not doing things well enough, okay?"

"You're doing just fine," Susan assured her. "We'll move upstairs once we're done in here."

"Is this what you always do on Saturdays? Clean the house?" Teresa asked.

"Usually, although I don't know if *Mamm* cleaned the upstairs every week while I was gone. She probably did her bedroom and the rest of the first floor."

Teresa paused to watch the snow blow against the windowpane.

"This is like a cleaning of the soul," she finally said. "It's like preparing to meet God tomorrow."

"The snow is?" Susan asked, stopping her work.

"No, the cleaning of the house. It's wonderful, this custom. It's like a reminder to also take time to clean the heart."

Susan resumed her dusting. "Well, I guess it kind of is. I hadn't thought of it like that before. *Daett* always makes sure things slow down on Saturday afternoon so we have time to catch our breath. There's a lot of work that goes into running a farm."

"Do you think I'll have time to read the Bible this evening?" Teresa said. "Do you have an *Englisha* one in the house I can use?"

"You can use mine," Susan said. "It has *Englisha* and German side by side."

Teresa's face shone with delight in the dim light of the bedroom. "Perhaps you can suggest what I should read. Something to prepare my soul for the meeting tomorrow."

"I don't know," Susan said after a moment's thought. "I suppose one of the psalms would do. King David had *gut* things to say about going to *Da Hah's* house."

"Then I will read from the book of Psalms," Teresa whispered, sweeping again. "I will cleanse my soul and go to meet God tomorrow."

"You really shouldn't make such a big deal out of this," Susan said. "It's just church. I've been going all my life. And God can be found in other places too."

"That's because you don't see how wonderful you have things," Teresa said, pausing to watch the snow move past the window. "Here in the community things are clean and spotless and new."

"Well, I guess they are," Susan said, realizing that Teresa would learn soon enough that no one in the community considered themselves perfect.

"Let's move upstairs now," she said. "This room is done. Not quite spotless, but *gut* enough. That's sort of the way we are too, Teresa. I hope you can learn to take us that way. We aren't perfect, you know. And we never will be."

Teresa said nothing but followed Susan out of the bedroom. At the kitchen doorway, Susan paused to say, "We're going upstairs, *Mamm*."

"Just a minute," *Mamm* said, standing at the kitchen sink and looking out the window. "*Daett's* bringing in more wood from behind the barn right now. He might need some help."

Susan walked to the kitchen window to glance at her *daett's* form struggling across the yard with an armful of wood. She went through the washroom and opened the outer door. "Do you need help, *Daett*?" she called.

He shook his head and kept coming.

"He's okay," Susan told *Mamm* when she went back into the kitchen.

*Mamm* nodded, still watching Menno coming across the yard.

"What's on our list for the rest of the day?" Susan asked, holding the stair door open.

Teresa stood by, waiting to follow her upstairs.

"I think we'll take the rest of the afternoon off," *Mamm* said. "Or we could bake, but this is Teresa's first Saturday here. Perhaps we'll save baking for another day."

"Don't worry about me," Teresa said. "I know I won't be much help with baking, but I'll be glad to watch and learn."

"We have plenty of food in the house," Susan said. "I'm for taking the rest of the day off."

"Some of your sisters will probably be coming over tomorrow to visit," *Mamm* said, her brow wrinkled. "Should we make something more? But I guess we can feed them popcorn and apple cider."

"They'll all be bringing something if they come," Susan said.

"I suppose so," *Mamm* replied. "I think I could stand a little time off myself."

"On a snowy day, that would be perfect," Susan agreed. "So let's get this cleaning done, Teresa."

As she followed Susan up the stairs, Teresa said, "Your mom's such a sweet person. I'll work extra hard next Saturday."

"You'll do no such thing," Susan said. "Now, let's start in my room, and then we'll move to yours if Samuel's awake by then. If not, we'll do the others first."

Following Susan into the bedroom, Teresa swept the floor. Pausing in front of the closet, Susan fingered through her dresses, stopping at a dark-blue one. "Teresa, come over here."

"Yes?" Teresa stepped closer. "What is it?"

"This is the dress you're wearing tomorrow," Susan said.

"But it's yours," Teresa protested.

"*Yah,* but it will fit better than my sister's old one you were planning on wearing."

Teresa stared at the dress. "I can't wear that one," she said. "Why, it looks like one of your best ones. Really, Susan."

"Come!" Susan motioned with her hand, holding the dress up beside Teresa. "A perfect fit I say. We won't even have to adjust anything."

"I can wear what I'm wearing now." Teresa pulled back. "I really can't take one of yours, and one of your best, I'm sure."

Susan giggled. "It *is* my best dress, Teresa. The one that makes Thomas swoon, and *you're* wearing it. Here, I want you to try it on now."

Teresa just stood there as Susan pulled the pins out of Teresa's work dress. She lifted her arms as Susan pulled the dress up over her head.

Taking the dark-blue dress from the bed, Susan gave it a gentle shake before she brought the dress over Teresa's outstretched arms. Pinning the dress in two places, Susan stepped back. "It's perfect!" Susan pronounced. "Just perfect."

"Oh, I can't stand this!" Teresa said. "It's so…not right."

"You need to stop making a fuss about everything," Susan said, pulling the pins out.

"I know," Teresa said, lifting her arms. "But right now I feel like a princess being dressed and undressed by her maid. And here I am the one who should be the maid."

"You *are* a princess, Teresa, and a very special one, so quit running yourself down," Susan said, handing Teresa the work dress and waiting as she slipped it over her head. Samuel's cry came from across the hall before Teresa was done sticking the pins in.

"Careful," Susan said moments before Teresa's muffled "Ouch."

"See, you should let me help you," Susan said. "There's a trick to this you haven't learned yet."

"I'll get it yet!" Teresa laughed. "Let me take care of Samuel. I'll be right back."

"Okay. Don't hurry," Susan called toward Teresa's retreating back. She continued her cleaning and then walked across the hall into the bedroom where Samuel was lying contentedly on Teresa's lap.

"He looks happy," Susan said.

"With his tummy full, and his mama with him, he should be," Teresa said. Then her face clouded over. "There's only one thing missing in his life—a daddy."

"Don't waste energy worrying about things that can't be helped," Susan said. "That's how we do things in the community. So relax this afternoon. You must be exhausted from all the new things you're learning. And tomorrow is Sunday."

"Yes, Sunday," Teresa repeated, getting to her feet and placing Samuel gently on the bed. She grabbed her broom as Samuel's eyes searched the ceiling. "I can hardly wait, Susan! Let's finish this room while Samuel's still awake."

"He's such a darling," Susan said, stopping to kiss Samuel before she began dusting.

When they were finished, Susan wrapped Samuel in his blanket and took him with her as they moved to the next room. Before lunchtime arrived, they had completed the last bedroom and gone downstairs where *Mamm* had sandwiches ready. Menno was already at the kitchen table. He motioned for them to be seated.

They bowed their heads in prayer and ate in silence. Susan kept her eye on Teresa to see if she would show signs of embarrassment as the silence continued. But Teresa seemed to be enjoying the peace.

"The snow's getting ready to quit," Menno said when he was done. He pushed back his chair and stood. "I think I'll shovel off the walk one last time. Even with the snow, we have much to be thankful for. It looks like it's going to be a beautiful Lord's Day tomorrow." Menno didn't wait for an answer. He went out the kitchen door into the washroom.

Moments later Susan heard the outside washroom door open and close.

"How can he tell what the weather will be tomorrow?" Teresa asked. "There's no radio or television."

Anna smiled. "Menno isn't always right, but it comes from years of working close to the soil and being outside. And he's got a barometer out in the barn. I would guess it's rising."

"That's still so awesome," Teresa said, watching a few stray snowflakes floating past the living room window.

"Oh no!" Susan gasped, following Teresa's gaze. "There's a buggy coming in from the north."

"Well, if you didn't give Thomas such rude welcomes, he wouldn't have to keep coming back so often," *Mamm* said.

"*Mamm*, it's not Thomas," Susan said, her voice rising. "It's Deacon Ray's buggy."

"Oh no!" Anna said, jumping to her feet. "I wonder what he wants?"

"You know what he wants," Susan said, grabbing Teresa by the arm. "Let's get you upstairs and out of sight."

"You shouldn't do that," *Mamm* said. "If the man wants to speak with Teresa, there's nothing we can do about it. You'll just be putting trouble off until some other day."

Susan let go of Teresa's arm and moved to the living room window.

"He's not coming in," Susan said after she'd watched awhile. "Looks like he's planning to speak with *Daett* in the barn."

"Come away from the window," Anna commanded. "It's not proper that he sees you staring out at him."

"Please invite him to come in," Teresa said, now seated on the couch with Samuel in her arms. "I don't want you taking anything bad for me. I'm the one who deserves whatever the man has to say."

"He shouldn't be saying anything," Susan muttered. "*Daett* already told him everything he needs to know. You would think they could give a soul a little peace around here."

Teresa's voice trembled. "I'm sure he's a man of God and knows what's right and wrong. I'm willing to speak with him and listen to what he has to say."

"That's very *gut* of you," *Mamm* said, her lips pressed together. "You already speak as one of our people should."

"Well, don't speak for me," Susan said. "I want to hear what he has to say first before I agree with him. I can't imagine that anything has to be done so quickly. We haven't even been to church yet. And it's not like I've brought the world home with me."

"Perhaps he thinks so," Teresa said. "You know what I've done."

"But we have all sinned," *Mamm* said, sitting down beside Teresa and holding her hand. "Perhaps Deacon Ray brings *gut* news for us all."

"I wouldn't be counting on *that*," Susan muttered, still standing at the window. "I saw how he looked at us the other day."

"Is he still speaking with *Daett*?" *Mamm* asked, still holding Teresa's hand.

"*Yah*, but it looks like he's getting ready to leave."

"Then it must be *gut* news he brings," Anna said, trying to smile. "He wouldn't be leaving without speaking with Teresa if it wasn't."

"That would be nice to think, but I don't believe it," Susan said. "Oh, *gut*, he leaving. He's climbing into his buggy now."

Silence filled the room as they waited, even Samuel holding still as if he felt the tension in the air.

"*Daett* is coming in," Susan announced moments later.

Menno entered by the washroom door, making bumping noises as he cleaned up.

Susan knew he was removing his coat and boots.

Her *daett* opened the kitchen door, appearing seconds later in the doorway, his hand stroking his beard.

"Well, sit down and tell us what Deacon Ray wanted," *Mamm* said, motioning toward his rocker.

"Perhaps I should speak with you first," Menno said.

"Perhaps you should," *Mamm* agreed.

Teresa held up her hand. "Please. If this is about me, will you tell me now? I need to know."

Menno looked at *Mamm* and nodded. "*Yah*, it might be for the best. We cannot hide what has happened."

"Menno, please," *Mamm* said. "Do not tell us there is bad news."

"I must say what I must say. The ministry has met this morning, and Deacon Ray has come to tell us what they decided. They are not allowing Teresa to attend the church services. If we wish to keep her in the house, then that is up to us. But she is not to mingle with the people."

"*Daett!*" Susan gasped. "This cannot be true."

*Mamm* had jumped to her feet, her face white.

"This is a hard thing, Menno," she said. "How can this be?"

Menno hung his head. "I don't know. But I do know I can do nothing about this."

Susan rushed over to Teresa. Surely her friend would burst into tears any moment.

Instead Teresa held up her hand, her face set hard.

"I will submit to whatever has been decided," she said. "But can Samuel go to the church services?"

Menno looked at *Mamm* and shrugged. "Deacon Ray didn't say…" He slowly nodded. "I suppose the child can go."

"Then that's good enough for me," Teresa said, tears now springing to her eyes.

Susan wrapped an arm around her shoulder as Teresa choked out a sob.

"At least my son will grow up to be an Amish man of God," she said. "What happens with me doesn't matter."

"See, she already speaks as one of our people," *Mamm* said, looking over at Menno. "Yet she isn't. Does that not count for something?"

Menno kept his head low, his eyes looking to the hardwood floor.

# Chapter Six

They all knelt around the living room for Sunday morning prayers. Menno's voice led out. "And now, our great Father in heaven, Master of the universe and full of glory, look upon Your humble children and grant us Your grace. Without You, oh mighty God, we are but dust that the wind blows away and like the grass that tomorrow is no more. Help us, oh God, and leave us not without Your Spirit.

"Give us now, if it pleases You, a day gifted with Your presence and food for our souls that we might be nourished and strengthened for our journey through this earth. Let us never forget that we are but pilgrims and strangers with no abiding presence on this lowly soil. We ask this all in Your most holy name. Amen."

Susan waited until her *daett* had risen to his feet before she pulled herself up and onto the couch. Beside her, Teresa followed every move. Tears stung Susan's eyes at the pain in Teresa's face. Even though she clasped them in front of her, Teresa's hands were trembling.

"It's time to leave, Menno," *Mamm* said, not looking at either of the girls, "or we're going to be late."

"I'll get Toby ready," he replied, turning to go.

Teresa now had tears running down her cheeks, and she made no attempt to wipe them away.

Susan hugged her friend.

Samuel looked up from *Mamm*'s lap. *Mamm* set him on the couch and disappeared into the kitchen.

"Oh, the little darling," Susan whispered through her own tears. "He has no idea what's going on."

"Thank God he doesn't," Teresa said, getting to her feet. "Is there anything I can do before you leave? I want Samuel to look exactly like he's supposed to for his first Sunday in church."

"He looks fine," Susan said, wiping her eyes. "And we can start sewing for him in a few months, but for now our old baby clothes *Mamm* kept around will do."

"My boy in a dress," Teresa said. "I never would have thought it, but I want to do what the others do because that's the only way Samuel will ever have a chance."

"Samuel has nothing to be ashamed of," *Mamm* said, bustling out of the kitchen with the baby satchel in her hand. "I have the bottles ready. They are still hot, but they should be cooled down enough to use by the time Samuel's hungry. You fed him before breakfast, didn't you, Teresa?"

Teresa nodded.

"Here, I'll take him." Susan reached for the squirming bundle.

"Take good care of him. I'll be praying all day," Teresa said.

Susan could barely look into Teresa's eyes. What was wrong with her people that they made such awful rules against a helpless young woman? Teresa was tenderhearted, but then Susan knew her and the others didn't. It was that simple.

"I'm so sorry about this," Susan whispered.

Teresa shook her head and followed them to the front door.

"This can't be helped," *Mamm* said over her shoulder. "Now come, we have to go."

Susan caught sight of her *daett* bringing Toby out of the barn as they walked across the front porch. He looked old and weary, and this morning perhaps even more than that. Likely they all looked worn out with the night they had been through. Teresa must have cried herself to sleep across the hall, the muffled sobs still audible when Susan awoke near midnight. For long moments she had stood in front of the bedroom door before returning to her own room. Sometimes sorrow needed to be cried out alone. If Samuel had been crying she would have gone on in, but he seemed the only undisturbed one. Now she held Samuel close to her chest. He gasped for breath when the blanket over his face shifted sideways and the wind blew over his face. Susan pushed the blanket back, holding it down with her hand.

"This is how life is," *Mamm* said, pausing to help Susan up the buggy steps. "We all love Teresa, but she needs to get used to how we live. There really is no other way."

Susan said nothing, wondering how *Mamm* could be so cold. Yet when she looked up, *Mamm's* eyes were also brimming with tears.

"I know. It's difficult for all of us." *Mamm* reached over to squeeze Susan's shoulder. "Now we really can't be late or this day will be even harder than it already is."

Settling into the seat, Susan pulled the buggy door shut and pushed the blanket back from Samuel's face. His eyes stared into space, his hands still under the blanket.

"*Da Hah* will see us through this," *Daett* said from the front seat as he slapped the reins gently against Toby's back and the buggy jerked forward.

Susan looked out of the small side window. Teresa was waving to them from the front porch, her hair worked loose from her *kapp*, the thin strands flying around her face. Susan waved back but *Mamm* stared straight ahead as they rattled out of the driveway.

They turned north, the bouncing of the buggy settling into a steady rhythm. Susan watched Samuel's face. A half smile played on his face. Perhaps Teresa was right, and her son would make a perfect little Amish boy. But even if that happened, Samuel would grow up and know he was different. He always would be simply because his mother wasn't Amish. The other children would know, and they would say the things that children say. And *Mamm* and *Daett* couldn't keep Teresa around forever. They were getting older themselves by the day. Susan shivered, drawing the buggy blanket up over her knees. Samuel looked at her as she pressed back the tears.

In front of her *Mamm* turned around. "Now, is the baby sitting with you or me?"

"I hadn't thought of that yet," Susan said.

"Nor had I with all the mess going on since last night," *Mamm* said. "Oh, why can't some people just be sensible for once? There would have been nothing wrong with Teresa coming with us this morning."

"We must not question the ways of our ministers," *Daett* said, his voice rumbling in the closed buggy. "Sometimes God speaks through their hearts as well as ours."

"Then how can there be such different things spoken?" *Mamm* shot back.

"*Da Hah* has His way of bringing them together," *Daett* said. "We must wait until *Da Hah* shows the way."

"Then I hope He hurries," *Mamm* said. "I can't take much more of this in my old age."

"If Susan hadn't gone rushing off to the *Englisha* world with her troubles," *Daett* said, "we wouldn't be going through this."

"Don't say that," *Mamm* told him. "She's sitting in the backseat."

"I haven't forgotten that," *Daett* said. "But it's something that needs to be said."

"It was because of Teresa I did come home," Susan said. "I wasn't going to tell you that, but I think I should. You owe my presence here to Teresa."

"Your heart would have brought you home in its own good time," *Daett* said. "It does for all of us. We can never be other than what we are meant to be. But I do wish you had settled this matter about leaving again before you returned."

"You shouldn't say that," *Mamm* spoke up. "Susan is home now, and that's *gut* enough for me."

"I'm afraid he's right," Susan said, a catch in her voice. It was true, and it might as well be said. Perhaps this was not the best morning to be saying such things, but broken hearts seem to spill things out easier than whole ones.

"Then there's the matter between you and Thomas, which is far from settled," *Daett* continued, still not done with his lecture.

"It's settled as far as I am concerned," Susan responded. "I want nothing to do with Thomas."

"I am sorry to hear that," *Daett* said. "I was hoping you would get things worked out. I am not that young anymore, and I really do need help on the farm. *Mamm* and I should have started building a *dawdy haus* this fall already."

"So you want me marrying someone I don't love?" Susan asked.

"*Ach*, you love Thomas well enough," *Mamm* interrupted before *Daett* could answer. "It's just your broken heart needs time to mend. You are getting things mightily confused, Susan. That's what I say."

"Thomas fell in love with Eunice, with my best friend," Susan said. "Tell me why I should trust him again."

*Mamm* didn't answer, and Susan looked down to see Samuel staring up at her with wide-open eyes. She had to keep her voice down or the baby would start bawling. That was all they needed when they pulled into Deacon Ray's front yard. How ironic that church was at his place today. Well, it served him right. He had kept Teresa away, and so they show up with her baby. Let him chew on that grass blade for a while.

"Sometimes we have to make the choice that is the right one," *Daett* was saying. "Even when our hearts are hurting and wanting something else. I don't know what all you learned out there in the *Englisha* world, Susan, but it couldn't all be *gut*. I advise you to forget anything you were told and submit to the ways of our people."

"And take Thomas back just like that?" she asked. "Even when he's got his heart set on Eunice?"

"You're wrong on that point, Susan," *Mamm* said. "The boy looks about as loyal as they come."

"You say that because you want to see me married off!" Susan shot back. "That's why you can't see what's in front of your own eyes. He was kissing Eunice! The boy is not fit for me."

"We should not think too highly of ourselves," *Daett* scolded. "I'm afraid for the thoughts that sometimes come out of your mouth, Susan. They speak of pride and self-exaltation. Thomas would make a *gut* husband for you."

"I'm not changing my mind," Susan said. "And as for leaving again,

I'll have to see what happens. The way people are treating Teresa isn't helping much. Everyone ought to be ashamed of themselves."

*Mamm* turned around in her seat. "Look, Susan," she said, "you have to hold that tongue of yours. I know how much you like your friend, and I know some of what you went through to bring her here. My heart goes out to you and to Teresa. But that is not what everyone else is seeing. They are seeing only Samuel and wondering about a young woman who shows up with a baby but no husband. They're piecing together why she's alone."

"*Yah*, and that's wrong of them," Susan said. "At least in the *Englisha* world people give girls like Teresa a second chance. They don't judge her harshly."

"*Ach*, so now comes your praise for the *Englisha* world," *Daett* said. "I can only hope things will get clearer for you the longer you're back home."

"Okay, enough of this," *Mamm* said, taking control. "You can preach about the *Englisha* some other day, Menno. We are almost there, and thankfully we aren't late. So Susan, who will keep Samuel during the services?"

"I'll keep him," Susan said, looking down at his little face.

"I don't think so," *Daett* said. "I think it's best if *Mamm* keeps Samuel with her."

"Are you afraid the people will think he's mine?" Susan asked.

"*Nee*, it's just not proper. It will be best if *Mamm* keeps the child," *Daett* asserted.

"I think he's right," *Mamm* agreed. "It will be more proper, and the people will feel better about it."

It was sad, but it was true, Susan thought. And it might help Teresa in the long run. If they saw *Mamm* with the baby, they would think she approved of Teresa in some measure.

"Whoa!" *Daett* called to Toby as he pulled the horse to a stop at the end of Deacon Ray's walk.

Susan pushed open the door and waited until *Mamm* got down and came over to her side of the buggy. She handed Samuel to her before climbing down herself. With the blanket protecting Samuel's face, they went up the walk to the house. Behind them the buggy clattered on toward the barnyard.

Miriam met them at the washroom door, reaching for the bundle in her *mamm's* arms.

"So you did bring him!" Miriam whispered. "I heard the news, and I thought '*Mamm* will still bring the child, as sure as I know her.'"

"It was the mother's idea," *Mamm* whispered back. "And Teresa is the girl's name. This is little Samuel."

More women's faces appeared in the kitchen opening. Susan smiled at them before taking off her shawl and bonnet. *Mamm* carried baby Samuel into the kitchen, shaking hands and greeting the women as she went. She looked just like she must have looked years ago when she arrived at church with her own children. Samuel was getting the best of treatment, Susan thought as she followed *Mamm* around the line of women.

## CHAPTER SEVEN



The four ministers came down the stairs, their heads bowed, as singing filled the house. Bishop Henry was in the lead, with Deacon Ray at the end. They seated themselves on the bench between the kitchen and living room, the line falling into place with order and grace.

A visiting minister rose to his feet, clearing his throat. His eyes swept over the congregation, and he clutched his hands together on his chest beneath his lengthy beard. "Dearly beloved brothers and sisters in the Lord, we have come together again on this our Lord's most holy day to refresh and encourage our souls unto holiness. I hope our hearts are all drawn toward heaven this morning and to the home that lies on the other side."

The minister paused, lowering his eyes to the floor as if to ponder the implications of what he had said. He cleared his throat again and quoted from Psalm 29: "Give unto the LORD, O ye mighty, give unto the LORD glory and strength. Give unto the LORD the glory due unto his name…"

Menno watched the minister's face, trying to draw his thoughts away from Teresa's baby across the room. The child stayed quiet, which was *gut*. What wasn't *gut* were the thoughts rushing into his mind. Thoughts that hadn't come while he was at home and should have been gone forever a long time ago. He had made his peace with the past, had he not? He had left behind the world and all its lusts. Had he not begged forgiveness from *Da Hah* many times? Had he not wept tears of regret? Why today, then, did seeing the baby in Anna's arms bring back what should have been forgotten—and indeed *had* been forgotten for so many years? His thoughts were too shameful to speak of. One expected such sin from the world's people, and from those who were weak among his own people. But he had not been known as a weak man. And yet he had been.

*Yah*, but there was forgiveness. There had to be. There was forgiveness for every other sin known to mankind. Even for murder, and he had not murdered. Pulling his thoughts back to the visiting minister, Menno kept his eyes on the man's face. What a *gut* job the minister was doing this morning. They could use new voices like him, speaking to them from time to time, warning against sin, and making valiant efforts to hold back the temptations of the world.

Moments later Menno's eyes wandered toward Teresa's baby again. Why should he be thinking of the baby now, or of Teresa? They had been here all week, had they not? Was it coming into the Lord's presence on His day that was causing this? Was the fear of *Da Hah* awakening what had been dead for so long?

Yet he had been coming in the Lord's presence for all these years, and there had not been this problem in his heart. No doubt the decision had been correct in keeping Teresa away from the gatherings. Look at what just having her child with them had brought into his heart. Perhaps it would be best if even the child were kept away. But such a thing seemed so wrong and would never be agreed to anyway. There were limits to where Bishop Henry would allow this to go.

Menno pressed his eyes together, rubbing them. Somehow he would have to live through this, but how? The emotions rose like a mighty wave in his chest, threatening to show on his face. That awful moment from the past rose up to stare into his eyes. He had sinned greatly. What if Anna knew? Or his daughters? Or Deacon Ray? It was too painful to consider.

But the child he had fathered so long ago had not lived. The *Englisha* girl had assured him herself. There was nothing for him to worry about, she had said. She had lost the child before it ever moved inside of her.

He had come home to the community from his service in the St. Louis Hospital, thankful that he was spared the worst of his sin. He was thankful to be accepted again by his people without anyone finding him out. He was thankful *Da Hah* was gracious and slow to anger. He had meant the girl no harm. And she had also been willing, had she not?

Perhaps he should have confessed to Old Bishop Bender back then, but it had seemed unnecessary since the child had not been born. And few questions were asked of Amish boys returning from their alternative military service. Was it not enough that they had withstood the temptations of joining the wars of the world and served in hospitals instead?

The pain of her beauty stabbed at Menno even now. *Yah*, she had been beautiful. A sheer vision of glory in her white uniform and short skirt. How he had longed for her, after growing up around girls and women wearing dark colors and long dresses. Could he be blamed for having fallen hard? *Yah*, he could…But he had repented, had he not?

Few people at the hospital had known he was Amish. He wore the same garb the other laundry people did, so there was really nothing to give him away unless it was his accent. That had been hard to conceal, as it had been for the other men who grew up speaking Pennsylvania Dutch.

An Amish man from Iowa worked at the hospital in the same department but on another shift. Here and there among the vast hospital were other Amish boys, but only one from his home community. Benny John Ray—known as Deacon Ray now. And he had never found out. Menno had made sure of that. And even if Benny had, there was a code of silence they kept among themselves about their time in the city. Were they not all aware of how hard the world was pulling on their hearts? So they freely granted each other the forgiveness they desired themselves. Was such forgiveness not *Da Hah*'s way? He sighed as his thoughts went back in time.

The woman came past his station often before he dared speak to her. He practiced English for hours at the apartment, trying to get his accent muted. Finally, after several weeks, he gathered his courage. "Hi, Carol," he said.

"Hi," she said, not even slowing her brisk walk down the hall.

The next day he tried again. "Hi, Carol." He smiled his best.

She slowed down long enough to glance at him. "You're one of those Amish boys, aren't you?"

"How did you know that?" he asked. "Do I have hay sticking out of my hair?"

She laughed. "I didn't notice any hay, but they told me we had some of those—what do they call them? Objectors of the war. I thought you might be one of them."

His face fell. "Do you have a problem with that?" he asked.

"No, I don't," she said with a relaxed smile. "I'm very much against the war myself. I'm glad to hear there are people willing to stand up for what they believe. You must come from a proud people."

He smiled. "My people do not think in those terms."

After lingering for a few seconds she said, "Well, I've got to be going."

He watched her until she turned the corner of the hall, her white uniform framing her slender figure. He saw her again a week later.

"We're having a get-together downtown this Saturday," she said. "I thought you might like to come."

He stood up straight, meeting her dark-brown eyes. They sparkled with excitement. "Of course," he said. "Where is it?"

She tilted her head. "You don't have a car if you're Amish. I know that much about you."

"No, I don't," he said. "But I can hire a taxi. I can pick you up. That is, if you wanted to go together."

She smiled. "Why I don't I pick you up in front of the hospital Saturday evening at six?"

"I'll be there," he said. And then she had disappeared like a dream from which he was sure he would soon awaken. Was this not the world the preachers warned us about for so many years? Was this not the pull the dark one used to tempt a man's soul down the wide and fallen road? *Yah,* it was. But he had been too excited and curious to pull himself back.

On Saturday morning he went out and purchased an *Englisha* pair of jeans and a dark shirt. At least it wasn't bright red or green. *I must keep some Amish sanity,* he decided. On schedule, she picked him up in front of the hospital in her car. He climbed in, shutting the door behind him with a soft click. *It sounds like the clanging of chains, like the closing of a lock upon my soul, like a bell warning of eternal damnation,* he thought. But then he lost himself in the sound of her voice, in the brightness of her smile, and in the toss of her beautiful hair.

"Have you heard of the Beatles?" she asked as she drove through town.

He shook his head and ran his hand through his hair.

"I doubted if they'd come to Amish country yet," she said with that sparkle in her eyes.

"What do they play?" he asked.

"Music that makes people feel alive and full of goodness and virtue."

"Must be something," he said, his mind on her hands. They were spread out as she gripped the steering wheel and made the turns on the streets.

"I hope you enjoy it," she said.

"I know I will," he said. "I certainly am enjoying being with you."

"Oh! Do people come right out and say things like that on Amish farms?"

"I don't know." He kept his eyes on the road. "I've seldom talked to girls."

"You look old enough," she said.

"I suppose so," he allowed.

"Someone break your heart?" she teased.

"No," he said, relaxing at the sound of her laugh. "I just didn't want to get involved before this thing was over."

She tilted her head, her face showing a question.

"My service to the government," he added. "Until after I've given my years for the war."

"Oh that," she said. "Well, it's not that awful, is it? You get to see me once in a while." She smiled.

He dared not look at her.

"It's better than shooting people, isn't it?" she insisted.

"Oh, much better," he agreed, not speaking his thoughts aloud. Anything was better than maiming and murdering human beings. Bishop Bender had stood in front of all of them on those many Sunday mornings warning the Amish young people of the dangers of war.

"Many of our people have given their lives for the faith in Europe rather than take up the earthly sword," Bishop Henry had said. "We must also be strong, and not give in to the carnal desires for vengeance which belongs only to *Da Hah*."

"This war is a great evil," Carol said, fitting right in with his thoughts. "The government has placed political and nationalistic policies ahead of human freedoms and dignities. What right do we have to tell the Vietnamese people what form of government they're happiest with?"

"I don't know about that," he said. "The Amish oppose all wars regardless of the reasons for it. Men were meant by God to live in peace."

"That's awesome!" she gushed. "That's absolutely awesome. I had no idea the Amish were such kind and thoughtful people."

"We try to live right with God," he said, "and love everybody as God commands us to."

Her face shone. "Is love not always right?" she asked quietly.

He smiled and nodded. He barely registered her comment about how wonderful the Amish were. All he could think about was what a sight she was, a vision dropped straight out of heaven. But was that not where the dark one had once been? Hadn't he fallen out of heaven? Bishop Bender had reminded them often of that fact too. He pushed the thought aside.

"Here we are!" she announced, breaking into his thoughts as she parked the car beside a well-kept white house. "We have the whole place to ourselves this weekend. Come on in, and I'll introduce you to everyone."

They were all nice enough to him when they went inside. He heard a dozen or so names he wasn't able to remember. He stayed close to her, even when some of the other young men paid her attention. The music started around dark, coming from a rotating machine he had never seen before. There was hardly a word in the music he could understand, but he quickly accepted her lead when she took him by the hand and led him to the middle of the living room with the other dancers.

He tried to follow her movements, his feet stumbling.

The smile didn't leave her face. "Just relax," she whispered. "Let your body feel the music."

He had thought then of the open farmland, the roll of the summer thunder across the horizon, the flash of lightning in the sky before a cloudburst. He leaned closer until their bodies touched. They moved together for what seemed like hours until he no longer cared about anything but her and the great passion for living that rose up in his heart. They finally stopped moving, and he pulled her aside to the couch. With both of his hands on her face he kissed her.

With a lurch, Menno came back to the present. He pulled his head up and glanced around. No one was staring at him. He hadn't fallen asleep or revealed anything during his reverie. Even if he had fallen asleep, that was an understandable offense. He looked ahead and listened, noting the first minister was wrapping up his thoughts before taking one last, long look over the congregation and sitting down.

Menno shook his head again, running his fingers over his neck. It didn't feel hot, but shame was running deep in his heart.

## Chapter Eight

A group of wide-eyed girls gathered around Susan after the church service. Behind them in the living room, the last of the smaller children were being served lunch on the long church benches. Susan held baby Samuel in her arms, teasing his cheek with her finger. He grinned, apparently none the worse for wear even after the three-hour service and the lunchtime afterward that he spent on *Mamm*'s lap. "We're going to make a little Amish man out of you yet," Susan cooed.

"Is that the *Englisha* woman's baby?" a girl behind her whispered. "*Mamm* said he and his mother might be here, but I haven't seen anything of her."

"She couldn't come," Susan said, not offering further explanation.

"What does she look like?" another asked.

"Just like you and me," Susan said. "She likes our ways and dresses like us. She's a very nice young woman."

"But where did she come from?" This question came from further back, and Susan didn't recognize the voice. "My *mamm* said she was a really wild *Englisha* girl. Is that true?"

"She lived the only way she knew," Susan said while smiling at Samuel.

"Did you live with her?" This question was asked quietly.

"*Nee*," Susan said. "I lived in an apartment over the bakery where I worked."

Silence settled over the group. Moments later the questions started again.

"When is the child's mother coming to church? You said she liked our ways."

"The ministers aren't letting her," another voice said before Susan had the courage to answer.

"Oh," someone else said. The silence settled around them again.

"Okay, girls," an older woman called from the kitchen doorway, "the last table is ready to clear. Come on."

The group broke up, leaving Susan on the couch holding baby Samuel. Tears stung her eyes, but she refused to wipe them away. People might misunderstand why she was crying, thinking she was just glad to be home. But in a way, that might be the best thought for them to have. Sympathy for Teresa and her plight could be misinterpreted. And what would they say if they knew she'd gone out to dinner with an *Englisha* man? That she had invited him to her apartment for supper? Sure, she had not done what Teresa had done, but still those occurrences would be hard to explain. Still, it didn't seem fair that she was allowed to come back and fit in again when Teresa was barred from even attending the services. The ministers hadn't even talked to her directly.

"Come, Susan!" *Mamm* called out. "*Daett* just left for the barn, and we need to get ready."

"Coming!" Susan called back, wrapping Samuel in his blanket. He squirmed and wiggled, a frown growing on his face.

"Susan," Miriam's voice whispered near Susan's shoulder as they walked toward the washroom, "is it okay if we come over this afternoon?"

"If you're not afraid of being polluted by Teresa!" Susan snapped.

"Ooooh…" Miriam said.

"I'm sorry!" Susan whispered. "I'm just a little angry right now. I'll try to do better. Of course you're welcome to come. We've been planning on it."

"Some of our sisters might come too," Miriam said. "Is that okay?"

"Of course," Susan said. "We'll be glad to have all of you come over." She left Miriam and headed toward the washroom, moving through the crowded kitchen. No one said anything or paid her much attention. The din of conversation in the enclosed area was a loud murmur.

*Mamm* handed Susan her bonnet and shawl when she arrived and then took Samuel from her arms. After slipping the items on, Susan and her *mamm* went out the door to find their buggy. *Daett* was waiting at the end of the walk. Susan climbed in first and reached down and took baby Samuel from her *mamm*. Anna got in beside Menno.

"Let's go," *Daett* called to Toby and then clucked his tongue. They were off.

An unusual silence hung over the buggy on the ride home. Susan's thoughts were on her *mamm* and *daett*. Surely they weren't agreeing with what had been done today. Or perhaps someone had spoken to them about other, more strident measures being planned. Was that possible? Maybe Samuel would be required to stay away from the services too. It did seem like the second minister had taken a lot of time talking about how the church must keep itself pure from the world. Susan finally blurted, "You don't think this can go on for long do you? It was simply awful today."

"I don't know," *Mamm* said. "It does seem kind of hard-hearted. For myself, I can't see what would be wrong with letting Teresa attend the services."

"I can't either," Susan said, relieved that at least *Mamm* was on her side. "Perhaps she can come with me to the hymn singing tonight. Nothing was said about Sunday nights." Susan waited. Her *daett* would surely have something to say on that, but he didn't offer anything.

*Mamm* spoke up a few minutes later, ignoring the not-so-subtle suggestion. "Some of the women asked whether Teresa is wearing our clothing. I told them she was, and they seemed surprised. I can't see what in the world they were thinking. Like I would allow the girl to show up in church in *Englisha* pants or something."

"We must not let disunity gather in our hearts," *Daett* said, clearing his throat. "The ministers know what is best even when we think sometimes they don't."

"So what do you think about this idea of Susan's?" *Mamm* asked. "Should Teresa be going with her to the Sunday night hymn singings?"

"We should ask Deacon Ray first," *Daett* said. "It makes little difference what I think about it. You know that."

"Then we might as well save our breath," *Mamm* said.

"You must not be too hard on the man," *Daett* said. "He is only passing on what the ministers decide."

"I know." *Mamm* turned around in her seat. "But at least we have Susan home with us now, and I can't say how thankful I am for that. *Da Hah* is faithful even when we doubt Him."

"I'm sure Teresa thinks so," Susan muttered, but *Mamm* had already turned around. The slow clop of Toby's hooves filled the silence again. Susan pulled baby Samuel close and whispered, "Mommy will soon be here. It won't be long now, and you can have some *gut* food instead of this stuff out of a bottle. Now won't that be just yummy?"

His face stretched into a grin as if he understood. Then he puckered up and let out a wail.

"*Ach,*" *Mamm* said, turning around again. "Here. Give him to me. Maybe he wants to see out the front."

"He wants his mommy," Susan said, handing Samuel across the backseat.

*Mamm* sat the baby on her lap, bouncing him up and down on her knee. His wails ceased at once.

"See, I still have the touch," *Mamm* cooed. "After all these years."

"You've raised enough girls," *Daett* said, keeping his eyes on the road.

"But no boys," *Mamm* added. "I always wanted a boy."

"We took what *Da Hah* gave us and were thankful," *Daett* said.

"You're surely not upset because we were all girls?" Susan asked, leaning forward. This was something she'd never thought of before.

A trace of a smile played on her *daett's* face. "I love all my girls," he said. "As well as I would have loved boys."

*Mamm* didn't say anything as she continued to coo to Samuel and bounce him on her knee.

Susan settled back into her seat and watched the countryside go past. *Now, if everyone would decide to like Teresa, how wonderful the world would be. Perhaps in time Teresa will be accepted into the community. It's possible. Wasn't liking almost anything possible with time? That's what Deacon Ray often said when someone had a hard time keeping the* Ordnung. *Perhaps it's time he applies his teachings to himself!*

They soon arrived at home and pulled into the driveway. Susan climbed down, turning to take Samuel from her *mamm.* She wrapped the blanket around his face and rushed toward the house. Before she arrived, Teresa came bursting out of the house, her arms bare in the afternoon cold.

"You're finally back with my baby!" she exclaimed. "I worried that you had all disappeared and gone to heaven."

"*Mamm* said it would be late in the afternoon before we made it back," Susan reminded her.

"I know," Teresa said, "but hearing it said and waiting all alone in the house are two different things."

"Here you go!" Susan said, handing Samuel over.

Teresa took him, her eyes fixed on Samuel's face. "Are you a little Amish boy already? Did you hear all the sermons?"

"I think he's mostly tired of cow's milk," Susan said as Samuel's face wrinkled up again.

"Oh, my little darling," Teresa comforted as she walked back to the house with him. Once inside, Teresa and Samuel disappeared upstairs.

*Mamm* came in the door behind Susan and sat on the couch. "Miriam said she might be coming over this afternoon," she said. "I told her to ask you in case you were too tired."

"I'm fine, *Mamm,*" Susan said. "And I think more of the family might be coming."

"At least something is normal around here for a change." *Mamm* sighed. "This turmoil is getting to be too much for me in my old age."

"You mean keeping Teresa here?" Susan asked, sitting down beside her.

"It's not just that," *Mamm* said, staring off into the distance. "It's going against the ministers' wishes. That's what troubles me the most. I can't live long like this, knowing they're opposed to what we're doing."

"But *Mamm*!"

"I know how you feel, Susan. But think about how we feel," *Mamm* said. "*Daett* and I are both older, and we are supposed to be examples for the younger people. And here we have a girl in the house who is not even allowed to attend our services. In my wildest dreams I would never have thought we'd be in this position."

"But it's not Teresa's fault," Susan protested. "She had Samuel because that's the way she was raised."

"I know, Susan," *Mamm* agreed. "But this is not the way *we* were raised. How much of Teresa's thinking has already influenced you? I have to wonder sometimes. Surely you saw Thomas making eyes at you today. The boy couldn't get enough of looking at you. Why are you holding back on him? *Yah*, he made a mistake, but he's such an upstanding young man and exactly who your *daett* wants to take over the farm."

"Thomas doesn't even know how to farm, *Mamm*," Susan countered.

"But the boy is willing to learn," *Mamm* said. "And it would work out nicely in the next year or so. Menno can teach him everything he knows, all while we're living in our *dawdy haus*."

"You don't have a *dawdy haus* built yet," Susan pointed out.

"That can be done right quick," *Mamm* said. "It can go up this spring in plenty of time for the wedding."

"I'm not doing it, *Mamm*," Susan said. "I don't love Thomas."

"You used to, Susan," *Mamm* said. "You know you did." *Mamm* seemed to sink deep into the couch.

Susan said nothing. There was nothing she could say that would convince her *mamm*. A moment later there was banging in the washroom, and a few minutes later Menno stood in the kitchen doorway.

"I think a good long nap would do you both wonders," *Daett* said, looking down at them.

*Mamm* groaned while sitting up straight.

"You're tired," *Daett* said, coming over to sit on the other side of the couch. Susan got up as he wrapped his arm around his wife's shoulder. "Anna, I know it's difficult, but we must do what we can to help the girl, even if it's hard. I'll try to do my part if you can stick it out."

She listened to their soft voices rising and falling in the living room, *Daett*'s deep tones and *Mamm*'s lighter ones running into each other.

Hopefully Teresa would stay upstairs with Samuel while they talked about her. *Daett* would win in the end, persuading *Mamm* to continue on. It was best that Teresa know as little as possible about the difficulties *Mamm* and *Daett* went through for her and Samuel.

It was going to be hard enough for the girl to keep her spirits up as it was. She faced such changes. Not that long ago Samuel had been born, and then Teresa had left her home in Asbury Park and all that she had known for the unknown world of the Amish. Teresa thought she knew the Amish world, but had she ever been wrong. And yet Teresa carried on with a strength and courage which put them all to shame.

Susan reached for the popcorn maker in the top cabinet. Perhaps popcorn would cheer them all up. Something was needed; there was no question about that.

# Chapter Nine

The late winter sun was setting. The last of the day's dim light seemed to hang from the clear sky outside the house. Deacon Ray lit a match, holding it up to the first of three lanterns before he opened the gas valve. With a soft burst of sound, light filled the room. He grabbed the lantern and hung it from the nail in the kitchen ceiling. The young folks' supper before the Sunday night hymn singing had started ten minutes ago.

Near the hiss of the lantern, Thomas stood behind his good friend James, Deacon Ray's son. They were standing in the line of boys winding their way past the food table. Thomas took a plate from the stack and shoveled on a large helping of mashed potatoes. He moved down the line, adding a generous pour of gravy from the dipper.

"Hungry tonight are we?" James asked with a laugh.

"I've got to be ready for all that singing coming up," Thomas answered.

"Ha!" James said. "You know that doesn't take much work. What you really need to get your strength up for is asking to take Susan home afterward and patching up all that mess you got yourself into."

"Who told you to mind my business?" Thomas growled good-naturedly, taking a large piece of meat from the simmering pot on the table.

"Just trying to help," James said, laughing again. "I thought you would have it all worked out by now. It sure looks to me like Susan came back home for something."

"Well, it wasn't for me," Thomas complained.

"Oh? So you've spoken with her?"

"Of course I have," Thomas shot back. "Now, would you put your mind on something else?"

"I don't think Susan is here." James glanced around.

"You don't know that for sure," Thomas said, but he also looked around the room.

"You really should keep better track of her," James teased.

"Just keep away from her," Thomas warned.

"Hmm…I hadn't really thought of that," James said. "Thanks for the idea since Susan seems to be so available now."

Thomas glared at his friend.

"Come on, move!" James ordered, punching Thomas in the ribs. "I wouldn't steal your girl."

Thomas stepped ahead. "If you're so anxious for a girl, you can have Eunice."

James grinned and gave Thomas a shove toward the desserts.

"I'll get pie later," Thomas said.

"If there's any left," James warned. But he too passed up the pies and followed Thomas toward the benches set up in the living room. As they passed through the line of girls forming behind the boys, Eunice glanced at both of them, her eyes lingering on Thomas.

"Hey, Eunice was looking at you," James teased when they'd seated themselves.

"Eunice you can have," Thomas said, digging his spoon into his mashed potatoes.

"Eunice is a nice enough girl, so don't go knocking her," James said out of the corner of his mouth.

"I didn't say she wasn't," Thomas said. "She's just not for me. So you go ask her home." When James didn't respond, Thomas continued. "What are you waiting for? You're not getting any younger, you know."

"I'm not that old," James retorted, "so don't start that on me."

"You're old enough to be married," Thomas said. "Instead, you've passed up a lot of *gut* chances. What happened with Rose from Geauga County?"

"It's none of your business," James said. "Let's just say it didn't work out."

"So there!" Thomas said. "A case in point. You really should think about Eunice. She's a nice girl."

"Maybe I'm waiting for the *perfect* girl," James said, his spoon stopping halfway to his mouth.

"You're going to have a mighty long wait," Thomas said. "Susan's the closest to perfect and she's taken—by me. So you're left with the pickings, I'm afraid."

James got a sober look on his face and leaned in close. "I guess you know that *Englisha* woman they have in their house isn't making things look *gut* for you," he said. "She might even be part of your problem with Susan."

"I know." Thomas grunted. "I wish there was something I could do about it."

"Maybe you should speak with Menno," James offered. "He might be able to do something. *Daett* says the ministers aren't backing down from their stand about the girl."

"Like Menno will listen to me," Thomas said. "And Susan will barely let me in the house."

James smiled. "You can talk with Menno in the barn, you know."

"So why don't the ministers take a stronger stand?" Thomas asked. "They should ask the woman to leave and take her baby with her."

James shrugged. "That does seem like the easy answer. *Daett* said they weren't going to take that step."

"Why not?" Thomas asked.

"Something about trying to help the woman the best they could, but the truth is I don't know. *Daett* seems to be holding back on sharing for some reason."

"Like that's going to stop Bishop Henry if he wants to move hard against the woman," Thomas muttered.

"Well, they do have to have unity," James offered. "I know that much from growing up with a deacon for a *daett*. Some of the ways of Amish ministers are mysterious, but that one's plain enough. They stick up for each other."

Thomas grunted again. "I wish something could be done."

"So why don't you think of something then?" James said. "There's always some way to do everything. Now, how about tying into some of that cherry pie back at the table?"

"I'm with you!" Thomas said, scraping the last of the gravy off his plate. As they moved across the crowded room, other boys were getting to their feet. A small line formed by the time they arrived back at the food table. James talked with a boy ahead of him, and Thomas stared out of the kitchen window at the falling darkness.

James could well be right, he figured. The *Englisha* girl might be having some influence on Susan. And he really needed this problem brought to some resolution, but how? As slow as things worked on the ministers' part, this could drag on all spring and well into summer.

The *Englisha* girl wasn't a church member, and if she faithfully stayed away from the services, there was little else which would be done. She might even win points for her obedience, and eventually gain acceptance among the people. All of which could take time. In the meantime Susan wasn't returning his attentions.

Ahead of him James pushed a large piece of cherry pie onto his plate, laughing at something the boy beside him was saying.

The *Englisha* girl needed to be married off, that was the solution, but how could that be done? She wasn't even a church member, and who would take her? There was already a child involved. If she were a widow, that wouldn't be a problem, but she wasn't a widow.

What Amish man would wish to involve himself with an unwed *Englisha* girl, even if she were obedient and eventually joined the church? Not even old Yost Byler, living in the northern edges of the community in his fallen-down house would want such a woman for a wife. Not that Yost Byler was that old, but living without a wife all these years seemed to make him old. That's what living without a woman did to a man.

Thomas stared at the hissing lantern on the ceiling, and the thought hit him like a streak of light. He was wrong…old Yost Byler probably *would* take the *Englisha* girl. He'd take anyone. Hadn't they made enough jokes about Yost's search for a wife? Old Yost made trips to other Amish communities all the time, attending weddings he wasn't invited to, paying respects at funerals of people he didn't know. All in his desperate search for a wife.

Yost claimed he went because he liked to travel, but that was a joke. His efforts to get a widow or any old maid who would consider his hand in marriage were well-known to the community. Thomas smiled at the lantern, squinting his eyes. Perhaps something could be done about the *Englisha* woman's problems. Old Yost might only need a small suggestion to get him going, and if he knew the ministers approved, this could all be brought to a solution rather quickly. The *Englisha* woman would have to accept his offer or leave the community. Few people would sympathize with her once they learned she turned down an offer of marriage—even if it was from Yost Byler.

Thomas pulled a piece of pie onto his plate, careful that the loose pieces didn't fall on the floor. Back on the bench, he jabbed James in the ribs with his elbow. "I just had an idea. I think I know how the *Englisha* woman can find herself a husband."

"Are you offering yourself?"

"No, of course not," Thomas said with a smirk. "But old Yost Byler would be perfect. All he needs is a bug in his ear."

"Now you're being mean," James said. "For all we know this woman might be nice and even good-looking."

Thomas shrugged. "She's an *Englisha* with a child. That's all we need to know."

"And how do you expect something like that to happen?" James asked out of the corner of his mouth.

"Don't worry about that," Thomas said. "Just drop the idea in your *daett*'s ear next week. Something about Yost Byler making a *gut* match for the *Englisha* woman. I'll take care of the rest."

"I'll do no such thing," James said. "You're not going to use me because I'm the deacon's son. I learned a long time ago—if you want something with *Daett,* you go talk with him yourself. Or break the *Ordnung,* and he'll come talk with you. But leave me out of it."

"Some people are not one bit helpful," Thomas groused.

"And tell me why I would help you out with Susan," James went on. "That would ruin my own chances."

"I know you're not serious." Thomas glared suspiciously across his plate at his friend.

"Susan's fair game," James said. "If the horse is loose on the road, who is to say who will bring her into the barn?"

"Just mind your own business," Thomas shot back, standing to his feet to take his plate back to the table. James was only teasing, but what if he wasn't? No boy could be blamed for being tempted with Susan. He really needed to do something and soon.

*Yah,* he would. The trip to Yost's place could be made tonight, instead of some evening next week when he was tired after a full day's work.

Thomas looked around. With a group this size, no one would miss him if he left now. The only problem was getting his sisters a ride home. Well, that could be taken care of. They could hitch a ride with someone going that way. They had often done so on the Sunday nights when he took Susan home.

Working through the group of boys, he moved toward the girls' side of the living room. Eunice caught his eye, giving him a big smile. He returned it without thinking and noticed an eager light flash across her face.

*All the more reason to resolve this issue quickly!* he thought, pushing on as he searched the group for his eldest sister. He eventually found Lizzie toward the back of the room. He waited a few minutes until she looked his way. Giving his head a slight nod, he motioned toward the kitchen. Lizzie got up and met him at the edge of the girls' benches.

"You girls need to find your own way home," he whispered into her ear.

"Why?" Lizzie asked, pulling her head away to look at him.

"I'm going to leave early."

"Oh? Is Susan here?" Lizzie teased.

"*Nee,* she isn't," Thomas said. "I just have to leave, that's all."

Lizzie shrugged and then nodded.

Thomas made a slow, unobtrusive retreat out of the house. Finding his way to the barn in the darkness, he kept his head down. The few boys going back and forth between the house and barn didn't say anything when he brought his horse out and hitched him up. Leaving the buggy lights off, he drove past the house and turned north on the gravel road. It would only be a friendly visit, and little would need to be said. Old Yost Byler would be thankful there was finally a woman available to work in his tumbledown house and wash his dirty clothes. The man could use a woman, there was no doubt about that.

And the *Englisha* woman should be thankful. Not that he knew that much about her, but she ought to be. A woman with a child doesn't have that many options, and Susan had said her friend really wanted to join the Amish. Well, now she would have her chance to show her willingness. If all went well...and why wouldn't it go well? Deacon Ray and the ministers surely wouldn't object to Yost Byler's desire. It might even be exactly the solution they had all been looking for. Thomas smiled in the darkness as he reached down to turn on his lower buggy lights. He slapped the reins and his buggy's wheels plowed through the loose gravel.

## Chapter Ten

Susan was bent over the sink, scrubbing a stubborn spot on a metal pan. Teresa was waiting beside her, a dish towel in her hand. Soft adult voices rose in the living room against the louder background noises of children playing just outside in the semidarkness.

"I'm so sorry you had to stay home from the Sunday night hymn singing because of me," Teresa said quietly.

"I'm okay," Susan said. "The only one who is probably really disappointed is Thomas. And that suits me just fine."

Teresa looked out the window into the dusk light.

"You have such a wonderful family, Susan," she said. "I can see where it wouldn't be too bad staying home to be around them. It's like a little touch of heaven on this poor, broken earth."

Susan glanced over at Teresa's face. "And I'm so glad to have you as part of it."

"You know that can't really be," Teresa said, wiping her eyes with the back of her hand. "I mean, your family is making me feel so welcome, but not everyone is like that."

"It'll be like this until people get to know you. Then everything will be okay," Susan said, rinsing the pan.

"Are you girls done?" *Mamm's* voice came from the kitchen doorway. "If not, we can come back in and help you finish."

"Last pan being dried," Susan said over her shoulder.

Teresa smiled as the conversation in the living room resumed its murmur. Behind her, the washroom door burst open, letting in a string of small children chasing each other. They raced through the kitchen and into the living room, the sounds of their happy cries blending in with the adult voices.

"I wish Mom could be here for this," Teresa said, a catch in her voice. "She believed in me when I told her what I wanted to do with my life, but she may never get to see how wonderful this really is."

"Maybe she could come and visit sometime," Susan suggested.

"I don't think that's such a good idea," Teresa said. "At least not yet. Look at the trouble I'm in. She wouldn't understand this. Mom doesn't believe much in God. She just supported letting me go after my dream. And wasn't that a wonderful thing for her to do?"

"It was," Susan agreed. "It was a very brave thing to do."

"And now I'm here," Teresa said. "I knew you were wonderful before, but you're even nicer here in your home. And your parents are so nice. And now your sisters are also here. And there are so many of them!"

Susan laughed. "That's not all of them, believe me. There are nine of us girls all together."

Teresa wiped her eyes again. "I don't see how there can be that many good people on this earth."

"We try to be," Susan said. *And it would be nice if some people in the community tried harder,* she thought. *But that's best not said aloud.* She asked, "Do you want to sit in the living room with the married folk?"

Teresa nodded, her eyes shining in the soft light of the gas lantern. She followed Susan into the living room and took a seat on the couch beside her. Susan's sister Betsy stood and took baby Samuel to Teresa.

"Here he is," Betsy said. "And such a *gut* baby. He hasn't made a sound since I've been holding him."

Teresa's face beamed as Betsy returned to her chair.

"Our two-year-old said his first word last week," Miriam announced, a smile spreading across her face. "I guess he's just a little late getting started."

"*Ach,* some of them are," *Mamm* assured her. "I wouldn't be worried."

"But all of the others were talking early," Miriam said. "Joe told me not to worry, but I still did. Now the baby seems to be trying to say '*mamm.*' Then on the ride to the sewing Wednesday he finally said '*horsey*' real quiet-like but perfectly. Yesterday he tried saying a whole sentence."

Ada, sitting beside *Mamm*, cleared her throat. "Does anyone know what to do with boys who aren't growing out of their stuttering? Duane and Joan both got over theirs right quick, but Lester isn't. I'm worried about him. It seems the more conscious he's becoming of the problem, the worse it gets. The teacher called on him with a question the other day, and Joan said he couldn't say anything. The poor boy."

Betsy and Esther looked at each other but didn't say anything.

"He'll be growing out of it soon," *Mamm* offered. "I wouldn't worry about it. At least no one was laughing at him, I hope."

"Joan said they weren't," Ada said. "But what if he doesn't get over it?"

"I expect your worrying about it just makes things worse," *Mamm* said. "Lester probably picks up on that."

"A girl in our class couldn't talk either when called on in school," Betsy spoke up. "One Christmas during the program practice time it was awful to listen to the poor girl trying. She had the beatitudes to recite and couldn't get the B's out. You can imagine how that went."

"Oh, no," Ada groaned. "Didn't someone do anything to help her?"

"You would think so," Betsy said. "The teacher finally gave her something without so many B's, but that took a while to happen."

"*Ach,* Lester's *gut*-looking enough," Betsy's husband, John, said with a laugh. "He'll be doing fine with the girls even if he can't talk."

"At least you don't have that problem," Esther's husband Henry said, and they all laughed.

"Milo is developing this nasty little habit," Esther said, bringing in another subject. "The boy discovered a while back that I scare easily when someone surprises me. Now he creeps up on me when I'm in the basement with the washing machine running and hollers real loud. It's gotten so bad I can't even relax while doing the washing. And to think that washday used to be enjoyable."

"He'll grow out of that," *Mamm* said. "*Daett* used to do that to me when we were first married, so I know little boys grow out of such things."

They all laughed as Menno turned red in the face.

"That sounds better than what our boys got into last week," Betsy said. "I do declare, it must be the winter weather or something. I would think they had enough chores to do besides all their schoolwork. But I heard the most awful bawling out in the barn soon after they came home from school. I thought for sure something was dying."

"You didn't think it was them?" Miriam's husband, Joe, asked.

"Of course not," Betsy said. "I can tell the difference. So I went running out to the barn, and here they were riding the yearling calf. I almost broke down laughing at the sight of those two boys on her back. I suppose they thought it was easier to stay on if they had each other to hang on to."

"I can imagine," *Mamm* said, but she wasn't smiling.

"They had a rope tied around her neck," Betsy said. "I didn't stand around laughing for long. I was soon yelling at them to get off. But a lot of *gut* that did. I think both of them were afraid to let go of the rope. They went around and around in the barnyard, the calf bucking for all it was worth."

"Now that's some young men!" Joe said. "How long did it take for the calf to get them off?"

"I don't know." Betsy covered her face with her hands. "I couldn't stand to watch. When everything was finally quiet I dared look again, and they were both lying in the mud, the calf panting over on the other side of the barnyard like it was going to fall over from exhaustion right then and there."

"My guess is you had some things to say," Ada ventured.

"I sure did!" Betsy said. "After I was sure they were alive, anyway. I thought they were crying at first, but they were laughing, the two rascals. That's when I really gave it to them. I don't think they'll be trying that stunt again."

"I wouldn't depend on that," Ada said.

"It'll be a whipping next time," Betsy said, with fire in her eyes. "I don't care how old they are. That's just a bunch of nonsense."

"That's something we tried as boys," Henry said, a sly grin on his face. "Only it was hogs."

"Did you mud them down first?" John asked, laughing.

"*Nee,*" Henry said. "But mine ended up breaking out of the pen with me on it. The neighbors must have talked about it for days afterward. I had gone a quarter mile down the road before I fell off."

"I'm sure your *daett* had something to say about that," Esther said.

"I got a good whopping," Henry said. "But it was worth it."

"Only a boy would say that." Betsy sighed.

"Now, now," John said. "I don't think you girls were exactly angels growing up."

"Of course we were!" Betsy glared at him. "What makes you think we weren't?"

"Oh, a little birdie told me things." John had a twinkle in his eye. "You have sisters, you know."

"We were all angels, weren't we?" Betsy asked, looking around the room. "And we wouldn't be telling anyway, now would we?"

"I didn't mean your sisters told me," John said.

"Then who did?" Betsy asked.

John didn't say anything but shot a quick glance toward *Mamm*.

"*Mamm!* " Betsy exploded. "Why would you be telling him things?"

*Mamm*'s hands flew to her face, hiding her laughter. "I couldn't help myself. You and Miriam were the funniest sight. It seemed a shame not to tell someone."

"So is this what I think it is?" Betsy asked, looking at Miriam.

"I expect it is," John said. "And it was funny."

"So why aren't we hearing the story now?" Joe asked.

"Because I don't want it told," Betsy declared.

"I think *Mamm* should tell the story," John said. "That way we can stay on speaking terms tonight."

"I think that would be wise," someone said.

Betsy was glaring at John again.

*Mamm* laughed out loud now. "It's really not much," she said. "One day the two girls took it upon themselves to dress up in their *daett*'s clothing when they thought no one was around. The pants and shirts didn't fit very well, which made for quite a sight."

"How come I was never told of this?" Menno asked.

"They didn't harm them," *Mamm* said, waving her hand at him. "And no one saw them except an *Englisha* neighbor who stopped by for something...I can't remember what, anymore. He came to the door and knocked while we were carrying on about how the girls looked. I told them afterward that he sees women in shirts and pants all the time, but they nearly tore the knob off the stair door getting out of his sight. I thought for sure they were going to break their legs on the stairs."

"Oh, that was a horrible day." Miriam groaned. "I was sure he thought about nothing but the sight of us in our *daett*'s clothing for days afterward."

"And to think I forgot this," Betsy said. "I must have buried the memory in the deep, dark corners of my mind, hoping it would never see the light of day."

"Well, see what comes from hiding your sins?" her *daett* said. "They always come out in the end."

"I guess so," *Mamm* agreed. "But this wasn't really a sin. They were just playing around."

"I know." Menno smiled. "I was just saying."

John jumped to his feet. "Well, enough stories. I believe we need to gather our children up and get back home. It's going to be late enough getting up in the morning the way it is."

Betsy got up with him, followed by the others. They stood around talking for a few more minutes as they gathered their children's coats and called the children indoors. The men went to the barn first,

getting the horses out and hitching them to the buggies. The women
followed with the children and helped the smaller ones up the buggy
steps.

Teresa stood with Susan by the living room window, watching the
buggies leave, their dim lights fading into the distance.

"Is it always this wonderful to have family around?" Teresa asked.

"I guess so," Susan replied, staring at the darkness. "I haven't really
thought about it."

"You have been given many things for which you can be very
thankful," Teresa said. "This evening was awesome."

"I think Samuel is wanting attention!" *Mamm* called from her
rocking chair.

Teresa went at once to pick up the baby, who was puckering up
his face.

"I'm glad you enjoyed the evening," *Mamm* said. "I hope all the
ruckus the children made didn't disturb you. I know you're not used
to that."

Teresa smiled. "It's something I could get very used to, believe
me."

# Chapter Eleven

Yost Byler threw the last of the hay bale into the rack. His horse pulled the long strings of dried grass through the wooden slats hungrily.

"That'll have to do for you, old boy," Yost muttered, noting again how the horse's ribs showed. "The hay mow's getting a little low already for this early in the winter."

The horse bobbed his head as if it understood.

"I reckon I'll go fix some supper for myself," Yost said, moving away from the stall. He paused to check the level of water in the barrel before walking out the barn door and making his way toward the washroom door of his small, two-story home. The paint was faded on the wooden clapboard siding, the tall, sagging windows were covered with plastic for the winter.

His stomach growled with hunger, but Yost paused to look up at the sky. Thomas Stoll's visit was still on his mind. He wondered again why *Da Hah* hadn't seen fit to send him a wife by now. Someone who would have a fire glowing in the old kitchen stove, the house warm when he entered, and a decent supper on the table. Was he so different from other men that he could live without a wife?

Pushing open the washroom door, Yost entered, tossing his weather-beaten wool hat into the corner on the floor. Dust rose from where the hat landed. He coughed. That was another thing a wife could do—sweep the place once in a while.

The last time he had tried sweeping the house was a day early in the summer when rain interrupted his hay baling. What an awful experience that had been, watching one's best crop of hay get soaking wet while he was doing housework. Now the sight of a broom was enough to bring back those sinking feelings. But a broom in the hands of a woman would be another matter entirely.

Yost sighed, splashing water into the dirty wash basin. Perhaps Thomas was correct, and *Da Hah* was finally remembering his years of distress. But an *Englisha* girl? How would she know how to cook? And she could not speak their language. But perhaps she could learn? Unless she was a total *dummkopf,* which Thomas said she wasn't.

She was young from the sound of it, which could mean children well into his old age. But that couldn't be helped and he must not let that bother him. Even if he couldn't work, there would be enough food to go around somehow. As long as the girl was a decent wife to him.

Thomas claimed she was nice enough, but then Thomas could be stretching the truth. He did have his reasons. But who wouldn't be tempted to stretch the truth when a girl like Susan Hostetler was on the line? How blessed some young boys were, and still they didn't have the sense to act decently. From what he'd heard, Thomas had tried to mow two hayfields at the same time. Like any man could do that? But at least it sounded like Thomas was seeing his mistake and trying to correct it.

Yost rubbed his face down with the towel, taking the time to dry his lengthy beard. *What would it be like,* he wondered, *to push open the washroom door right now and know a woman was waiting for him?* He rubbed his beard a little longer before dropping the towel back on the countertop.

*Yah*, there must be something *wunderbar* about it. Too wonderful for him, but perhaps that was about to change. Impossible as the idea seemed, the chance simply couldn't be passed up. Hadn't he spent untold amounts of what little money he had on trips to far-flung Amish communities in search of a wife? *Yah*, he had, and it had been all for nothing. What could be wasted with a buggy ride down to Deacon Ray's place? The horse was fed, and he could easily stand the trip and still be rested up for the Sunday morning drive to church.

Yost pushed open the washroom door and stepped inside. The kitchen table still had the breakfast dishes in place, with last night's supper dishes pushed to the side. He picked up a handful, rinsing them under the faucet at the sink, scrubbing with his bare hands at the dried egg crusted on the plate. Sighing, he gave up, taking the plate back to the table. He found a meat casserole his youngest sister, Susie, had brought over last week and cut cold slices off with a table knife. Opening the bread bag, he took a piece out, placing the meat across the bare top. Getting a glass and filling it with water from the faucet, he sat down, bowed his head in silent prayer, and ate.

After he was done, he grabbed his coat from the hall closet and went outside. He took the horse out of the stall. It whinnied and snorted in protest, but Yost kept going. He threw the harness over the horse's back. Leading the animal outside, he held up the shafts of the buggy. Making the swing with one hand, his beard snagged on the shafts. He jerked back, leaving a few hairs hanging on the wood.

Fastening the tugs, Yost rubbed his chin before throwing the lines through the open storm front and climbing in. The horse shook its head but took off when Yost tightened up the lines and clucked. Once he was on the road, the doubts and fears came rushing into his head.

How old was this girl? And what would Deacon Ray think about him? Not that it mattered, but still…The whole community could end up laughing when they found out. Well, let them laugh. He needed a wife even if she had once been an *Englisha* girl. Would not an Amish baptism, with a little training, and a decent dress make all the difference in the world?

He slapped the reins. *Yah*, it would, and Deacon Ray would even be thankful for his help if Thomas Stoll had things straight. Settling back into the buggy seat, Yost allowed the cool winter air to flow over his face. He pulled the buggy blanket up to beard level. The miles passed as he drove ever further south, turning left several times on the gravel roads. His horse's head was drooping when he took the buggy into Deacon Ray's lane and rattled to a stop by the barn.

Thankfully there was still a light in the barn, so perhaps this would be even easier than he'd imagined. He wouldn't have to go calling at the house where everyone could hear him ask about the *Englisha* woman. Climbing out of the buggy, Yost tied the horse to the hitching post and shuffled toward the barn. Pushing open the barn door, he looked in and saw the surprised look on James's face when the boy looked up from shoveling out the last of the gutters from the evening milking.

"*Gut* evening," Yost offered.

"*Gut* evening," James said, continuing his work. "What brings you all the way down here?"

"I need to speak with your *daett*," Yost said, stepping inside. "Is he still out here?"

"*Nee,* he's gone into the house," James said, pausing to look at him. "Shall I tell him you're here? Or do you wish to speak with him in the house?"

"Ah, if you could call him, that would be nice," Yost said. "I wish to speak with him in private."

"Then I'll finish this and head into the house," James responded with a smile.

"That would be *gut,*" Yost said, his hand on the barn door.

James was still looking at him. "Is one of your cows down?" he asked.

"*Nee,*" Yost said.

James knew good and well his cows weren't down, but the boy would just have to remain curious. James wasn't even dating a girl, so what did he know about marriage? And this was none of his business anyway.

"I see," James said, placing the manure shovel against the barn wall. "I'll go call *Daett* then."

Yost watched James stride across the lawn. At the house, the outside door slammed, followed by silence. Yost stayed by the door, listening to the soft stirring of the barn life around him. He kept an eye on the faint outline of the house. A rat poked its head out from under the manger, looked in his direction, its long whiskers casting dark shadows across the concrete floor. When Yost stamped his foot, the creature dashed out of sight, only to appear on the other side of the manger before scurrying off into the darkness.

The door slammed at the house, and Yost jumped, moving away from the barn door. It would not be *gut* if Deacon Ray thought him too eager, like a young boy taking his girl home for the first time. He took a deep breath and waited.

Moments later, Deacon Ray stepped into the barn.

"James said you wanted me," he said, closing the door behind him.

"*Yah,*" Yost said. "I need to speak with you about a matter."

"I see. Have you been breaking the *Ordnung*?" A smile played on Deacon Ray's face.

Yost ignored the tease, rubbing the toe of his shoe on the concrete floor.

"*Nee,* it is about the *Englisha* woman," he said.

"I see." Deacon Ray's voice was hesitant. "And how does the decision the ministers made concern you?"

"Oh no," Yost said. "I would not be speaking against the ministers. I was thinking you might be looking for an easy way out of this problem, as the *Englisha* woman apparently has no plans to leave anytime soon."

"Really?" Deacon Ray said. "So now you have instructions for the ministry?"

"Well, it's like this," Yost said. "Will you be able to keep her away from the meetings for years to come? And how will this look to the people? Menno and Anna are quite up-building members, you know. Their word might begin to have an effect."

Deacon Ray shrugged. "I see you have a point, but we already knew this."

"And have you men come up with a way of solving this problem?" Yost probed.

"*Nee*. But we're still talking."

"Then perhaps you would be willing to listen to my way of taking care of this problem," Yost said.

"You have an answer?" Deacon Ray said, astonishment on his face.

"I wish to marry the woman," Yost said. There was no sense in beating around the bush. He might as well just come out and say the words.

"You wish to take this woman as your wife?" Deacon Ray gasped.

"If she is willing to have me," Yost said, his shoe circling in the dirt on the floor again.

"Then you have spoken to her of this?" Deacon Ray was staring at him now.

Yost shook his head. "I have come to speak to you first. And you know why."

"*Yah*." Deacon Ray ran his hand over his beard. "I see that you are a wise man, even if you cannot find a wife."

"*Da Hah* has not seen to bless me now for these many years," Yost protested. "Am I to be blamed if I take what He does offer?"

"So you see this woman as a blessing from *Da Hah*?"

"If I choose to see it so, would you hold it against me?" Yost shot back.

"But what if she leaves you, even after the vows have been said? Have you thought of this?"

"I had not thought of that," Yost admitted. "But I have thought of other things, and my mind is made up. If you approve of this, I will speak with Menno about this matter, and he can speak with the woman."

"If the *Englisha* girl leaves you, do you understand what that means?" Deacon Ray asked, wanting to make sure his point was made. "You could never marry again, Yost."

"Is that worse than what I have now? Do you see a woman who wishes to live with me?"

Deacon Ray chuckled. "*Nee,* I do not. And I am sorry for laughing. I guess it is not that funny," he said, noting the look on Yost's face.

"*Nee,* it's not funny," Yost agreed. "Not to the one living without a wife."

"You know I will need to speak with the ministers on this matter," Deacon Ray said. "This is a grave question and may take some consideration."

Yost shook his head. "There will be no speaking on the matter. We all know that when it comes to such hard things as this, Bishop Henry depends on you. He will agree with what you decide."

"But he has a mind of his own. Surely you know that," Deacon Ray corrected.

Yost nodded. "*Yah*, but I have said enough. Do you agree to allow me to speak with Menno at least?"

"I must think on this," Deacon Ray said. "You are catching me by surprise. But what if we should agree to this and the girl agrees to marry you, and then she changes her mind after she has been baptized? What kind of shape would that leave us in? An unwed Amish woman living in the community with no one to wed—at least no one she finds acceptable."

Yost scratched his beard. "I hadn't thought of that," he admitted. Seconds later his face lit up. "Perhaps she would agree to marry me on her baptismal day. That would solve your problem, would it not?"

"Perhaps," Deacon Ray admitted. "But you cannot require this of her."

Yost went back to scratching his beard.

"It's not like she will have much of a wedding anyway," Yost finally said. "She has no parents in the community to give her one. So I think it would be worth asking her if she will do this. Would that not ease your mind greatly?"

"*Yah*, it would," Deacon Ray said. "This is a grave matter of concern to the church. And if this causes further disunity amongst us, then you know where that could lead."

Yost's face brightened. "Then I may speak with Menno? You are agreeing to this?"

"*Yah,*" Deacon Ray allowed. "And may *Da Hah* give you an answer of peace. Perhaps if all goes well, this may bring peace for all of us."

"I will go then." Yost turned to walk toward his buggy. He untied his horse, climbing into the buggy even as he slapped the reins against his horse's back.

# CHAPTER TWELVE

Teresa was holding baby Samuel on the couch, tracing her finger across his cheek until a broad smile broke over his face. *Mamm* watched from her rocker, finally laying aside the weekly copy of *The Budget* she was reading to get to her feet.

"I'll hold him for a bit," *Mamm* offered. "That is, if you want to do something yet before bedtime. We've worked you pretty hard today, and now the baby wants your attention."

"I feel all tired and happy at the same time, so don't worry about the work," Teresa said as she handed over Samuel. "But perhaps I could walk outside. The stars are so beautiful. We don't get much of a chance to see them this way in the city."

"I'll come with you," Susan said, appearing in the kitchen doorway. She took their coats out of the front closet, slipped hers on, and handed the other one to Teresa.

As they stepped outside, Susan took in the sweep of the sky. "It's so beautiful."

"The stars are so bright and twinkling," Teresa said. "Can we see them even better away from the house?"

"You can see more of them, but they don't get much brighter," Susan said, following Teresa across the lawn.

"Is that a star over there toward the road?" Teresa asked, pointing.

Susan laughed. "That's a buggy coming. Probably some boy out snooping around where he shouldn't."

"Perhaps it's that boyfriend of yours coming to see you," Teresa suggested. "Should I go back inside so you can speak with him in private?"

"Stay right where you are!" Susan ordered. "Thomas doesn't have that much nerve. And if he does, I want you with me to help throw cold water on his plans."

"I can't do that." Teresa giggled. "I don't know how to speak with Amish men."

"They talk like everyone else," Susan said. "So don't worry about that. They can understand you."

Standing still in the yard, the two watched the approaching lights. Soon the sound of horse hooves in the gravel reached their ears. Susan took Teresa's hand and pulled her toward the barn. "Let's hide in case the buggy pulls in here."

"I'm not hiding," Teresa said, standing firm. "You think it's about me, don't you? Well, if it is, there's no sense in making it worse by hiding."

"The buggy is coming to our house. There's no time to hide anyway."

"Then we'll meet what comes out in the open," Teresa said.

They waited as the buggy clattered into the lane and came to a stop near them. The door slid open. The interior was too dark to see the occupant. The horse snorted. "It's not Thomas or Deacon Ray," Susan whispered. "I don't recognize the horse."

"*Gut* evening," a man's voice said from the buggy.

"*Gut* evening," Susan replied.

Teresa said nothing but pulled her coat tightly around herself.

A man's pant leg came out of the buggy, followed by the rest of him, his back turned to them while he climbed down the steps. He turned, his bearded face now visible in the dim buggy lights.

"Yost Byler! What brings you here this late?" Susan asked in surprise.

Yost blinked several times. "I wish to speak with your *daett*," he said. "Would he be in the house?"

"*Yah*," Susan said. "Shall I tell him you're here?"

"That would be *gut*," he said. "I will wait for him here."

"Come on, Teresa." Susan turned to go and pulled on Teresa's hand.

"He wouldn't even look at me," Teresa whispered on the way to the house. "He must be very ashamed of me."

"That's Yost for you," Susan said. "He doesn't know his way around women. He barely speaks to me, let alone to an *Englisha*. You probably scare him half to death."

"He didn't look scared," Teresa said. "I thought you said the other day this fellow was *old*."

"Well, he is old."

"He didn't look *that* old," Teresa protested.

"That's because it's dark, and you can't see anything well," Susan said.

"So how old is he?" Teresa asked.

"Oh, about forty or so. I don't know for sure. Just *old*."

Teresa laughed. "I guess that is old for us young women. What do you think he wants?"

"I have no idea," Susan said, holding the front door open until Teresa was inside.

"Who's out there?" *Mamm* asked, looking up from the rocker.

"Yost Byler," Susan said. "He wants to speak with *Daett*."

"Yost?" *Daett* looked puzzled, but he got to his feet, dropping *The Budget* he was reading on the floor.

"He's outside waiting for you," Susan said.

"I'll go see what he wants then," *Daett* said. "I can't imagine what it could be."

Susan opened the door for her *daett* after he pulled on his work coat. She shut it behind him, glancing out the living room window after him. Turning toward Teresa, she shook her head and went into the kitchen. Moments later she was back, standing in front of *Mamm* with her hands on her hips. "I don't like this one bit!" she announced.

"Like what?" *Mamm* asked, not looking up.

"Yost Byler out there talking with *Daett*," Susan said.

"I'm sure it's nothing serious, Susan," *Mamm* said. "Maybe he wants to borrow something."

"At this hour of the night? I don't think so," Susan said. "I'm afraid it has something to do with Teresa."

"With me? The man wouldn't even look at me. I'm sure he's glad I didn't say anything to him so he wouldn't have to lower himself to talk with the likes of me," Teresa stated.

"Teresa, please!" *Mamm* said. "I know people are being hard on you, but it's our way of dealing with problems. It's not meant to harm you."

"I know that's what I am—a problem," Teresa said. "And I'm sorry for the way I've lived my life, but I didn't know any better. I really am trying to live right now. That should make a difference."

"We know that," *Mamm* assured her. "And somehow it will work out. It always does in *Da Hah's* own *gut* time."

"I still don't like it," Susan said. "Look how long they're out there talking. Yost can't have that much to say."

*Mamm* got to her feet and looked out of the window. "It does seem a little strange," she admitted.

"*Daett's* coming in now," Susan announced moments later. She opened the front door and paused to watch Yost's buggy go past, its dim lights moving toward the road.

"So what did he want?" *Mamm* asked as soon as Menno appeared in the doorway and pulled off his coat.

"Perhaps we should speak in private," Menno said, his face troubled.

"It's about Teresa, isn't it?" Susan asked.

"You shouldn't jump to conclusions," *Mamm* reprimanded. "We all want what is best for Teresa."

Teresa got to her feet with Samuel in her arms. She spoke in a choked voice. "Apparently the man has some complaint about me, and I'm very sorry about this. I certainly didn't plan to cause so much trouble for you folks. I'm going up to my room now, and if there is anything I can make right, please let me know."

"You had better stay," Menno said, choosing to sit in his rocker. "The man has no complaint against you."

"Then what did he want?" Susan asked.

"Susan!" *Mamm* said. "I don't like that tone of voice. He may be Yost Byler, but you will still speak respectfully of him and be respectful of your *daett*."

"He wanted to ask for Teresa's hand in marriage," Menno said. "After she is baptized, of course. He has already spoken with Deacon Ray. It seems the ministers would allow Teresa to attend church if they knew there was such an arrangement. And Yost is suggesting the wedding be the same day as the baptism. That is, if Teresa agrees. Yost is willing to wait a bit for an answer."

"Yost Byler!" Susan shrieked. "The nerve of that man!"

"Susan!" *Mamm* said again. "Please. Your *daett* is not finished speaking."

"Surely you don't approve of this plan, *Daett*?" Susan asked.

"I don't know what to think," her *daett* said. "And it really isn't up to me. I'm only passing on the offer. Teresa will have to decide."

"Teresa has already decided," Susan said. "She's having nothing to do with Yost. That man's house is a disaster. He hasn't worn a washed pair of pants for years. He can't find an Amish wife high or low, and now he wants to pick up a helpless *Englisha* who can't do anything about her situation."

"Susan!" *Mamm* scolded. "Teresa *is not* helpless. She can speak for herself."

"So what do you say?" Susan asked, turning toward a white-faced Teresa, who was staring wide-eyed at the wall. "Please tell them you will have nothing to do with this."

"Teresa," *Mamm* said gently, jumping to her feet and taking Samuel from Teresa's arms with one hand. With the other she helped Teresa to the couch. "Oh my, we have scared the poor girl half to death with this talk. I'm so sorry, Teresa. I should have spoken with Menno alone as he suggested."

"The man is willing to marry me?" Teresa squeaked.

"It's not going to happen," Susan insisted, sitting down and taking Teresa's hand in hers. "Believe me, it's not going to happen. This is the sick idea of a sick old man who has nothing to think about but sick thoughts."

"He wants to marry me?" Teresa broke into hysterical laughter.

*Mamm* quickly placed Samuel on the blanket on the floor, grabbed Teresa's other hand, and felt her forehead.

"Teresa," Susan whispered, "he's not going to marry you."

"The shock has driven the girl out of her mind," *Mamm* said.

Susan stroked Teresa's hand as *Mamm* rushed into the kitchen, coming back with a cold cloth that she immediately pressed to Teresa's forehead.

"It's the perfect solution!" Teresa muttered, little streams of water from the cloth running down her cheeks. "Samuel would have a father, and the Amish community would accept me."

"You're not doing it," Susan whispered. "Never!"

"I will do it!" Teresa sat up straight. "Of course I'll do it. This is the only chance I'll ever get, and I can't pass it up."

"Menno! Please help us here," *Mamm* said.

Menno shook his head and spoke, his voice strained. "I haven't seen such a thing in all my life," he said. "The people aren't understanding Teresa at all or considering what she wants to do. And there seems no way to convince them."

"See?" Teresa said to Susan. "He agrees with me."

"I didn't say that," Menno corrected.

"But this is all I deserve," Teresa said. "He's a man and I'm a woman, so what difference does it make if we marry? Samuel will have an Amish father. This Yost man isn't mean, is he? He won't abuse me?"

"*Nee,*" *Mamm* said. "I doubt if he would do that."

"Please, Teresa," Susan pleaded. "Think about this for a while. You don't even know him."

"I've seen him outside this evening, haven't I?" Teresa asked.

"But that was in the dark," Susan said. "You haven't seen him in the daylight."

"But…he wasn't awful," Teresa said. "And he'll make a good father for Samuel, right?"

"Oh, this is awful!" Susan moaned. "I can't believe this is happening."

"Look," Teresa said, "remember how wrong you were in Asbury Park about me wanting to join the Amish? You never thought it would come this far, did you? And remember how ignorant I was of all the problems ahead of me? And yet God placed a great desire in my heart to join your people and find peace among them. Now here I am, and God is again supplying a way through the hard times. Sure, I don't love the man yet, but I can learn to love him. Look, Susan. I'll clean his house. I'll cook for him. Oh, I know I'm not as good at it as Amish women are, but it sounds as if he doesn't have much now anyway. So what is there to lose?"

"There's more to marriage than cooking and cleaning," Susan said.

"I already know something about that," Teresa said, looking over to Samuel.

"You deserve better than Yost," Susan said. "Much better."

*Mamm* cleared her throat. "Perhaps we should allow Teresa to make her own choice on this matter," she said. "If Teresa does agree to this, she can attend church and start the instruction class for baptism. If she changes her mind before her baptism, she is free to leave."

"I like that plan," Teresa said. "Can you give this Yost my answer at once?" she asked, looking at Anna and then at Menno.

*Mamm* shrugged and looked over at her husband. "You will tell Deacon Ray about Teresa's answer?" she asked.

He nodded.

A flood of relief crossed Teresa's face. "Does that mean I get to go to church on Sunday?"

"Does it?" *Mamm* looked to Menno again.

"I believe it does," he replied. "Yost can then come over for a proper introduction to Teresa whenever he wishes."

## Chapter Thirteen

✦

The late Saturday night snowstorm blew squalls against the window of the old farmhouse, driving in through the cracks between the windowpanes and dusting the sill with a coating of white. Menno stirred in bed, still wide awake, listening to the steady, even breathing of Anna beside him. Cautiously he swung his stocking-clad feet out from under the covers. He pulled his pants on over his long johns. *Who would have thought things with Teresa would take such a turn?* he mused.

Tiptoeing into the living room with his flashlight, he held a hand over the lens to keep the light dim. He found the basement stairs and made his way down, the treads creaking at each step. At the bottom, he took his hands off the flashlight lens, opened the furnace door, and added a fresh supply of wood.

When he was done, he stood erect, listening. The soft swish of snow against the basement window drew his attention. He walked over to check the latch. It turned a little tighter under the steady pressure of his fingers. Moving back up the stairs, he closed the basement door, and turned off the flashlight. With his hand held out in front of him, he found his way into the living room and sat on the couch.

Menno's eyes followed the shadowy movements of the snow squalls racing across the front window glass. This was Yost Byler's fault really. If he had kept his wild, harebrained idea to himself, things would never have come to this. But then how long would the community have tolerated the presence of Teresa?

It was hard to tell, because already whispers had begun here and there. Little suggestions that perhaps the ministers were being too harsh. So now thankfully Teresa would be in church this Sunday and the matter would be resolved as far as the community was concerned. Word would move among the people about the agreement between Yost Byler and the *Englisha* girl. Some would be concerned, others would perhaps wish it wasn't so, but when they heard that Teresa had agreed on her own free will, hopefully they would see the wisdom of the matter.

Menno sighed, moving to the other end of the couch closer to the warm heat rising from the floor register. Why was he so troubled then? Standing to his feet, he paced the floor in the darkness. Because it wasn't right somehow.

He shivered and sat down on the couch again. This pacing had to stop, before his foot hit a piece of furniture, and he awakened the whole house.

What if Teresa really didn't want to marry Yost? That was what bothered him. And who deserved Yost? Certainly not a young *Englisha* girl who figured she had no other options.

Hadn't he been given another chance by *Da Hah* after his great sin? Were there not decent children in the community who called him *Daett*? Were there not grandchildren who sat on his lap, enjoying his attention? Why should he be so blessed and yet now help others in condemning another who had sinned like he had to a marriage with Yost Byler?

Should he speak up and object? And even if he did, it still wouldn't bring a halt to this. He would only cause trouble for himself. And was this marriage a bad thing, really? Perhaps Teresa would have a happy life with Yost. He was after all a *gut* man at heart, and would take care of her.

Menno stood and began to pace again. In his mind's eye he saw the face from his past and dug his fingers into his hands. Why was there to be no peace on this matter? And how much worse would this be if she hadn't lost the child? He would have been a father of an *Englisha* child, and there would have been no hiding the sin.

He thought of how it would have been. No returning to the community, no fresh start, no young, blushing bride named Anna standing at his side, no children to raise in the faith, and no hope of returning to farm the land he loved. He shuddered. His past must remain buried. It must never be known to anyone. How could he continue living the life he now had if his sin got out? He couldn't. No mere church confession would repair the damage. Even on his knees in front of the church, his sin would not be forgotten. There might even be excommunication.

Yet the child had not been born. The woman had told him so. She'd spoken the words with tears running down her face. She had trembled while he held her, unable to find words of comfort to speak while the horror of what he'd done raced through his mind.

Her eyes had filled with longing, bursting out in fresh sobs over her great loss. It had also been his loss, had it not? But then hadn't he been secretly glad the child would never be born? Had he not rejoiced in his heart? Had he not taken pleasure that his offspring would never see the light of day or call him an *Englisha* father? That surely was the sting of his guilt…that he could ever have felt so about his own child.

His toe caught the edge of the couch, and he groaned, catching his foot with both hands. He sat down hard on the rocker. After the pain subsided he listened to the silence of the house. A creaking bedroom door or a snap in the hardwood steps would give him time to gather his thoughts. Perhaps he could even light the kerosene lamp before Anna arrived from the bedroom.

When there was only silence, the thoughts returned. What would his *Englisha* child look like now had the baby lived? Was the child in heaven awaiting his arrival? He fell to his knees beside the rocker, pressing his head against the floor.

Why had Teresa come to stir this horror in his life? He'd spent years pushing this away, hiding the thoughts, seeking peace through repentance. He had never sinned so again, not even when the desire for Anna had been great before their marriage. *Does that not count for something?* he pleaded. *Is not my sin long past? Has not love sprung up in my heart for the things of home to replace or counter my wrong actions?* His love for *Da Hah* and the ways of his people had always been present, only momentarily forgotten when the world called so strongly. And his memory of the world faded once he returned.

Yes, the guilt had pounded in his heart for weeks, his fears rising that someone would know he had defiled a woman. But he hadn't been found out. And the memory of his first woman had grown dim, replaced with the face of another. The love for Anna grew in his heart with a wonder that took his breath away. He had been allowed a chance again after what he'd done. How clean he'd felt when he had taken Anna to speak with the bishop a few Sundays before they were published to be married.

"Are you free from each other?" Bishop Bender had asked.

They had both nodded, their faces open for all to see. And he had hidden his past behind a door through which no one else had ever gone. And it had remained tightly closed all these years…until an *Englisha* girl coming in from that world brought the memory of it with her. Is that not what he should be concerned with? Should he be warning others of what lies behind the kind eyes of *Englisha* girls? No, he had only his own sin to deal with. Pressing his head against his hands, he prayed. "Oh great God in heaven, You who know best the weakness in all our hearts. Forgive me, I pray, even as I have forgiven others their sins. Find it in Your most gracious and tender heart to overlook this, my sin again. Wash me clean with the blood of Your dear Son, who gave His life a ransom for many.

"I am but dust, oh God. I am but a weak man who fell and sinned greatly. I confess that I cast my eyes upon the beauty of the world. I lusted after the forbidden and have sinned greatly. Let not my sin bring others to destruction. Let not my sin continue on into eternity.

"Speak now, oh God, to the child who lies on the other side of Your pearly gates. Tell the child I am the father, but that I have sinned and sorrowed greatly over my misdeed. Will You not in Your great mercy make all things work together for good? Tell the child that though I have sinned, yet through my sin, he or she has avoided the temptations of this world. The child is safe with You, surrounded by Your glory and suffering none of these things that beset the frailness of our flesh. For my child this world is forever over even before it began. The child is with You, even as I long to be with You someday.

"Have mercy, oh God, and remember not my sin any longer. Set it not before my mind in remembrance. But if this is not Your will, and You desire in Your great wisdom to bring this suffering near to my heart again, then I ask not that You take it from me, but that I might be given the strength to bear it."

Drained of words, Menno slowly rose to his feet and walked to the window to watch the snow race past the glass. Lifting his fingers to touch the cold, the sting ran up his arm, reaching his shoulder. He didn't take his hand away. He saw her in the distance, her car parked outside the hospital in St. Louis, her face turning to look at him before she climbed in. She pulled the door shut with a soft clunk. Suddenly he jumped. Behind him the hinges on the bedroom door creaked, and footsteps came from the bedroom. He stood still and waited.

"What are you doing up at this hour of the night?" Anna asked.

"My heart is troubled," he said simply.

She slipped her arm around his waist, nestling her body close to him. "Why are you standing here, staring out of the window?"

"Because it is *gut* sometimes for a man to think and to pray," he said. "*Da Hah* begins to seem far away when life presses hard on the soul."

"Is it of the children you are thinking?" Anna asked. "Have you heard news that troubles you?"

"*Nee,* our children are okay."

She leaned against him. "The world seems just beyond the door, does it not?" she asked. "Always ready to come in."

"*Yah,*" he agreed. "It lies not far away for all of us."

"Come then," she said. "You will be in no shape for church tomorrow if you don't get some sleep. Your side of the bed was cold, so you must have been out here for some time."

"I don't know how long it was," he said, "but I think I have found peace."

She pulled on his hand, and he found her face in the darkness.

"You are too *gut* for me," he whispered.

# CHAPTER FOURTEEN

Susan held baby Samuel as Teresa climbed into the backseat of the buggy. Once settled, Teresa reached to take Samuel from Susan's arms, her face lighting up with happiness. Susan pulled herself up to sit beside the two of them.

"Are you ready, Anna?" Menno asked as he climbed in next to her on the front buggy seat.

"Yes, all set."

"Get-up, Toby!" Menno called from the front seat, slapping the reins.

The buggy jerked forward, and Teresa's smile widened. She whispered, "We're really off!"

Susan nodded but didn't say anything.

"Do you think he'll be there today?" Teresa asked as they rattled out the lane.

"Yost Byler?" Susan whispered back.

Teresa nodded.

"I don't know, but I would expect so," Susan said.

Teresa's face turned serious.

"Are you perhaps getting some sense into your head?" Susan asked.

"I'm just thinking he'll be better-looking than I remember from that night," she said. "So it won't be so bad. But I will have to speak with him soon, so I'm preparing myself."

Susan sighed. "You know I don't like this one bit," she said. "But if it's any comfort, I doubt Yost will be coming around anytime soon. He's too scared of women to be rushing into this thing. You notice the other night he didn't even speak to you. *Daett* had to bring in his message."

"Well, I'm ready when he comes," Teresa said, forcing a smile.

"You know," Susan said, "I was just thinking...you can have Thomas if you want him."

Teresa laughed. "Now you're being funny!"

"Well, somebody has to find some humor in this dark story," Susan replied.

"It's not dark, Susan," Teresa said. "Now, tell me again about the service. I don't want to do anything wrong."

Susan took a deep breath before beginning. "We arrive at the place where church is being held," she said, "which happens to be at Benny Zook's place today. We climb down from the buggy after *Daett* stops near the front door of the house. We pull our shawls around ourselves. We walk inside. We take off our wrappings and go around shaking hands with everyone."

Teresa shivered. "Please, God," she whispered, "don't let me do something wrong. And I can't afford to faint on the first Sunday they let me come."

"Do you want to hear the rest?" Susan asked.

"Perhaps you'd better not," Teresa said. "You told me yesterday, and I guess I'll learn as I go along. I feel a little light-headed already."

"You can stick close to me until church starts," Susan said, reaching over to squeeze Teresa's hand. "And when the time comes for you to feed Samuel, *Mamm* will know where the women are going with their babies and she'll point the way."

"We're almost there," *Mamm* spoke up from the front seat.

Teresa peered out of the small buggy window. "There are so many buggies here," she said. "They're everywhere."

Susan nodded, reaching over to pin the top of Teresa's shawl shut just as *Daett* brought the buggy to a halt. She opened the buggy door and, once on the ground, reached back to take baby Samuel from Teresa.

Susan, still holding the baby, followed *Mamm* up the walk, Teresa right behind her. Miriam and Esther met them inside the washroom door. Miriam took Samuel, and Esther helped Teresa take her shawl and bonnet off, showing her where to place them on the table.

"You have to be able to find them after church," Esther explained. "Everyone's looks about the same so note where you put them."

"I would say so," Teresa said, looking wide-eyed at the stack of almost identical bonnets and shawls.

"I'll help you find yours when church is over," Susan said. "Everybody's looks a little different if you look closely. You'll learn with time."

"I expect so," Teresa said absentmindedly.

Teresa and Susan followed *Mamm* into the kitchen. Miriam and Esther were close behind with Samuel. Susan noticed that Teresa wasn't quite as white-faced anymore, which was good.

*Mamm* was shaking hands, exchanging *gut meiyas* as she moved down the line of women.

"This is Teresa," Susan introduced, making a point to keep Teresa close to her.

"And this is Samuel," Miriam said, showing off the baby as she shook hands.

"*Gut meiya*," the women said one after the other as they shook Teresa's hand.

Teresa's smile was tense at first, but she relaxed as she received honest smiles in return to her *Englisha* "good morning."

"I have to learn how to say good morning in German," Teresa whispered to Susan when they arrived at the end of the line.

"It's easy," Susan assured her. "And it's doesn't have to be perfect. Everyone will understand. It's '*gut meiya*.'"

Teresa took a deep breath. "Okay, here goes."

Susan watched Teresa out of the corner of her eye as the next woman approached with her young daughters in tow. There was no question about it, Teresa had more courage than she did out in the *Englisha* world. She had waited for weeks before she dared turn on electric lights in her apartment. And it had been like a knife cutting into her heart to flip on that switch. But Teresa was bravely taking giant steps into the Amish world in such a short time.

"*Goot mayer,*" Teresa managed, a look of pain on her face.

The woman smiled. "*Gut meiya.* So you must be Teresa, the young woman staying at Menno's place. I do declare, I wouldn't have recognized you as an *Englisha* girl. You look right Amish to me."

"I'm sure you could tell when I opened my mouth," Teresa said with a nervous laugh.

"Oh, you did pretty *gut,*" the woman told her before moving down the line.

"Don't even tell me how awful that was," Teresa whispered out of the corner of her mouth in Susan's direction.

Susan whispered back, "Just take the *er* off the end and say *a,* '*gut meiya.*'"

Teresa nodded and tried again with the next woman.

"Really *gut!*" Susan encouraged as the line of women moved toward the living room.

"What happens next?" Teresa asked. "I can't remember."

"It's time to go in for the start of services," Susan said. "Remember, you can't sit with me. You have to sit with my sisters or *Mamm* since you have a baby. They will take care of you."

Teresa kept going as Susan stepped out of the line of women to join the young girls in the front rows. Silence settled throughout the house once everyone was seated. Susan held still, not looking over her shoulder to where Teresa was probably seated. *Mamm* would take *gut* care of her.

The song leader shouted out the first song number and Susan jumped. Seated beside her, Mandy Schrock looked over. Susan avoided her glance. What Amish girl jumped when the song leader gave out the number? Mandy had plenty of reason to be curious, but this wasn't something that could be explained with a whispered answer. Some man in the living room burst into song. The song leader's soaring voice led out, drawing the notes into mighty swirls of sound that were swallowed up as the congregation joined in on the second syllable.

As the ministers got to their feet to file upstairs, Susan dared look over her shoulder. She found Teresa's face in the benches full of women and babies. Teresa was sitting in full view, her face lifted in rapt attention, her lips moving as the sound of singing filled the house. There was no way Teresa could know the words, but she was trying. Susan kept on watching as another verse started. Teresa was now looking down at the page of the songbook. Tears were welling up in her eyes and soon ran in little streams down her cheeks.

Turning back, Susan followed the black and white words in her own songbook, mouthing the words from memory. She listened to the sounds of the singing. The words were so familiar, so often heard, and yet were moving Teresa to such depth of emotion. Had Susan missed something in the years of her childhood? The singing had always been enjoyable and beautiful, but one did not cry during the songs.

It was simply too much to understand. All of it was. What had brought this girl to them? What made her so determined to stick this out at all cost? There was no doubt Teresa had been determined. But now she was even willing to marry a man she didn't love for the sake of her child. And here she, Susan Hostetler, had run away from this life, rushing into the arms of the world with hardly a thought of the dangers involved. Dangers which the ministers had often warned about.

Yet *Da Hah* had spared her the evils of that world, sending Teresa to bring her home again. Was Teresa an angel? Susan sat bolt upright on the bench at the thought. But angels didn't have babies with earthly fathers, so that couldn't be the answer. Teresa must be exactly who she said she was. An *Englisha* girl sick of her world, who wanted to become part of another world. A world where she hoped to find peace.

Susan glanced up from the page again catching the eye of Thomas. The old love for him rose in her, but she pushed it away. Thomas could not be trusted. Teresa could marry whoever she wanted to, but she was not going down that path.

But what kind of an example was she setting for Teresa? The thought came with a sting. Did her actions line up with Teresa's courage? And how could Teresa's love for the community be so strong, even when they treated her wrong?

Susan pulled her eyes away from Thomas's face, catching a glimpse of Eunice seated on the row in front of her. Eunice was looking in Thomas's direction with a slight smile on her face. Well, let Thomas look at her, Susan thought. The two deserved each other.

The singing came to a halt with silence settling over the house. Susan kept her head down until another song began. Stealing another look in Teresa's direction, Susan saw that Teresa was still sitting with her face uplifted, joy written on every feature.

Some thirty minutes later when the ministers came down from upstairs, the singing stopped, and the first speaker soon rose to his feet. He spoke for thirty minutes or so, using a singsong voice, and following no certain path, jumping from Scripture quotations to short exhortations and back again.

Deacon Ray had the Scripture reading, and Bishop Henry soon rose to begin the main sermon. Forty minutes later, heads were nodding here and there in the men's section, and Susan took another peek over her shoulder. Teresa was gone, with no sign of either baby Samuel or Miriam. So they must have gone to the bedroom where the children were tended to.

When she turned around, Thomas was looking at her. Susan glanced away at once. But guilt feelings had crept unbidden into her heart, the earlier anger gone. Perhaps she should reconsider her hard-hearted rebuff of his advances? Did not her people teach that forgiveness was one of the highest forms of grace, given freely from *Da Hah* to each of them, and from each of them back to the other?

Yet, she had forgiven. But surely that didn't mean she had to take Thomas back. Thomas would say she had to, but he had a reason to say so. The question really was, what did *Daett* need? The farm needed help, and *Daett* had his heart set on Thomas taking over for him. But was that reason enough to marry Thomas? No, it was not.

Bishop Henry was wrapping up his sermon, asking for testimony on what had been said. He named a few men, sitting down to wait while they began speaking in the order they had been called. Susan looked towards Teresa again, who was now back and holding Samuel in her arms, a look of total peace on her face.

How did Teresa do it? In all her months among the *Englisha,* such peace had never found her. Sure there had been *gut* times with Robby, during the times she was learning how to drive a car and getting her driver's license. Even taking the test for her GED had been fun and so had been her *Englisha* "dates" with Duane Moran, but there had been little peace.

Susan almost gasped aloud, as she remembered. The driver's license was still sitting at home in her dresser drawer, hidden under her clothing. If *Mamm* or *Daett* discovered the license, it would break their hearts. They were so hoping she was home to stay, and they would see that little piece of plastic as her link to the other world, making it easy to return at a moment's notice. Perhaps it was time to cut her ties to the outside world and follow Teresa's example of submission and humility?

The house was silent again, interrupting her thoughts as Bishop Henry got to his feet.

"We can give thanks today that *Da Hah's* word has been given to us free from the errors of men," he said. "This is not within our power to do, but only by the grace that *Da Hah* gives to weak men filled with the frailties of this earth. So we have one announcement to make today. In two weeks pre-communion church will be held at Johnny Chupp's, and communion—if there are no objections—will be held two weeks after that."

Bishop Henry sat down, and the last song number was given out.

# Chapter Fifteen

✦

Susan took Teresa's arm and guided her through the rush of women and girls coming in and out of the kitchen. The men were sitting at the long tables in the living room, the steady murmur of their voices filling the room. Near the back wall, Benny Zook was bending over Bishop Henry, whispering into his ear.

Susan's hand tightened on Teresa's arm. "Shh…we have to wait right now," Susan whispered in her ear.

Teresa's eyes got big.

"It's prayer time," Susan whispered.

Bishop Henry's voice rang out, reaching throughout the house. "If we have now been seated at the tables, let us give thanks."

Everyone bowed their heads. Susan watched out of the corner of her eye as Teresa looked around for a moment before bowing her head.

"For this food set before us by Your great and compassionate mercy," Bishop Henry prayed, "we now give thanks. We humble our hearts before You at this noon hour, beseeching Your grace upon our gathering and upon each one who is here. Let us not sin against Your holy name or against our fellow man. And for each of these favors and blessings, we give You thanks. Amen."

When the murmur of voices resumed, Teresa asked, "Do they always pray like that?"

"It's the normal thing," Susan said. "Come, you can help me serve the tables. You'll learn things, and it will help the people see you in a *gut* light."

"But I don't know how," Teresa objected, hanging on to Susan's arm.

"I'll show you," Susan said. "It's not that hard. You carry peanut butter bowls to the tables and pick up the used ones."

"That's all?" Teresa asked, almost sounding disappointed.

"Well…" Susan laughed. "There's also bread to carry, butter, red beets, cheese sometimes, water, and coffee, of course."

"To those men back there?" Teresa looked over her shoulder.

"*Nee,*" she said. "I think we can get the women's table."

"Is *he* here today?" Teresa asked as they went into the kitchen.

"Who?" Susan responded without thinking.

"You know who!" Teresa whispered back.

"Oh…" Susan said. "Here I've been in my own little world all day and I nearly forgot about him. *Nee,* he's not here. I promise we'll stay away from the men's table."

Teresa's face fell. "I was hoping I would see him," she said. "But I didn't dare look very hard. Maybe I wouldn't recognize his face anyway, since I only saw him that night in the dark."

"You know you don't have to marry him," Susan reminded.

"And leave instead?" Teresa said. "Do you want me to do that?"

"Of course not!" Susan said. "But this just isn't fair."

"It'll be worth it in the end," Teresa said. "I did hope to see him today. Does he look much different than the rest? I think they all start to look the same after a while. Maybe it's the beards."

Susan laughed for a second and then pulled on Teresa's arm. "Come! They need help at the tables."

Teresa shrugged and followed her. Entering the kitchen, Susan guided Teresa to the counter where two girls were dishing peanut butter into smaller bowls.

"We'll take some," Susan told them. "Which table?"

"The boys' table," one of the girls said. "The women's and the men's are taken care of right now."

"Oh…" Susan paused before she turned to Teresa. "Here, take these." She turned back to fill her hands again. With Teresa behind her, Susan led the way down the basement steps.

"Where are we going?" Teresa asked, taking her time on the steps.

"To the boys' table," Susan said.

Teresa was silent, balancing peanut butter bowls with care.

"Hi, Susan," several of the boys greeted when they arrived. Susan ignored them, leaning between their shoulders to exchange the peanut butter bowls.

"We need bread over here," a boy hollered from the end of the table.

"I only have so many hands!" Susan retorted.

"I think everyone has forsaken us down here," a skinny boy said. "How are we to get enough food if no one serves us?"

"I guess you can go get some yourself," Susan said to roars of laughter from around the table.

Teresa followed Susan's example, leaning in between the boys' shoulders and coming out with empty peanut butter bowls.

The girl was *gut* at most everything. There was no doubt about that, Susan decided.

"We'll be back with more food for you poor starving creatures," Susan told them.

Laughter rose again.

On the way upstairs, they met two girls coming down, their hands filled with more peanut butter in bowls.

"I think they need bread and cheese," Susan mentioned while passing.

"They're trying to find more people to help," one of the girls said. "They're a little shorthanded right now."

"Do we have to go back down there again?" Teresa asked at the top of the stairs.

"*Yah,*" Susan said. "As long as they need help with the food."

"Who was the boy sitting beside that lover boy of yours?" Teresa asked.

"Teresa!" Susan said. "Don't talk like that about Thomas—especially here."

"Sorry," Teresa said.

"That was Deacon Ray's son," Susan said. "His name is James. Why?"

"He was looking at me like I was a ghost or something. Do I look awful? Can they see I'm not Amish? I mean…I prayed to God last night—really hard, that I would look exactly like the rest of you."

"You look just fine," Susan said, her eyes traveling up and down Teresa's outfit. "You look exactly like the perfect Amish girl. So ignore the boys however they look at you."

Back in the kitchen they filled their hands with plates of bread and cheese, traversing the basement steps again. The other girls had completed their transfers and were waiting at the bottom of the steps for Susan and Teresa to pass.

"I see someone has mercy on us," the skinny boy said as the girls approached the tables again. "I've only had one piece of bread so far, and they're going to chase us off the table soon."

"Then you'd better be stuffing your mouth right quick," Susan told him as she handed him a piece of bread.

Again laughter filled the space around them.

Susan placed another bread plate on the table and motioned for Teresa to place her bread and cheese in the middle of the table before moving to the other end. When she returned, she saw Teresa standing with her eyes cast down, her hands clasped in front of her.

Looking across the table, Susan saw James staring at Teresa, his dark eyes intense, his eyebrows pulled downward.

"Come," she whispered in Teresa's ear, taking her arm.

To the creaks of the stairs they made their way back up, meeting the two girls waiting at the top, their hands filled with platters again.

"I'll be right back down," Susan told them.

"I'm not going back down there," Teresa whispered. "I'll go take care of Samuel."

"That's a good idea," Susan assured her. "It wasn't nice of James to be looking at you like that."

"Do I look so sinful?" Teresa asked, tears welling up.

"You look like a very *gut* Amish woman," Susan said, squeezing her arm. "Don't let a boy's stare scare you off so easily."

Filling her hands again, Susan made her way back to the basement door, passing the two girls at the top of the stairs. They nodded as they passed. Thomas and James were engaged in deep conversation, their heads together when Susan arrived. Looking up, a soft, hopeful smile broke across Thomas's face. Susan looked away. With her head held high, she deposited the bread plate and peanut butter bowl at the other end of the table, returning to the top of the stairs just as Bishop Henry's voice vibrated through the house. "If we have all eaten now, let us give thanks." Susan paused as the people in the house quieted.

Bishop Henry's voice continued from the living room. "And now we give thanks, oh mighty God, for what we have eaten. As our bodies have been strengthened, so let our spirits also be strengthened by Your great mercy and grace. Be with us through this coming week, and keep us from evil. In the name of the Father, the Son, and the Holy Spirit. Amen."

As the women began moving around in the kitchen again, Susan took one of the bowls filled with soapy water and washcloths set out on the counter, following the two girls back down to the basement. The last of the boys' backs were disappearing out the door. Their knives and forks were strewn everywhere, and drips of peanut butter and beet juice dotted the table.

Beginning at the end, Susan washed each utensil and glass, wiping the area clean before setting everything back where it belonged. One of the girls brought a water pitcher and refilled the washed glasses.

"So how's it like to be back home again?" the oldest of the girls asked.

"Oh, *gut*," Susan said, smiling. Both of them were too young for boyfriends. They were obviously curious about the world she'd lived in. The less said about that time, the better.

"So you really lived in New Jersey?" The question came with a quick glance over the shoulder at the basement stairs.

"*Yah,*" Susan said. "With the sister of the woman I cleaned house for in Livonia."

"Are there Amish people living there?"

"I saw two couples once," Susan said, "on the day the town had a festival."

Behind her the basement door slammed, admitting the first of a long stream of younger boys for the next table setting.

"Then there were only *Englisha* people living in the town?" the older girl asked, her eyes large. Obviously she already knew and must be wanting to confirm her information.

"It was a big city," Susan replied, not really answering the question as she held up her hand to the onrushing line of young boys. "We're not quite ready yet."

"But we're *hungry!*" the first boy in line insisted. "You have some places clean."

"I'll sit anywhere," the one behind him seconded.

"Then help yourself," Susan said, motioning toward the places behind her with a wave of her hand.

When all the places were clean and set, Susan carried the dirty bowls of water to the basement sink where she and the eldest girl emptied them.

"What is it like to live amongst the *Englisha* people?" the girl asked in a whisper.

"Very different," Susan said, "but you kind of get used to it."

The girl's eyes got even bigger. Susan led the way upstairs, placing her empty bowls on the counter. She fled into the living room, where she found Teresa holding baby Samuel. They were surrounded by older women.

"Give Samuel to *Mamm,*" Susan said, bending over to whisper in Teresa's ear. "We get to go eat now."

"Oh!" Teresa said. "I hadn't thought about eating."

"Well, you should think about yourself more," Susan advised,

waiting until Teresa got up before guiding her over to where *Mamm*
sat on the couch. Wordlessly *Mamm* held out her arms, and Teresa
handed her the baby. With Susan at Teresa's side, they moved toward
the girls' table. They had just seated themselves when Bishop Henry
made the announcement for prayer and led out.

"My first Amish church meal," Teresa whispered when the prayer
was done. "What do I do? I've been watching the tables, and I still
have no idea."

Susan smiled. "You take a piece of bread, spread butter on it, and
then add the peanut butter. In between bites you chew on the cheese
or red beets, whichever fits your fancy. And coffee is either while
you're eating or afterward."

"I'm going to be a real Amish woman yet," Teresa asserted, spreading butter on her bread eagerly.

# Chapter Sixteen

✦

The late afternoon sun shone through the living room windows, sending long shadows across the thick, homemade rugs covering the hardwood floors. Deacon Ray sat in his rocker, reading the week's edition of *The Budget* while eating from his bowl of popcorn.

"*Daett*!" James called, coming out of the upstairs doorway. "So what's up with this *Englisha* woman?"

"Nothing is 'up' really. Why? Did you notice her in church today?"

"*Yah*," James said. "She was serving tables with Susan."

"That's *gut*," Deacon Ray said. "Thankfully the Hostetlers are teaching her how to work."

"Is this true about her planned wedding with Yost Byler?" James asked.

"You shouldn't worry your head about the *Englisha* woman," Deacon Ray said. "You have your own troubles with girls, I should say. What happened with that Geauga County girl you were interested in?"

"Rose?" James frowned.

"Whatever her name was," Deacon Ray said. "I can't keep track with how fast you keep putting them through. Maybe you should think about settling down soon."

"I'm still young, *Daett*," he said. "You know that."

"Perhaps, but soon the *gut* ones will be gone, James. You know they don't keep lying around if no one picks them up."

"Thomas said I could take Eunice off his hands," James offered.

Deacon Ray laughed. "I see he's not offering Susan."

"*Nee*," James said. "But that would be a catch now, wouldn't it?"

"Are you doubting yourself, James?" Deacon Ray looked up from his popcorn. "Perhaps you'd be the one to tame her down. It sure looks like Thomas hasn't been able to. The girl is an unsightly mess, the way she trotted around the *Englisha* world. And now she's brought home this unwed woman with a child. Thankfully for all of us, Yost is interested in marrying the *Englisha*. Of course, even then the woman might up and leave. I noticed Yost wasn't in church today. He probably doesn't want to scare her away."

"So it is true then?" James asked again.

"Is what true?" James's *mamm* asked, coming up from the basement. "I thought I heard you two chattering up here."

"Yost and the *Englisha* girl," Deacon Ray replied, transferring another piece of popcorn to his mouth.

"Oh that." Ruth sat on the couch. "It all sounds a little impossible to me. But the woman did seem nice enough today. She even helped with the boys' table in the basement. Susan seemed to be taking *gut* care of her."

"I think they're both up to something," James said.

"Oh?" Deacon Ray looked up from the newspaper.

"Surely not, James," Ruth disagreed. "Susan seems right settled down since she's come back."

"I don't know." James shrugged. "It's all a little fishy to me. Susan disappears suddenly, supposedly over a little fight with Thomas. I mean, what's the big deal? Who doesn't fight with their girlfriend?"

"You just quit yours," Ruth said. "Why do you do that? I thought Rose was a *gut* match for you."

"Maybe she quit me," James said with a smile.

"I suppose she could have," Ruth allowed. "But I don't believe it. And you could still write the girl a nice letter and get things straightened out, couldn't you?"

"I don't think so," James said. "Things didn't go too *gut* with Rose."

"Well…" Deacon Ray rocked, his eyes on the magazine. "Things might not work out quite like Yost thinks either. I'd be surprised if the girl even makes it to the instruction classes that start right after communion. And mind you, we're not putting them off for her, nor are we waiting until she can speak German. She either learns fast or waits for the fall classes."

"I wouldn't be too hard on her," Ruth interjected. "And the articles of faith are written in English, so she'll be understanding those. It's only the ministers' questions that may be asked in German."

Deacon Ray grunted his agreement.

"I think I'll get ready for the hymn singing," James said, getting up. "There's supper served tonight for the young people."

"Maybe we'll come afterward," Deacon Ray said. "But I wouldn't worry about the *Englisha* girl. The ministers are aware of what problems might lie ahead."

"I just hate to see Thomas involved with all that mess," James said. "He ought to take Eunice up on her interest and forget about Susan."

"Now, James," Ruth said, "we all have to come to our own understanding of things. So don't go pushing Thomas away from Susan."

"He's not listening to me anyway," James said as he went up the stairs. Once in his bedroom he quickly changed his clothes. He walked back downstairs and out to the barn. After hitching his horse to the buggy, he drove out of the driveway, turning toward the hymn singing. He gave his horse its head. With a rattle of wheels, he didn't slow much at the next turn, sliding the buggy sideways on the gravel. With a smile he let the reins out again. Perhaps this was why he couldn't keep a girlfriend, although he never drove like this when he had a girl along. But perhaps she still picked up on his reckless ways or saw how tight the reins went out the storm front. Girls were like that.

*Nee,* he decided. It wasn't that at all. Whatever kept him and girls from getting along, he simply wasn't going to worry about it. The right girl would come along when she was supposed to. *Mamm* was right though. Rose had been a nice girl. True, she came from another community, so there might have been some adjustments, but Rose would have made them. She had made that fact abundantly clear.

Still, he had not asked to see her again on his last trip to Geauga County.

Ahead of him a buggy appeared, the horse plodding along. James slowed his horse and pulled out, staying well on the other side of the road. A brief sideways glance as he passed revealed the bearded face of Yost Byler. James pulled back to his side of the road. *Wow!* he thought. Things had to be serious between Yost and the *Englisha* girl if the man was coming to supper at the Sunday night hymn singing.

So the poor man must have fallen hard for the *Englisha* girl. Yet he had barely seen her or she him. That was the strange part about this whole thing. Yost was just desperate, but that didn't explain the girl's part. Who would agree to a marriage with so little information about the man? She couldn't have seen much of him. Unless Yost and she had had some secret meeting to talk things out, but that would have made matters worse. Talking with Yost would decrease, not increase, a girl's willingness to marry him. At least among the girls he knew.

Susan and the *Englisha* girl were hiding something. There was no doubt about it. But what? And strangely no one else seemed to care. Not even *Daett*. He usually was the first to care about such things. Bishop Henry placed great stock in *Daett's* opinions on serious matters, and this was serious if there ever was anything serious. An *Englisha* unwed girl was making her way into the heart of the community. Would there be trouble following after her?

Well, he decided after a long moment of hard thinking, it was none of his concern. Why darken his brow about this matter, when no one else cared? Pulling into Benny Zook's driveway, James stopped by the barn beside the other buggies. Thomas saw him arrive and ran over to help unhitch.

"Taking Susan home tonight?" James teased as he undid the tugs.

"You know I'm not," Thomas said. "So quit it."

"Yost Byler is coming to supper," James announced. "How about that? I passed him a ways back."

"Looks like the plan is working," Thomas said, a pleased smile spreading across his face.

"Now what would an *Englisha* girl want with an old man like that?" James asked.

"Don't worry your head about it," Thomas said. "I'm just glad it's working. After a while Susan won't have any reason to put me off."

"I still don't think Susan's telling you everything about her time out there with the *Englisha,*" James said. "Anything could have happened, Thomas. And you know it. I think they're covering something up. Something bad enough to marry an old Amish man over."

Thomas laughed. "Are you trying to get me out of the way so you can make your move on Susan?"

James snorted and shook his head.

"Come on now, be honest," Thomas said. "You'd leap at a chance for Susan Hostetler's affections. I've known that since our school days. It's just that you've never had a chance, and you're not getting one now."

James chuckled. "I'm not getting in your way, believe me. This has to be a two-way street, you know. And Susan's never paid me much attention."

"That's how I want it to stay." Thomas held the buggy shafts as James led the horse forward. Behind them Yost Byler's buggy banged into the driveway. Thomas smiled and turned to walk toward him. James shook his head and led his horse to the barn.

When he returned to the yard, Yost had just finished unhitching with Thomas's help.

"*Gut* evening," James greeted him.

Yost grunted, "*Gut* evening," hauling on his horse's halter as he pulled the beast toward the barn.

James looked Yost over as he passed. His beard had rough scissors marks over the entire surface. At least the result was a shorter beard, which would have helped his looks except for the chop marks. His pants looked washed for a change, but his feet were bootless and his shoes muddy. Didn't the man know that muddy shoes wore out quicker, costing more in the long run than the money spent on boots? Perhaps the man was past caring about such things.

"Should we wait for him?" James asked Thomas as he looked over his shoulder at the barn.

Thomas laughed. "I think he can find his way to the house."

James shrugged and followed Thomas through the front door. Inside, they tossed their hats on the pile. A group of boys already sat around the bench table, laughing and talking.

"Do you think Susan brought the *Englisha* girl?" James asked, motioning toward the kitchen.

"I'd expect so," Thomas said. "All I care about is if she comes herself."

"Come on now. Sit down. Don't be shy," one of the boys hollered at them, making room at the bench table. "The girls will be coming out soon enough for supper."

They both laughed and walked toward the table. Behind them the front door opened and Yost entered. He took his hat off, fiddling with the rim. A hush settled on the room as the boys turned to look at him. He nodded, the edges of freshly trimmed beard even more pronounced in the shadowy light of the gas lantern.

"Evening, Yost," someone said, and Yost tossed his hat sideways. The edge of the rim stayed on the floor, the hat bouncing against the others. It wobbled out across the living room falling over against a chair. James stood and retrieved the runaway hat. Yost stood unmoving by the front door.

"Hey, there's room over here," someone called, and Yost moved in that direction.

James waited until Yost was seated before he took a seat at the end of the table. The conversation resumed, rising and falling in the living room. James listened to their opinions on horses, on spring, and on the coming summer's hay crop, but he watched Yost's face. It soon lost its tense look as he joined in the talk. Only when a girl's name was mentioned, accompanied by laughter and good-hearted humor, did Yost look away.

James kept quiet, thinking things over. Was this what the *Englisha* girl was after by joining the Amish? This common everyday living they all experienced? But was not the *Englisha* world so much more exciting? Was it not a place with movies to watch, with television in the house, with an automobile outside to drive when one wished to? Something wasn't right here. No one would willingly leave that world for this. And no one would marry Yost Byler over nothing. The girl was running from something, and Susan knew what it was.

The thought hit him like a bolt of lightning out of a dark summer's thunderstorm. This was why Susan had returned. She was helping the girl run away from her past. It was the only thing that made any sense. Lost in his thoughts, James jerked his head up at the sudden quieting of the room around him. Boys were standing to their feet, and he jumped up himself.

From the kitchen doorway, the girls were streaming out into the living room. Their white coverings were outlined against the pale blue wall, framing their cheerful faces. James searched the line, finding Susan toward the end with the *Englisha* girl beside her. Both of them looked happy, as if they had finished sharing something funny in the kitchen. What could the two be hiding?

"We're glad all of you could come," Benny was saying as he stood at the kitchen doorway with his wife, Naomi, beside him. "It's always a privilege to have the young folks over for supper on a Sunday night. The chance doesn't come around but once a year, and it's not often enough for me. Thank all of you for coming. So let's pray and then we can eat."

Silence settled across the room as they all bowed their heads.

When the prayer was over, James looked in Susan and the *Englisha* girl's direction. Both had their heads turned in his direction. James glanced away. It would not do to be caught staring at them. And if he was not mistaken, the *Englisha* girl had just caught sight of Yost Byler, and she looked quite pale. Indeed, something very strange was going on.

## Chapter Seventeen

✤

Susan watched from the upstairs window, pushing the dark-blue curtains aside as her *daett* drove the team of Belgians around the corner of the barn. He looked tired and weary, his face drawn after the day of spring plowing in the fields. Susan's hand trembled on the drapes between her fingers. How could she even be thinking about leaving?

Of course they wouldn't be running away. They would inform *Mamm* and *Daett* of where they were going, but they definitely needed to leave. Things were simply getting out of hand, and Teresa was not coming to her senses. Across the hallway, the cry of baby Samuel startled her.

Susan walked over to the dresser, pulled open the drawer, and dug under the clothes. She picked up her driver's license and stared at the picture. Her hair had been done up in a high knot, unadorned with the usual white *kapp*. Her *mamm* and *daett* would pass out if they knew Susan even obtained a license, much less kept it around. But what did they expect? That she had behaved herself perfectly as an Amish woman while living among the *Englisha*?

*Mamm* had to know she hadn't, and so did *Daett.* They both knew, and that was the problem with so much of what was going on. Everyone knew, but no one was talking. Susan sighed. This might be the Amish way, but it didn't mean she had to cooperate. That much she had learned from her time with the *Englisha*. She could do what she thought was right. Talking with Teresa about leaving would be the first step. The idea might still be a little too much for her friend, but Teresa simply had to have some sense talked into her head.

Slipping the driver's license back under the clothes, Susan closed the drawer and then walked across the hall. She knocked on Teresa's bedroom door.

"Come in," the soft answer came.

Teresa was tending to Samuel when Susan entered.

"I thought it was you," Teresa said. "I'm almost done feeding Samuel. Then I think it's time to start supper, isn't it?"

"*Yah*," Susan said. "But you've worked hard enough today with the wash and the housecleaning. You should let *Mamm* and me take care of supper."

"I wouldn't think of it," Teresa said. "I'm enjoying every minute of this and wouldn't trade it for the world."

"Aren't you ever going to get tired of this, Teresa?" Susan asked. "I'm tired by the evenings, and I'm used to this work. And you're studying German on top of it all."

"But it's *a gut shvacheit*," Teresa said, her smile spreading across her face. "Did I say that right? *A good weakness?*"

"Just like one of us!" Susan sat down on the bed beside her.

"So why are you so dark-looking?" Teresa asked.

"I'm thinking about you…about us, I guess," Susan said. "Teresa, I think we should leave."

"Leave?" Teresa gaped at her. "Why in the world are you thinking of something like that? That would be absolutely awful. You're just letting dark thoughts float around in your head, Susan. Throw them out."

"Maybe I am," Susan protested. "But don't you realize what lies ahead? Marriage to an old man like Yost Byler. Do you know what that means? You'll have to live with him, not with us. And it won't be the same. His house is a wreck, and you'll have to deal with that every day. And his bed, Teresa. Have you thought about that? He's never been married before. If he had, that might be a little different."

Teresa laughed. "You make it sound as if I will die shortly after arriving at his house."

"Well, it feels like that sometimes," Susan said. "Doesn't it bother you?"

Teresa sobered. "It does sometimes," she said. "I'm not going to lie about it. There are times I lie awake at night wondering how I've gotten myself into this situation. And I wonder if my heart is leading me correctly. Then I look over to where Samuel is sleeping, and I know I'm doing the right thing."

Susan sighed. "Think of really living with him, Teresa. The reality of it."

"I have thought of that, Susan," Teresa said, looking at Samuel. "But you're forgetting that I have been with a man. I know things that you don't. Believe me, Susan, I'm sure Yost is a decent man under all that grime and dirt you claim is at his house. And the place will clean up and his clothing will wash. He's what I deserve, Susan. I'll be content with that. I have to be."

"I can't believe you're saying this, Teresa," Susan objected. "You don't have to just be content. You deserve to be *happy*—and that means marrying a man you love."

"I will love him," Teresa said, touching Susan's arm. "I will love him in my mind, and someday I'll make him a *gut* wife. Yost will be a better man for it. I know that because I don't think God would deny me that since I'm asking for Samuel and not for myself."

"I think you're wrong-headed and thinking in circles," Susan said. "Yost Byler is an awful man. And it will take more than you to change him."

"I don't agree about the awfulness," Teresa said. "But *God* will change him if he needs changing. It will be my job to love him."

Susan gasped, standing to pace the floor. "You're talking like *Mamm* now—when she speaks to me of Thomas."

Teresa laughed. "You and Thomas are another matter. I think you ought to make up with him. And why are you even thinking of leaving again? You should burn that driver's license you have hidden in the bottom of your drawer."

Susan stopped her pacing.

"Why do you remember about the driver's license?" she asked.

"You told me earlier you still had it," Teresa said, "and isn't a dresser where all Amish girls hide things?"

"I hope *Mamm* doesn't think like you do," Susan said, smiling just a little as she resumed her pacing.

"I'm sure she does, Susan. But I think she's giving you space to work through these things on your own. You ought to help her. Why aren't you joining me for the baptismal class coming up next Sunday?"

"I can't," Susan said.

"Even if that Thomas of yours joins?" Teresa asked.

Susan stopped and stared at her.

"How do you know he's joining the class?"

Teresa shrugged. "Whispers here and there. The girls don't think I can understand German yet, and I guess I don't a lot, but they use enough English words so I can follow along. That Eunice girl thinks Thomas is joining, and she also has plans."

Susan laughed. "Then you can forget about me even thinking about joining."

"So what did Thomas really do to you that has you so upset?" Teresa asked.

Susan didn't take long to answer. "He broke my heart. He betrayed my trust. He shattered my dreams. Shall I go on?"

"Then why don't I see little pieces of your broken heart lying around on the ground? Susan, you're getting along quite fine. And you didn't hold back from considering love out there in my world. Let's see, what was his name? Duane Moran?"

"That was different," Susan allowed. "Duane was just someone I met. Here I had plans to marry Thomas since our school days."

"People seem to make a lot of plans around here," Teresa said. "Is that what was broken, Susan? Your plans instead of your heart?"

"That's not a nice thing to say, Teresa," Susan remarked. "And I did love the boy. He was the cutest thing in eighth grade, a charmer right down to his bare toes. Thomas could smile at the blackboard and make my heart beat faster. So you can imagine what he did to it when he really smiled at me. I often dreamed of our little farm-house sitting on top of a hill, where we would love each other forever and ever and never leave. It seemed so real, Teresa. And his affections felt like they could never be broken. Then *bam!* They were. Just like that. I caught him outside the hymn-singing house one night, laughing and talking with Eunice. Those smiles he gave me were all over his face—giving *her* what I thought he was only giving me. And then there was the kiss. That did it for me."

"That *is* a sad tale," Teresa agreed. "And I'm sorry for accusing you."

Susan came over in the silence that followed and sat beside Teresa, taking her hand. "And I'm sorry for carrying on about my own troubles. They must seem like nothing compared to what you've been through. And don't try to deny it because I was there. I saw the place you lived in. I saw the area. All that trash in your yard. It's a wonder you don't still have nightmares."

"It's okay." Teresa wiped her eyes. "The trash in my life wasn't the worst thing. But at least you understand. I'm so glad you were there to see why I'm acting the way I am."

"I'm still not sure I understand totally," Susan allowed. "Still, you don't have to go back to that life. We could stay with Laura."

"And what would I do with Samuel?" Teresa asked, sitting straight up. "Do you know what my world holds for him, Susan? Even in Laura's world I'd have to hold down a job. Samuel would be in daycare somewhere. Other people would be taking care of him instead of me. Then how would he turn out? Would Samuel drift toward the life I used to know? He would, Susan. I know he would. All my prayers wouldn't keep him away from that evil. And all because I would have decided that I wanted life a little easier for myself. No, Susan. I'll take Yost Byler any day rather than see my son grow up like that."

"Okay." Susan touched Teresa's arm. "I wouldn't want you to do something you think isn't right."

"I'm just sorry for your sake," Teresa replied, wiping her eyes again.

"Why should you be sorry for me?" Susan asked.

"Because I'm keeping you here," Teresa said. "That's why. You never would have come back in the first place if it hadn't been for me."

"I don't know about that," Susan said. "I would have come back sometime. Eventually."

"Then don't leave now, Susan," Teresa pleaded. "Stay with me. And your *mamm* and *daett* need you more than I do."

"I'm not going to leave," Susan said. "I just have dark thoughts sometimes. Maybe you're doing me more *gut* than you think. What if you end up helping me to stay?"

Teresa laughed. "I don't know about that. But either way, I think I'll hurry up and get baptized."

"You know that your wedding day will be right afterward?" Susan asked.

Teresa picked up baby Samuel. "I haven't forgotten. I'll be okay. The Lord will be with me."

"I suppose you know that Yost will be by to talk with you—once you start instruction class," Susan said.

"Has he told your dad this?" Teresa asked.

"No, it's just my educated guess," Susan said. "The two of you will have to make some kind of plans."

"There's not a whole lot of plans to make," Teresa said, laying baby Samuel on the bed. "We get to our feet after I'm baptized, join our hands, and say 'I do.'"

"Mostly you say *yah* to the bishop's questions," Susan said. "And then you're married."

*Mamm's* voice interrupted them, calling up the stairs, "Are you helping with supper, Susan? *Daett* will be in soon."

"I'm coming," Susan hollered toward the bedroom door.

"I'm coming with you," Teresa said, picking up Samuel. She followed Susan out the door. At the bottom of the stairs in the living room, Teresa placed Samuel in the crib by the stove before joining Susan in the kitchen.

"Teresa, you don't have to help tonight," *Mamm* said. "You worked hard enough around here today already."

"That's what Susan told me," Teresa admitted. "But I want to help."

"Well, we'll try not to work you to death," *Mamm* said, laughing. "And if you need more encouragement, I think you're doing really well with your German studies. Your accent is getting *gut*. Soon no one will tell you from a real Amish woman."

"I tried a few words out a while ago." Teresa beamed. "And I think Susan almost thought I was Amish!"

"She's already picking up conversations among the girls," Susan said. "Maybe I ought to tell everyone to be careful."

"I'd let them find out on their own," *Mamm* said. "It will teach them to be careful about what they say. Which is a *gut* lesson for all of us."

"I've definitely decided to join the instruction class," Teresa said. "Is that still okay with you and Menno?"

"We have no objections," *Mamm* said. "But are you sure about the marriage with Yost Byler? I hope you understand enough about our ways to know that the ministers are serious about the agreement."

"I understand," Teresa acknowledged, busying herself with setting the table.

"I still think it's wrong," Susan muttered.

"It doesn't matter what *we* think," *Mamm* said. "Are you planning to join the class, Susan?"

"I don't think so, *Mamm*," Susan said. "I don't think I can yet."

"I wish you would consider it," *Mamm* said. "This would be a *gut* time to do it, with Teresa going. And I heard that Thomas is also joining. It would make both of our old days so much easier to see you settled in the faith, Susan."

"I'm sorry," Susan whispered. "But I just can't."

## Chapter Eighteen

The singing had started and James sat on the hard bench watching as the boys who were leaving for instruction class rose from their seats and followed the line of ministers upstairs. After a respectful pause the first girl got to her feet, moving with quick steps. Another girl stood to follow, and another, until four of them formed a line behind the boys.

James's head jerked sideways as the *Englisha* girl rose from the women's section, pushing through the aisle of women and babies. When she arrived at the bottom of the stairs the last girl was already halfway up. Teresa's cheeks were bright red, her eyes on the floor. So the *Englisha* girl was going to instruction class? How about that? That could only mean she really was willing to marry Yost Byler.

Teresa looked young as she dashed up the stairs after the others. James watched in horror. She obviously didn't know Amish tradition where no boy, let alone a girl *ran* up the stairs to attend instruction classes. A low gasp rippled through the women's section, as Teresa caught her shoe on the edge of the steps and ended up on her knees. Susan rose to her feet, sitting down again when Teresa continued on as if nothing had happened.

James shook his head. She had looked so helpless for a moment, her dress splayed across the steps, her hands white on the handrail. But she wasn't helpless, was she? How could she be helpless and have a baby without a husband? Girls didn't get in such situations without knowing what they were doing. And how could she be helpless and travel all the way from the *Englisha* world to the Amish community?

No one did that without courage or perhaps a great dose of stubbornness. But Teresa didn't look stubborn.

The song leader bellowed out the first syllable of the next line, and James looked down at the little black songbook he was holding. The boy seated next to him held on to his side of the page. Taking a deep breath, James joined in with the others.

His thoughts kept racing though. Why had Teresa looked so frightened at the Sunday night hymn singing when Yost had been looking at her? Hadn't she agreed to marry him? Yost was here this morning, seated in the men's section even though he was not married. That's how old the man was.

This was a puzzling situation, and it wasn't that Teresa wasn't *gut*-looking. She was quite striking, especially this morning with her cheeks flushed from the embarrassment of lagging behind the others. Why was Teresa doing this?

At this moment she was upstairs sitting on hard-backed chairs listening to the ministers reading the first two of their eighteen articles of faith. That would leave nine lessons to go and five months, followed by baptism and then marriage to Yost. That was if she went through with the plans, which from the way she bounced up from that spill on the stairs it was obvious she would.

So why did that bother him? That was the real question. James concentrated on the page in front of him. He really shouldn't be thinking these thoughts, especially about an *Englisha* girl. Why was he even admitting that Teresa was *gut*-looking? Had he no sense in his head at all? Didn't temptations come in the world's *gut*-looking packages? The preachers never grew tired warning of that danger.

Glancing up, his eye caught Eunice seated in the girls' section. She was looking at him, and smiled when she caught his eye, the contact lingering for a long moment. Now there was also a *gut*-looking girl and available to him. She'd take up his offer to drive her home in a heartbeat. Perhaps he should, he thought, letting a hint of a smile creep onto his face. Eunice brightened considerably before looking back down at her own songbook.

James kept looking at Eunice's face. There was no hint of blushing. Eunice was a confident girl. That she would consider him an option ought to be a compliment. It would be nice, wouldn't it, to have a girl like that? A girl who knew what she wanted, and who would go along for the ride. They could grow old together, never trying to get anywhere, just living a simple life.

Allowing the thought to linger, James glanced away from Eunice. His life could be like that, if he wanted it to be. Why then was he thinking about the *Englisha* girl?

In front of him in the women's section, Susan's *Mamm* got to her feet carrying Teresa's baby toward the bedroom. He was wrapped in a blue blanket; his little face turned upwards, one hand waving around as if he was trying to reach something on the ceiling.

After what seemed like a long time, but was only several songs later, the first of the returning boys appeared on the stairwell. Thomas watched as the line of identical black suits came down the stairs, followed by the girls in their plain dark dresses. Teresa brought up the rear, her face tense, almost pale, each foot seeking for the step before she took it. The others had left her several steps behind by the time they reached the bottom of the landing.

James watched her face as Teresa moved down the aisle in the women's seating, finding her empty place on the bench. Another song was given out, and she kept her eyes on the page, her lips moving. Did the girl already know how to sing German? That could hardly be possible, but she was clearly trying.

The bedroom door opened and Susan's *Mamm* came out, carrying the baby. Approaching Teresa, the baby must have caught sight of her, turning its head in her direction. A light seemed to come on in Teresa's face, moving outward from her eyes until she beamed. She reached her hands out to take the baby.

James looked away. Obviously, Teresa loved the baby, but what mother didn't? This was not unusual, and yet it was. He searched his mind for the reason, but found none. Would not any of the Amish women do the same? Yet none of them had a child outside of marriage. Was that not the difference? An illegitimate child would be an awful thing for them and scarcely endurable.

They might even reject the child. And Teresa could have done so, could she not? She was an *Englisha*, and they had their ways which an Amish girl did not have. Horrible ways of removing a child from existence before it was born, and beyond that there were easy ways of placing a child with other parents. Teresa did not need to be here, accepting this situation.

A vision of Yost Byler rose in James's mind, standing in line with the men earlier this morning, his tattered black hat pulled down over his ears, minute traces of straw clinging to the bottom of his pant legs. Teresa was willing to accept that? She was willing to marry Yost? And for what?

The answer glowed before his eyes, shining out of the joy of Teresa's face when she looked at the child. She was doing it because she loved her baby with a depth quite beyond explanation.

James drew in his breath, concentrating on the pages in front of him. A soft click of shoes on the hardwood steps above him brought the singing to an end. The ministers were filing down the stairs. When they were seated, the first speaker got to his feet and began speaking. But James was watching Teresa's face as she held the baby. One little hand was sticking out of the blue blanket, the little fingers wrapped around one of hers. A smile was spread across Teresa's face as she looked down at him, joy written on every feature of her face.

James pulled his eyes away, turning toward the preacher. But the words kept running together in his head, his mind unable to pull away from the sight he had witnessed. This was a very *gut*-hearted woman. An equal in love even to his own *mamm* and her seven children. So now the question really needed to be answered. What in the world was Teresa doing marrying Yost Byler?

Because she had sinned? *Yah*…but more than that. Because she loved her son. James stared at her, both hands clenched on the edge of the bench. Such love did not deserve to be given to Yost Byler. The man could not return that kind of love to a wife.

Moments later, the first minister concluded his remarks and knelt down to lead them in prayer. At the "amen," they got to their feet and remained standing, as Deacon Ray read the Scriptures. James kept his balance, light-headed, staring at a single spot in the floor. He should never have started wondering about this *Englisha* girl. That's what came of minding other people's business.

What if *Daett* found out about his questions, let alone his conclusions? James glanced at his *daett's* face, now studiously reading from the pages of the Bible. There would be trouble indeed, much trouble. *Daett* was behind much of the current treatment of Teresa, and if his own son came to her defense, it would be a serious matter indeed.

His sympathies would likely be viewed as rebellion at best, and falling for the forbidden things of the world at the worst. But was that true? James searched his heart. Was he falling for the allurements of the world? Daring to glance at Teresa again, he shook his head. She was *gut*-looking, but not enough to risk one's reputation over.

Out of the corner of his eye James caught Eunice watching him. Eunice's eyes were filled with questions, a slight frown on her face. James met her look, and she raised her eyebrows. Had he been found out? He smiled, and Eunice's face softened. Hopefully no one would believe her if she said that Deacon Ray's son had been looking at an *Englisha* girl that way.

But Eunice didn't seem to be suspecting anything, so he shouldn't have to worry about her. She looked away and he did likewise.

Deacon Ray finished reading and everyone sat down, the house rustling with the sound. James tried to listen to the next sermon, refusing to turn in the direction of the women's section. Eunice was still visible out of the corner of his eye, and she obviously was keeping an eye on him, her gaze coming his way every few minutes.

Well, let Eunice think what she wanted to. She had no evidence, and he had done nothing wrong. Toward the end of the sermon, when Eunice was looking away, he dared glance toward the women's benches, but Teresa was gone, the spot empty. By the time Eunice looked back, James was watching the minister who was wrapping up his sermon. Moments later he was asking for testimonies.

When those were completed the minister turned to Bishop Henry, who cleared his throat and said, "We're so grateful today that all which was spoken and heard could be declared as the Word of God. This is what all of us strive to do each day with our words and actions. Let us now be dismissed with the Lord's blessings. Church will be back here in two weeks, and we have no further announcements to make."

The smaller boys jumped to their feet, moving toward the front door as fast as possible without drawing stern looks from the men's section. James stood when his turn came, ignoring Eunice's gaze on him as he walked by her.

Outside in the barnyard Thomas sidled up to him. "Did you see Eunice making eyes at you? She could hardly look at anything else!"

James allowed a soft smile to spread across his face. "I did. But you ought to be upset, I would think. Aren't you afraid I'm stealing your girl?"

Thomas laughed. "So why don't you take her home tonight? Eunice is a sweet girl."

"So why don't you?" James shot back.

"Because I'm waiting on Susan; you know that," Thomas asserted. "I was so hoping she would come along to instruction class today, but she didn't. She's so stubborn. But not more stubborn than me. I'll wait her out if it takes years."

"How do you think Teresa did?" James asked.

Thomas raised his eyebrows. "Not bad, I would say. Your *daett* didn't bother her with any German questions."

"Maybe *Daett* wants this thing to work between her and Yost Byler," James said.

Thomas laughed. Then he stopped suddenly. "Whoa! What's this interest in the *Englisha* girl? Are you after her yourself?"

"Of course not," James said. "But it still doesn't seem right. She deserves better than Yost."

"My, my." Thomas slapped James on the back. "If I didn't know you better, I'd say you had it bad. But don't worry, Teresa will make it. I feel a little sorry for her sometimes, but what can we do about it? The important thing is that everyone's trying to find a way out of the troubles she's caused—which, I might remind you, she brought on herself. You'd be much better off taking Eunice home tonight and forgetting your troubles with her charming smiles. How about I line her up for you?"

"I don't think so." James shook his head. "I can ask my own girls home."

"There you go!" Thomas led the way toward the barn. "That's much better. Just step right up and ask her."

# Chapter Nineteen

Susan sat in the back of the buggy with Teresa and baby Samuel as the family drove home from church. *Daett* held the reins in the front seat. *Mamm* was seated beside him, the doors of the buggy open. Rattling down the dirt roads, the early spring weather poured inside the vehicle.

The baby was awake and wiggling under the blanket that was keeping him warm.

"He wants to see the nice day," Susan asserted.

"I don't want him to catch cold," Teresa said, looking down at the squirming baby. "It's nice out, but there's still a chill in the air."

"It'll do him good to get his head out," *Mamm* said, turning around to watch as Teresa cracked the blanket open. Samuel blinked his eyes and ceased his struggles.

Susan laughed and closed the buggy door on her side.

"There's no use taking chances, I guess," *Mamm* said, closing her own door.

"What's all the talking about?" *Daett* asked. "Am I also supposed to be closing my door in this nice weather?"

"Please don't," Teresa said. "I'll pull the blanket back over Samuel's head if it gets too breezy back here."

*Daett* slapped the reins, nodding his head with the bounce of the buggy.

"So how did the instruction class go today?" *Mamm* asked Teresa.

"Very good, I think," Teresa said. "The ministers were quite nice.

There were a lot of us, so I hope I blended in. That was after falling on the stairs. I'm sorry if that caused any disturbance to the church time."

"That's okay," Susan said as *Mamm* nodded in agreement. "I was going to come up and help, but you got up by yourself."

"You looked okay when you came back down," *Mamm* added.

"I can't believe I was so clumsy," Teresa said. "And on such an important day."

"Did you understand the questions the ministers asked in German about the instructions?" *Mamm* asked.

"Not all of them," Teresa said. "Oh my, I just thought of something. Is there an exam at the end of this thing?"

Susan laughed. "I don't think so. The ministers will just be interested in whether you agree with the instructions."

"I'll agree with anything," Teresa said.

Susan groaned but didn't say anything.

"You are learning your German fast enough, from what I can tell," *Mamm* offered. "I know I'm not worried. You're a smart woman."

"Too smart for Yost Byler," Susan muttered, but *Mamm* didn't act like she heard.

Teresa held her finger to her mouth. "Shh…"

Behind them the rattle of another buggy could be heard. Menno leaned forward and slapped the reins again, urging Toby on.

*Mamm* laughed as a buggy pulled out and passed them. "You look like you're standing still there, Menno."

"I'm too old for that kind of foolishness," Menno said, settling back into his seat.

"I saw you trying to speed up," *Mamm* teased. "And don't you think about buying a faster horse some week when that shifty *Englisha* horse trader comes around. You know it wouldn't work anyway. He'd sell you some horse that might have some speed but comes with a bad shying habit that'll land us all in a ditch."

"I'm leaving all that to the young boys," Menno assured her. "No more fast horses for me."

"Just keep remembering that!" *Mamm* said, pulling her bonnet strings tighter under her chin. "One never knows when wild ideas will spring into a man's head."

"Did you see who that was going around us?" Susan asked Teresa, keeping her voice low.

"No, I didn't see," Teresa said. "Who was it?"

"That was Deacon Ray's boy, James," Susan said. "He was staring at you all during church. I wonder what that is all about."

"Shh…" Teresa said again, her face growing bright red.

Susan raised her eyebrows but didn't say anything more.

*Daett* pulled back on the reins as he turned into the driveway, coming to a stop out by the barn.

Susan climbed down, taking Samuel from Teresa's arms while *Mamm* got down and helped *Daett* unhitch.

"We're going inside," Susan hollered over her shoulder, ushering Teresa ahead of her and then upstairs.

"What is going on?" Teresa asked as they entered her room. "Why the rush?"

"That look on your face, that's why the rush. Now let's get to the bottom of this, Teresa!" Susan said, laying baby Samuel on the bed. "Why is James watching you? And why did you turn red when I mentioned it? Has he spoken to you?"

"Of course not!" Teresa sounded horrified. "I wouldn't dream of such a thing. I'm an engaged woman, remember?"

"*Yah,* but that's not how it seemed today," Susan said. "Although I couldn't see your face, James couldn't stop looking in your direction. And I'm sure Eunice noticed. You should have seen the look she gave James. That's all we need—rumors floating around that you and the deacon's son are making eyes at each other. Do you know what people will say about that?"

"But I wasn't doing anything!" Teresa protested. "Believe me. And for part of the time I was in the instruction class trying to do good."

"And you said they were nice to you," Susan said. "Did anyone make trouble?"

"No. Susan, please," Teresa said, "it was fine. Even that Deacon

Ray was nice, and the bishop couldn't have been nicer. He even asked if I could understand the questions being asked about the *Ordnung*. I kind of nodded and muttered something. I'm not lying to him, but at the same time I did understand words here and there."

"Understanding German is not the problem, Teresa," Susan said. "Making eyes at an Amish man is. If anyone notices, they will descend upon your head with a fury like you have never known."

"Is everything okay up there?" *Mamm*'s voice came from the bottom of the stairs.

"*Yah*," Susan replied, getting up and closing the bedroom door. Below them the stair door also clicked shut.

"So you think I'm up to my old ways?" Teresa accused, sitting down on the bed. "You think I'm trying to lure men in?"

"Look, Teresa." Susan took both of her hands. "I don't think that, and no one thinks like that around here. It's different than it is out in your world. Here we're thinking about marriage, about children, and about what is the right thing to do. Do you understand what I'm saying?"

Teresa answered, "*Yah*, I do and I also understand who I am and what is to become of me. For a few moments, yes, it was delicious to think otherwise. But how can I undo the life I have lived? I know I deserve Yost Byler. I deserve everything about him. In fact, I know that it's right that I should be thankful he even deems me worthy of his attention. That's the real me, Susan. Have I made that plain enough for you to understand?"

"Oh, Teresa..." Susan sat down on the bed again. "I'm sorry. This situation is really horrible. I know you're not the kind of person who would try to lure a man. You're very wonderful, and sweet, and beautiful. You deserve a good husband. And that's what makes it even more difficult."

"In my dreams, I do," Teresa said. "But I know what is real, and this is what is real, Susan: Yost Byler. Not that young man who was looking at me today. So you don't have to worry about him and me."

"Sometimes I think you should go back to your own world and

find yourself the kind of husband you deserve," Susan moaned. "There has to be one out there, Teresa."

"Susan, you still don't understand yet? Not after all this time? I *can't* go back. My life was awful and growing worse. Even Mom couldn't have saved me from it. If I went back, in no time at all I'd be just another sad statistic in the newspaper. And someday so would Samuel. That's not going to happen to us! It just isn't!"

Susan sighed. "There has to be some way out of this mess, but I have racked my brain and haven't found one."

"Come, come," Teresa said. "Don't worry your head about it. I'm going to be fine."

"I hope so. I pray so. But please know that one of these Saturday nights Yost will come by now that you're attending the instruction classes. And if for any reason you want to call this whole thing off, I'll take you to the bus station and buy you a ticket to Asbury Park. I'll write a letter to Laura, and I'm sure she'll take you in. I might even go with you!"

"You are very sweet," Teresa said, a tear running down her cheek. "All of you are, but I'm not turning back. I know where my place is, and I know what's good for Samuel."

"Then I'll come with you to clean that old bachelor house of Yost's," Susan declared. "I can do no less, even if it stinks to high heaven in there. And it probably does!"

Teresa relaxed and smiled. "Aren't you thinking a little far ahead? I just had my first instruction class."

"Your wedding will come before you know it," Susan said. "And keeping that man's house will take all the help you can get."

Below them they heard the sound of the stair door opening again.

"I have popcorn made!" *Mamm* hollered up. "Come get some if you want."

"I don't feel like eating popcorn right now," Susan said.

"Come!" Teresa picked up Samuel. "I think popcorn would cheer us all up. Now wouldn't it, little man?" she said as she smiled at her son.

Baby Samuel wrinkled his face into a broad smile.

"He's such a little darling," Susan commented. "Maybe even I would marry Yost Byler if Samuel were my child and needed saving."

"You know you would," Teresa said, holding Samuel against her shoulder. "*Your* sweetheart was in class today. Are you sure you don't want to join us? I really don't see why you're holding back."

"Well," Susan said, "you do make my troubles seem kind of small."

"I wouldn't say that," Teresa said, opening the bedroom door. "Just different, that's all."

Susan said nothing as she followed Teresa down the stairs. In the living room *Mamm* had bowls of white fluffy popcorn sitting by the couch, along with two glasses of orange juice.

"I'm going to be spoiled and pampered yet!" Teresa said, seeing the bowl and drink set aside for her.

"I doubt that," *Mamm* said with a laugh. "Sit down and eat while the popcorn is still warm."

"Teresa and I are not going to the hymn singing tonight. Or to the youth supper," Susan said.

"Why not?" *Mamm* looked up in surprise.

"Too many things going on." Susan shrugged and looked away.

"Teresa, do you want to stay home?" *Mamm* asked as she glanced over at her guest.

"I think so," Teresa said after a moment's thought. "Susan is right. It's been a little stressful today with the class and my falling on the stairs and all."

"You're not changing your mind, are you, Teresa?" *Mamm* asked.

"I'm not changing my mind about anything," Teresa said. "I'm not even thinking about changing my mind." She shot a glance at Susan.

# CHAPTER TWENTY

Three weeks later on a Saturday evening, Yost Byler drove south along the gravel roads, allowing his horse to take its time. At each stop sign the horse lingered, hanging its head before Yost slapped the reins again. What was it going to be like, he wondered, to actually speak to the *Englisha* girl? Not that Teresa was *Englisha* anymore. She had been through two instruction classes now, and looked very Amish in the dresses Susan and Anna made for her.

Still, she was an *Englisha* girl. And with that knowledge came fears, even though he was determined to marry her. What if after the vows were said she decided to up and leave him like many of the *Englisha* women left their husbands? There could even be children by then, many of them, since he was an old man and she was a young woman. He would lose them all besides losing his wife. Didn't *Englisha* women always take the children with them when they left home?

Yost combed his beard with his fingers, holding the reins with the other hand. Well…things didn't look too comforting, but neither did his present state. Marriage to an Amish girl wasn't going to happen, so he might as well take this chance. And Teresa was *gut*-looking, much too *gut*-looking for him, but that could not be helped. He would have to be thankful for what *Da Hah* had sent him.

Yost combed his beard again. Teresa was still a little skinny. No doubt she was hanging on to some of her *Englisha* eating habits. But this was nothing that good Amish cooking and a couple of children couldn't take care of. That was, if Teresa could cook.

His fingers stopped combing his beard. Surely Anna and Susan would be teaching the *Englisha* girl the ways of the community? A wife who couldn't cook would be too awful to even think about. His hands grew cold at the very thought.

And what about how young Teresa was? Teresa would be bearing children for many years. Would it be wise to have a wife who was still bearing children when he could no longer farm the land? They would starve once he could no longer work. Yost pushed the thoughts away and slapped the reins. These were things *Da Hah* would have to take care of. He was going to marry the girl.

Ahead of him, Menno and Anna's farm came into view. No one knew he was coming, but they surely expected him. It was, after all, Saturday evening, and the time for these things. Work would be slowing down on the farm in preparation for tomorrow's day of rest. Teresa would have time to speak with him.

He should have waited longer perhaps, but there were many things to speak of with their wedding coming up so quickly. He drew his breath in. How fast *Da Hah* worked once His will was understood. Yost really had nothing to offer but thanks even with his many fears. Turning into the Hostetler driveway, he pulled up to the hitching post and climbed down.

It would not be wise to unhitch, Yost decided. That could look like he wanted to stay for supper—which he did—but one didn't go asking for an invitation. This was his first visit, and he hardly knew the *Englisha* girl. He should not be staying long. Taking the rope out from under the seat, he tied the horse to the wooden crossbar.

The washroom door behind him opened, and Yost nearly lost his hat turning around. Menno was walking across the yard toward him, a slight smile on his face.

"*Gut* evening," Menno greeted him.

"*Gut* evening," Yost said. "Nice weather tonight."

"*Yah*," Menno said. "And if it holds, I ought to get my plowing done this week."

Yost looked around, "Are you still taking care of the farm on your own?"

Menno laughed. "I'm afraid so. I've been waiting on Susan and Thomas…but you know how young people are these days. They can't make up their minds. In our day and time we would have had the vows said a long time ago."

Yost cleared his throat, his mind on other things than Menno and his trouble with Susan. "Is the *Englisha* girl available to speak to? I was thinking it is time she and I spoke with each other."

"I don't suppose Deacon Ray would have any objections, what with her attending instruction classes," Menno said.

"Has the girl been speaking of doubts?" Alarm flashed across Yost's face.

"No doubts," Menno said shaking his head. "Teresa seems to have fully made up her mind. I must say you will be getting a *gut* wife. The girl is learning our ways rather quickly."

"Has she been…learning to cook?" Yost asked, staring at Menno's face.

"I can't say that I've been keeping track," Menno chuckled. "But she spends time in the kitchen with Susan and Anna. I suppose she's helping cook. You wouldn't be worried, now would you?"

Yost swallowed hard. "I was just thinking, that's all."

"She couldn't do worse than your own, now could she?" Menno teased.

"I guess not," Yost agreed. "But she is an *Englisha* girl."

"I wouldn't worry about Teresa," Menno said, slapping Yost on the shoulder. "But why am I jabbering with you? I'm sure Teresa will come out if you take a seat on the swing over there."

"I'll do that," Yost said, watching Menno's back as he went inside. Yost walked up to the porch. The swing creaked as he placed his weight on it, holding the seat steady with his feet.

Yost turned to look across Menno's open fields. Happy thoughts ran through his mind. With his marriage to Teresa, he would fatten up in the years ahead until these porch springs not only squeaked but groaned when he sat down. Wasn't that what happened to married men? With even half decent cooking around it would also happen to him. He would grow old with his middle swelling from added pounds.

There would be cherry and apple pies. Perhaps the *Englisha* girl could even learn how to make shoofly pie. Although that could be expecting a lot. Fresh bread on Saturdays would be enough to be thankful for. Of course all of this would cost more in groceries. He would have to work the farm a little harder, but it would be worth every effort. Perhaps the back field could be plowed this spring yet, and a large garden begun. Yost smiled, looking out across Menno's fields.

"Good evening," Teresa's voice said behind him, and Yost jumped to his feet.

"*Gut* evening," he said, extending his hand.

What else was there to do, he wondered. How did one greet an *Englisha* girl, especially one that was to be your *frau*?

"I'm glad you came to visit." Teresa shook his hand.

Her touch was soft. That wasn't *gut*. Amish women's hands were toughened by hard work. But perhaps he was jumping to conclusions too quickly. Teresa hadn't been in the community long, and might not have had time to show the effects of her hard work.

"I thought it was time we spoke," Yost said, sitting down again. She lowered herself onto the swing beside him.

"Was it a nice drive down in your buggy?" Teresa asked, with a warm smile. "It's been beautiful weather all week."

"*Yah*, it has." Yost cleared his throat. "It makes for good working conditions in the fields."

"Where is your farm located?" Teresa asked. "Susan said it was north of here."

"It's on the edge of the community," he said. "Land is cheaper up there, but not by much. I hope it's not someplace you don't wish to live. I mean, our people like to live close by each other."

Teresa's cheeks blushed, but Yost didn't take his eyes off of her face. This was an important question, he figured. But surely Teresa wouldn't be putting on airs, wanting to live in a more convenient place?

"It doesn't matter where I live, Yost," Teresa said smiling again. "Just as long as it's part of the community."

"Oh it is," Yost said. "It's only a little inconvenient."

"I'm used to inconvenient," Teresa said. "Were you born here in the community?"

"*Yah*," Yost said, leaning back on the swing. "*Mamm* and *Daett* used to live here, but they have moved away to a community in Iowa. I decided to stay. Most of my brothers and sisters also have stayed. I guess we like it around here."

"I'll have to meet your family sometime," Teresa said giving him a quick sideways glance.

Yost smiled. The girl was definitely on the right track with things. She already wished to meet his family.

"We have our reunions once in a while," he said. "And there's Sundays of course. At the church services."

"Perhaps Susan can point them out sometime," she said.

Silence settled on them, broken only by the soft squeak of the swing. It was time they got down to talking about what was most important. Yost cleared his throat.

"I hope you understand about you and me—how this arrangement came to be," he said. "I know that you are an *Englisha* girl, and that your people do things differently. So perhaps I should ask you to marry me like they might do it."

"It is a little different around here," Teresa said, not looking at him.

"Are you willing then to *wed* me on the day of your baptism?" he asked. "I know Menno has already asked you, and that is *gut* enough for me—if you don't wish to answer."

Teresa sat unmoving, her hands clasped in her lap. "Is this how your people ask each other to wed?"

"I don't know," he said. "I have never asked a woman to wed me."

"I see." She raised her eyes to his face. "And are you asking me now, even when I have already given my answer?"

"*Yah,* I thought this might make it easier for you," he said.

"Perhaps if we should speak of this to each other, instead of through others."

"It would be best if we didn't do things through others anymore," Teresa agreed. "And I am agreeing to wed you on my baptismal day."

Yost stared off across the plowed fields, his eyes taking in each clod of turned dirt, lingering on the rich darkness of *Da Hah's* great creation. This was so much easier than he had ever imagined. All that work he had put into traveling to other communities. All that work trying to get widows and old maids to allow him to take them home from the hymn singing. Now here was an *Englisha* girl, agreeing to be his *frau* the first time he spoke with her. Surely *Da Hah's* compassion had finally reached him.

"There is only one requirement that I have," Teresa said, her voice jerking him out of his thoughts.

"*Yah*, what is that?" he asked.

"That you must accept my son, Samuel, as your own," she said. "That you raise him as an Amish boy and give him your name. I don't know how such things are done, but I've been here long enough to know that a strange name among the Amish will raise questions. I want him growing up without any doubt in people's minds as to who his father is."

Yost didn't think long.

"*Yah*, that is possible," he said. "I have no objections to such a request."

"Even with what you know about me?" she asked. "That I have been with a man, and borne a child by him? This does not bother you?"

Why did the *Englisha* girl have to speak so plainly? Already there was red creeping up his neck at such open thoughts, but she was to be his *frau* and likely she didn't know any better.

"I have accepted the will of *Da Hah*," he said after a few seconds. "If Deacon Ray and Bishop Henry approve of your baptism, then I will also agree. None of us are without sin, and *Da Hah* is always merciful."

She nodded. "I wished to hear the words from you. Remember, we are not to speak through others anymore."

"Samuel will not be a problem," he said. "You will have been baptized by then, and both of you will be a part of the community."

"It is good to hear you say these things," she said. "For a long time I've dreamed of living among your people, of finding peace among them. But I never dared think I could be a part myself. I thought my son could, but not me. That seemed too high a thing to even pray for, yet it is happening. I can't tell you how happy I am, Yost. To think that someone like me, with my life so messed up, could turn around and start fresh again, is a very wonderful thing. I know you may not understand all of that, but I thank you for listening. And I will try to be the best Amish wife for you that I can be."

Yost nodded, still looking across the fields. She spoke tender words but he wished to know about something else.

"Can you cook?" he asked

Teresa laughed. "What? Do you think I'm going to kill you?"

"*Nee*," he said, a slight smile crossing his face. "I was just hoping Susan and Anna were teaching you our ways."

"They are, believe me," she said. "I'm even learning how to bake bread. Now how strange is that? I'm a city girl, and here I am with my hands up to the elbows in bread dough."

A pleased smile spread across his face.

"But I don't see that you're eating that well by yourself," Teresa said. "So I don't think I'll make things any worse."

"I don't think you will either," he said, getting to his feet. "Well, I really should be going. I have kept you long enough, but I need to ask you before I go, is it okay if I visit again sometime soon?"

Teresa nodded. "Or we could visit your place," she said. "Susan could drive me up."

"That would be *gut*," he agreed. "Either way. Perhaps Menno could tell me on the Sunday before this visit would happen. And I will return when I think it wise."

"I will do that," Teresa said, as he turned to walk across the yard.

Reaching the buggy he untied his horse and climbed in, giving a little wave of his hand as he passed her standing on the front porch. There was no question about it. The *Englisha* girl would make him a very *gut* wife. Anna and Susan were teaching her the ways of the people.

# CHAPTER TWENTY-ONE

S usan paced the floor in her bedroom, pausing every few minutes to look out the window. When was that awful man leaving? And to think that Teresa was down there making her wedding plans with him. It was all too much to even think about. How had things ever come to such a state? It really was her own fault for ever agreeing to bring Teresa home.

Yet how convincing Teresa's passion had been. First for her unborn child—wanting to see him raised so as to avoid the kind of life she had. And then Teresa's own desire to be a part of her Amish dreamworld. Well, Teresa's dreamworld had turned into Yost Byler rattling out of the driveway at the moment. Susan raced to the window to watch Yost leave, seeing him give a little wave of his hand just before he turned north.

So much for any hopes that his deal with Teresa had fallen apart. The man looked quite pleased with himself, and he should be. Teresa was way too *gut* a woman for him. No doubt Teresa had given Yost her word to wed him even after James had been making eyes at her again on Sunday. Oh sure, James was being much more careful than he had been that first Sunday, but his attention certainly often wandered in Teresa's direction.

Clearly Teresa had found James's attention attractive, and just as clearly she was ignoring him. At least on the surface. Susan stepped away from the window, frowning. Regardless of how exciting the thought might be, Teresa and James speaking of love with each other would have the whole community in an uproar.

Perhaps Teresa was as confused as she was? Maybe she should show Teresa the letter from Robby which came last week, and speak plainly about what the options were.

Susan was willing to return to Asbury Park with Teresa, after speaking with *Mamm* and *Daett*, of course. They would be heartbroken, but she had to make her own choices in life. And watching Teresa accept this impossible arrangement was not pulling her heart closer to her home and people. In fact, it was driving her heart farther away.

Going down the stairs, Susan entered the living room where her *mamm* and *daett* were seated.

"Is Teresa still outside?" Susan asked.

"*Yah*," Mamm said. "On the porch swing."

"It's best that we not think too much about this," *Daett* said. "There is really no other way if Teresa wishes to remain in the community."

"I know that," Susan said. But she went to the door and stepped outside.

Teresa looked up as Susan approached, a weak smile flitting across her face. "Hi," Teresa greeted.

"I see he's left," Susan said shortly as she sat down beside her. "Is the big event still on?"

"Don't be mean to me," Teresa said as a tear slid down her cheek. "This is hard enough already."

"Then why didn't you just tell Yost to leave?" Susan asked. "You know I would have supported you."

"You know why," Teresa said. "And he wasn't as bad as I thought he would be. He's really a nice man on the inside. It's just that no one has been taking care of him for all these years."

"*Yah*, years is right!" Susan snapped. "He's old enough to be your *daett*. Well, almost."

"Please don't make me feel worse than I already do," Teresa said.

"Then what about plan B since plan A—sending the man home on his own—doesn't seem to be working?" Susan asked, pulling the letter from Robby out of her dress pocket and waving it with a flourish.

"A letter? Who is it from?" Teresa stared at the envelope.

"Mr. Robby himself," Susan said. "Laura's son," she reminded. "Shall I read it to you? It confirms everything I've been telling you."

"Where did you get that letter?" Teresa whispered. "I've been here every day, and you didn't get anything like that."

"I stuck it in my pocket when I picked up the mail one day last week," Susan said. "No one else knows anything about it."

"You hide things from your family—from your mom?" Teresa asked in horror.

"Well, maybe I shouldn't," Susan admitted. "But why worry *Mamm* with this yet? Robby just wrote a nice letter, and I've already answered with a breezy, newsy letter in return. He only wants to know how we're doing, and he tells us we both are welcome back anytime. So shall I read it to you or not?"

"It won't make any difference." Teresa's voice was low and hard.

"Okay, I won't read it then," Susan threatened.

"Please read it!" Teresa whispered.

Susan smiled and pulled the white paper out of the envelope and unfolded it:

> *Dear Susan,*
>
> *This is old Robby. Remember? The long-haired, godless fellow. Your sort of adopted brother. I know I'm not Amish and all, but we did seem to hit it off pretty well while you were here. And you do owe me for all the time I invested in carting you around town. But fear not! I am not collecting on the debt. We shall leave that for another day.*
>
> *Mom says hi since she knows I'm writing. I had to ask her for your address.*
>
> *The tourists are starting to trickle back to Asbury Park with the nice weather we're having. I haven't been out on the ocean since the night I took you out. That was a grand time—if you remember, but perhaps you've already forgotten with all that's going on upon your return to your hometown.*

*Please tell your old beau hi for me. I'm sure you've patched up
the fence with him by now. With your indomitable spirit and
sweet charm, I'm sure you have him licking the salt block and
then some. A little farm lingo there, although I hope he is not
quite on a level with the cows. That, of course, more for your
sake than his. But I am being mean. I'm sure anyone you consider for marriage is well worth your attention.*

*I think all your advice has finally borne fruit. I have a girl
now. Mom is charmed with her, so that helps. She's the sweet
girl from church I told you about before you left. I've mended
my fences with her, so to speak, and with the church. The
broken fence seemed to be mostly on my side of the property.
Mom couldn't be more pleased on both fronts, and I think she
gives you a lot of credit. Which you fully deserve, I must say.*

*Anyway, I thought I would write and let you know how
things are going. Yes, I am a little lonesome. It would be great
to see you again, so stop by sometime. Like that would be possible, I know, but just sayin'. Our house is always open, and
for Teresa also, if things get too rough for her there. I can't
imagine you not taking good care of her, but things do happen sometimes.*

*Yours truly,*
*Robby*

Susan folded the paper and slipped it back inside the envelope.

"I wish I were taking better care of you, Teresa," Susan said. "But
I'm afraid things have gotten a little out of control. Don't you think
it's time we go back? I'll go with you, and Laura will put us both up
until you can get on your feet."

"You don't know what you're asking," Teresa said. "I wish you'd
quit thinking about going back. I can't go back there! Not under *any*
circumstance. And I'm certainly not taking Samuel back."

"Laura would help you get away from the life you used to know,"
Susan countered.

"Stop thinking about such things, Susan!" Teresa grabbed her friend's hand. "Look what you have here. Your mom and dad love you. You're surrounded by a whole community who loves you. There is a nice boy just waiting to drive you home on Sunday nights. There is no way you're giving that all up for me."

"It wouldn't be just for you," Susan said. "I don't think I like what's going on around here."

"They are treating me the best way they know how," Teresa said. "I mean, what would you do with someone like me? A woman who has a baby but no husband."

"I wouldn't make you marry Yost Byler, that's for sure," Susan promised.

"But he's not a bad man," Teresa said. "And no one is making me do anything. I *want* to marry him."

"James was watching you on Sunday again. I saw him," Susan pointed out. "And you noticed. I know you did."

"I'm not good enough for that man," Teresa whispered. "And you yourself said it would be a disaster."

"Oh, yes you are," Susan insisted. "And if you're going to stay, I think I'm changing my mind about something. I think you should at least consider that option. Even with all the trouble it would cause. *Let* there be trouble. There already is plenty anyway."

Teresa turned toward Susan. "You've always had your head in the clouds," she said. "I've had mine in the gutter, Susan. And Yost Byler is a whole lot better than what I've seen. He's all I can ask for, Susan. Please don't go making trouble for me."

"Is this all your heart is asking for?" Susan asked.

"Susan! Please don't ask such awful things. Following my heart is the reason Samuel was born. Look what it's costing me to straighten out that problem."

"Samuel isn't a problem," Susan said.

"Of course he's not!" Teresa said. "*I'm* the problem. And I wish you wouldn't try to push me into things I shouldn't be doing. It's hard enough already. Believe me." Teresa turned away, and the swing rocked under them as their feet dragged lightly on the porch floor.

Finally Susan reached over and wrapped an arm around Teresa's shoulder, pulling her close. "I'm sorry," Susan whispered. "I shouldn't be speaking to you this way. I should be more supportive. Shall we go inside now? It's getting cold out here."

Teresa nodded as she got to her feet. They entered the house, and *Mamm* jumped up to offer Teresa the couch.

"I think we'd better eat supper," Susan said. "Teresa must be starving after that visit."

"Was it bad?" *Mamm* asked, looking concerned.

"He *is* a nice man," Teresa said. "He's much nicer even than I was expecting."

"Well, I'm glad to hear that," *Mamm* said. "Come, sit at the table while Susan and I get supper ready."

Teresa followed them into the kitchen but didn't sit down. "I think I should help," she said. "It sounds like I need to learn all I can, and as quickly as I can. Yost is worried I don't know how to cook."

"The nerve of the man!" *Mamm* said, waving her hand toward the kitchen chair. "I don't care what Yost wants, you're going to sit down. I can see clearly he has worn you out with his questions. No doubt he wants to know if we've been teaching you how to bake bread and wash clothing."

"Something like that," Teresa admitted. "I reassured him, but I'm not sure how much he believed me."

"I wouldn't worry about him," *Mamm* said. "Yost will be happy enough with whatever food you make. I can't imagine he's getting much right now anyway."

"I told him that," Teresa said, a smile playing on her face. "I don't think he cared much for the remark, although he agreed."

"Men!" Susan exclaimed, wringing out the washcloth until her fingers turned white. "I would think Yost ought to be grateful instead of worrying about what kind of food he will be getting out of the deal."

"He's probably worried I might starve him or poison him with *Englisha* food," Teresa offered.

"It's more like he thinks you don't know how to cook," Susan said. "He's thinking about microwaves and restaurants. He probably thinks that's all *Englisha* women know how to do."

A smile crossed Teresa's face.

"I can't imagine Yost in a restaurant," she said. "He'd pass out from astonishment."

"He's certainly no Mr. Moran and his fancy Italian restaurant," Susan said absently. She paused suddenly, realizing what she'd said. She noticed *Mamm* staring at her from beside the counter.

"I went to a nice restaurant with Duane Moran," Susan reminded. "I already told you about him, so it's not something you didn't know."

*Mamm* looked away but remained where she was. "I wonder sometimes how much of the *Englisha* world is still in your heart, Susan," *Mamm* finally said. "You know how dangerous that life can be. Little things get hold of a person. And now you won't even join the instruction class. Why don't you go to Deacon Ray and tell him you still want to join this spring? You could finish with Teresa and Thomas and be baptized this fall. It would be a comfort to our hearts to see that you have really left the world behind, Susan."

"*Mamm*," Susan reminded, "the instruction class has started already."

"Bishop Henry will understand and make room for you," *Mamm* insisted.

Susan shook her head, continuing to clean the tabletop.

Teresa cleared her throat. "Yost wants to know if Susan can come with me sometime for a visit to his place," she said, obviously wanting to change the subject. "Do you think that would be okay?"

"I don't know why not," *Mamm* said.

Teresa jumped to her feet right after a cry from Samuel came from upstairs. "I'll go get him," Teresa said, "and then I'm going to help with supper."

"Susan, I wish you'd try as hard as Teresa is," *Mamm* said after Teresa disappeared upstairs.

"I see things differently than she does," Susan said. "And there's nothing to be done about that."

## Chapter Twenty-two

$\maltese$

James sat on the front row, keeping his eyes on the songbook as the sound of the young people's voices filled the living room. Supper had been over for an hour, and the sun outside the living room windows had sunk below the horizon. Above his head two gas lanterns gave out warm light, along with two more hung further back. Emory Yoder believed in having plenty of light when the young people had the Sunday night hymn singing at his house. Perhaps he thought this would hold back the darkness that threatened their young hearts

James turned to look at Teresa again. He shouldn't be looking, but he couldn't seem to keep his eyes away from her. *Yah*, Teresa might be an *Englisha* girl from birth, but right now her face had joy written all over it as she followed along with the German words. There was no way she could be understanding all of them, but she was clearly enjoying the effort.

Teresa glanced up from the songbook page, meeting his eyes, and the joy disappeared, replaced by a look of fear. She turned away, streaks of red spreading up her neck to where the strands of hair hung out from under her white *kapp*.

Why did he keep disturbing the girl, James asked himself. Was his heart flirting with darkness? James looked back to the songbook page. Everyone knew the *Englisha* girl was promised to Yost Byler, and should be off-limits to any other boy's attention. Why then could he not stop looking at her?

It had to be more than her face. There were Amish girls he knew who were better-looking. Even Eunice would pass that test—if good looks were what he wanted. But it was more than good looks that was drawing him to Teresa. It was the softness and tenderness of her heart which seemed to shine through her face in moments when she didn't know anyone was watching. He had noticed this on the first Sunday she had attended the instruction classes. Teresa couldn't possibly know what her face was showing, and that made it even more *vundahboah*. Yost Byler certainly didn't deserve a wife this *gut*.

Glancing at Teresa out of the corner of his eye, James felt the boy beside him nudge his ribs.

"You can ask her home," the whisper came, delivered with a slight smile. "She's available."

James kept his head still, his heart pounding. Obviously the boy thought he had been looking at Eunice. If he knew the truth there would have been no smile in the teasing.

"I don't want to," James whispered back, and the boy's smile got broader. Clearly he was not believing the story.

This whole situation was becoming intolerable. Should he speak to his *daett* about this? *Nee*, that wouldn't do any good. But then what was he to do? Speak to Teresa? That was even more out of the question…or was it? His head ached with the thinking. What could the preachers possibly do to him? There would be some fuss, that was for sure. His *daett* after all was the deacon.

James blinked hard, trying to clear his mind. Why did Teresa have to marry Yost Byler once she was baptized? The answer was obvious of course—no one trusted her, but they were wrong. Clearly wrong, and things needed to change. Could he be the one to change them? He was Deacon Ray's son, though. That made it all the harder.

Yet Yost and Teresa's wedding day was coming up before long. And it would simply be awful to stand by and watch Yost Byler taking the vows with Teresa. And all the while Teresa would have that deep tenderness shining out of her eyes, mixed in with fear and trust. There might even be tears. He doubted he could bear to see that.

*Nee*…this couldn't be allowed to continue. He had to speak with

Teresa. He had to tell her she had other options. That he would be willing to consider a courtship with her. Because he was willing, wasn't he?

The question stared him in his face. *Was* he willing? Was he willing to say the vows with an *Englisha* girl? Vows from which there could never be any going back? What if she left him after the wedding? What if she became tired of being Amish and longed for the worldly things she had left behind? That was possible was it not?

James looked at Teresa's face again, and she raised her eyes as if she knew he was looking, meeting his gaze without blushing. There was sorrow written in them, and deep, deep pain. James tried to smile, the effort failing, and she lowered her eyes to the page on the songbook.

Beside him the boy's elbow dug into James's ribs again and he jumped. This had to stop somewhere, he told himself, but what was he to do now? Did all these questions about Teresa have to be decided tonight? Maybe he was taking things in giant steps instead of in the order in which they should be taken. He was thinking of marriage, and she might not even wish to be his girlfriend, let alone his wife. He could speak with her about Yost, and they could always part as friends if nothing else. Like some of the other Amish girls he had dated. But she should at least be given the option. That was the important point.

"I can ask her for you," the boy next to him whispered close to his ear. "That is, if you're scared."

James shook his head, forcing a smile. Behind them someone hollered out the last song number of the evening, an *Englisha* song they all knew by heart: "God Be with You Till We Meet Again." Concentrating, James sang along, keeping his eyes away from the bench full of girls.

Low chatter filled the room as the young people talked with each other. Every once in a while the conversation reached across the space between the boys and girls, but James didn't join in. The steadies soon left, the boy leaving first, followed closely by his girlfriend a few moments later.

James waited until Susan and Teresa rose and walked out to the washroom. Slipping outside, he went to the barn. He found Susan's horse in the second stall and led it outside.

"Oh, it's you, James," Susan said, meeting him at the buggy. Teresa hung back in the shadows. "I was hoping some kind soul would bring Toby out for us."

"You wouldn't expect us to leave two lovely girls to hitch their own horse," he joked.

Susan laughed, the sound ringing in the night air, but Teresa moved deeper into the shadows and around to the other side of the buggy.

"Susan, um, I need to speak with Teresa," James whispered, motioning toward her with the rim of his hat.

"With Teresa?" Susan questioned.

"*Yah*, but don't make a racket about it," he said. "I wish to speak with her in private. Here, hold the horse for a moment, please."

"She doesn't wish to speak with you," Susan said. "And you're not allowed to anyway. It will make all kinds of trouble."

"I don't think you want this thing with Yost Byler to go forward either, now do you?" he shot at her.

"No, I don't," she snapped. "But this isn't the best way to handle the problem. You can't just go and talk with her. You can talk with your *daett* if you really care. That might do more good."

"I just might do that," he said. "But first I wish to speak with her."

"You're not going to unless Teresa agrees—and she won't," Susan retorted.

"Would you speak more quietly?" he asked. "Someone will hear you! Of course I won't talk with her if she doesn't want to. But I'm going to find out from her, not from you. So hold the reins while I do that."

"What's going on?" Teresa asked, her voice coming from the edge of the darkness.

"I would like to speak with you in private," James said, trying to see her face in the dark.

"You don't want to talk to him," Susan asserted. "I know what I'm saying, James."

"I think I'd better," Teresa said. "Have we got time?"

"Well, make it quick then!" Susan said. "You can't be seen with him for very long."

"Come," James said, stepping behind the buggy.

Teresa's face still wasn't visible, and he didn't dare take her hand. Hopefully she could see well enough to follow. He kept walking until he reached the wooden fence that separated the barnyard from the field where the rows of buggies were parked. He heard soft treads behind him, and then saw her body take shape beside him in the dim lantern light coming from the house.

"I'm sorry if this is inappropriate," he said. "But I simply have to speak with you. First of all, my name is James."

"I know," Teresa said. "You'd better tell me what you want to say. Susan is waiting."

"Susan can wait," he muttered. "It may be hard for me to get a second chance to speak with you, so I plan to take my time."

"Why are you watching me all the time?" Teresa asked.

"Because I care about you," he admitted. "And especially about this Yost Byler situation."

Teresa stumbled over her words. "Thank you, James. But I'm a young, unwed woman with a child. Your people are doing the best they can for me."

"I don't think I agree with that," he responded.

"I think it's nice that you have a soft spot in your heart for the poor *Englisha* woman who plans to marry Yost Byler. But there's nothing that can be done. This is what's best and what I deserve."

He didn't say anything for a long time. "You aren't who they think you are, Teresa," he finally said.

Teresa wouldn't look at him. "I...I...really should go," she said. "Talking to me will only cause trouble for you. I don't want that. And it could mean worse trouble for me. They might not allow me to join the community. Your father wouldn't allow it. And the ministers and

Menno and Anna support the arrangement with Yost. It's the only way for me to stay, James."

"But you deserve better than Yost Byler!" he protested.

"Why don't you tell me how else it might be done?" she said. "You're Amish. You know the rules better than I do. You know how the ministers—and your dad—feel."

He fell into silence again.

She moved closer to him.

"Is it really that important to you?" he asked. "That you join the community? Is it because of your son?" He searched for her face in the darkness, and this time she turned her head toward him, the light from the house playing on her damp cheeks.

"I would do anything for Samuel," she said, her voice choking.

"Is it that bad out there, out in the world?" he asked. "Bad enough to marry Yost Byler so you can stay here?"

She was silent for a few seconds before saying, "Yes."

"I'm sorry it's so hard for you," he said, his hand touching his hat. "I only wanted to know for sure. I've thought about this...about some things. There is another way out, Teresa. I am willing to help you."

"I thank you for the thoughts and effort, but there really is nothing you can do."

James looked at the moon and then turned his gaze back to Teresa. He looked directly into her eyes. "I am willing to take you home on Sunday nights—to be your boyfriend, to be whatever you call it in the *Englisha* world. Then once you are baptized, you can do as you wish."

"You would play with my heart, James?" Teresa responded. "You would deceive the ministers with such a trick?"

"*Nee*, Teresa," he protested. "I play with no one's heart. But neither do I ask for promises from girls who say they have no choices."

Teresa gathered herself. "I can't do it. That's all there is to it. There would only be trouble, and I cannot have more trouble."

"Hey!" He laughed, trying to lighten the mood. "Things get a little boring around here anyway, so what's wrong with a little excitement? I can handle it."

"Perhaps you can, but I can't," she said, turning to go. "I have my son to think about. I won't forget your kindness though."

"Teresa!" he exclaimed, but she was already on her way back to the buggy.

He leaned against the wooden fence, resting his full weight on the top rail. *Well, that went really well*, he told himself. *What a tumble fingers I am with girls. I can't do anything right.*

## Chapter Twenty-three

Susan followed the line of buggies out to the main road, her hands clinging to the reins as she held Toby back. Just shy of the turn, he reared. In the darkness of the buggy, Teresa clutched her shawl and sobbed.

"What a nasty boy!" Susan stated. "I think our men are nothing but a big, grand mess. The nerve of him! I'm sure several boys walking past saw him talking with you."

"James didn't do anything wrong," Teresa defended, sniffling. "He was trying to help. And I'm sorry if you think I was out of line, but I needed to hear what he had to say and make myself clear to him."

"And are things clear now?" Susan asked.

"I'm afraid not," Teresa said, starting to sob again. "It's a lot worse than I imagined."

"What did James say?" Susan asked. "Will you tell me or do I have to go back and ask him myself?"

"That's the last thing I want to talk about right now," Teresa said. "I want to forget all about it. I know now I should have listened to you and never even looked at him."

"If you don't tell me," Susan warned, "I really am going back to ask James."

"He offered to see me, to take me home on Sunday nights,"

she whispered. "That's what he said. James said I didn't have to go through with the marriage to Yost."

"Like he's going to prevent it?" Susan snapped. "So did his *daett* okay this little scheme of his?"

"I asked him the same thing—or something like it," Teresa said. "He didn't say anything."

"That takes the cake and the frosting," Susan said. "I can't believe this. So James is attracted to you, and you obviously are to him or you wouldn't have gone to speak with him. I sure hope you didn't give James encouragement."

"None at all," Teresa said, a catch in her voice.

Susan made the next turn, leaving the last buggy behind them. Toby slowed down. Taking both reins in one hand, she wrapped her arm around Teresa's shoulder. "I'm so sorry. I don't know what to say. I'm mad at James, at his *daett*, at my *mamm* and *daett*, at the situation. But what *gut* does getting angry do?"

Teresa wiped her eyes. "It's my own fault that I'm attracted to him, Susan. You know that's the real problem. James is only feeling sorry for me."

"Well, I don't blame you," Susan said. "Not that I find him attractive. But anything would be better than Yost Byler. But you do know we have to tell *Mamm* and *Daett* about your conversation."

"No, Susan, you can't!" Teresa wailed. "It's too embarrassing."

"It may be," Susan said. "But they will understand. What they won't understand is when this rumor comes floating back to them and they don't know anything about it. And believe me, it will. James was completely out of line talking to you like that—out where everyone could see both of you."

"But it was dark!" Teresa protested.

"People figure things out," Susan said. "It's not that hard. If James had anything decent to say, he could have said it in front of me."

"Will you please tell your mom and dad when I'm not around?" Teresa begged. "I don't think I can stand admitting this in front of them."

"If you want me to, but they have to be told. That is, if you are to stay in the community. Did you give James any encouragement?" she asked again.

"I didn't," Teresa said weakly. "And I don't think he can read my heart."

"I don't think he can either," Susan said as the horse settled into a slow trot. "What a glorious mess. Are you ready now to go back to Asbury Park?"

"I'll never be ready to go back—you know that," Teresa said.

They drove in silence, surrounded only by the soft hoofbeats of Toby and the steady crunch of buggy wheels on gravel. Susan pushed open the buggy door and leaned out to look at the star-speckled sky. Teresa did the same on her side. When the moment had passed, they sat straight in their seats, the doors still open as they watched the low clouds before them scurry across the horizon.

"This is what I missed when I lived in Asbury Park," Susan said, her voice low. "These quiet moments when a person feels so close to the land that it takes on a life of its own. It's almost as if there are whispers on the night air that speak to my soul about deep things too hard to place into words. This is when the heavens are a sound that roars in my ears. Here, in this country, life is never really silent."

"I didn't know you thought such things," Teresa said. "You say it well. Much better than I could. Can you understand why I don't want to leave?"

"Yes. I guess I was foolish to try to convince you to go, but surely there is something like this elsewhere in the world?"

"I've been in the world, Susan," Teresa said. "And, no, there's nothing like it."

"But there are millions and millions of people and places. We can't be the only ones who feel like this."

"Well, I never met any of them who did where I grew up," Teresa asserted.

The buggy wheels rattled on through the night, the light from the Hostetler living room window soon glimmering in the distance.

"Will your parents ask me to leave," Teresa asked, "when you tell them about James?"

"Of course not, Teresa," Susan replied. "They like you."

"You've been wrong before," Teresa reminded her. "About me... about the people in the Amish community."

"Perhaps," Susan admitted. "But I'm not wrong this time. I'll leave with you myself if they ask you to go."

"I don't want people sacrificing themselves for me," Teresa said. "And I wish James would understand that. I want to be left in peace with Yost."

"I will tell them, and they'll be okay with it," Susan assured her again as she turned Toby into the driveway.

Teresa climbed down when the buggy came to a stop and helped to unhitch.

Susan took the horse into the barn with her flashlight, looking back over her shoulder at Teresa standing beside the buggy gazing up at the stars.

*The poor girl,* she thought. *Why couldn't everyone leave well enough alone?* The truth was, she couldn't either. It simply was too hard to watch. It was too much of a shame. James really wasn't having that different a reaction from what she had herself. James's interest was just more explosive.

And she really couldn't blame James for his interest. Teresa was a nice girl. Anyone could see that she had a heart of gold. But then perhaps they did see, and were as unable to do something about it as she was. James was trying but sure wasn't helping. He was only making things worse. Much worse.

Susan pulled the harness off Toby and hung it on the wall. Slapping the horse on his rump, she shooed him into his stall, made sure he had some hay, and then left, shutting the barn door behind her.

"There!" Susan said, returning to where Teresa was still watching the stars. "All done. We can go inside now."

"It's so beautiful out here," Teresa said. "I could stay out all night."

"My guess is Samuel will be more than glad to see you," Susan reminded her.

"He's probably soundly sleeping, the little darling," Teresa said as she followed Susan across the dark lawn. "He likes his bottle more all the time."

"He *is* growing up fast," Susan acknowledged, holding the door open while Teresa entered. They pulled off their shawls and bonnets, hanging them in the closet. *Mamm* and *Daett* were up, reading in the living room by the light of the hissing gas lantern.

"You're a little late," *Mamm* noted, looking up with a questioning smile.

"A little," Susan agreed.

"I'll go check on Samuel," Teresa said, heading for the stair door.

"He's been sleeping for the past hour," *Mamm* said. "He settled down really nice. I think he's starting to like me."

"Samuel has always liked you," Teresa said just before disappearing through the door and up the stairs.

"Did I see tears in her eyes, Susan?" *Mamm* asked when Teresa's footsteps had faded.

"James spoke with her tonight," Susan said. "He's got Teresa all disturbed. I can't believe this is happening. It's not like Teresa doesn't already have enough problems on her mind with the wedding to Yost coming up."

"Please sit down and talk sense, Susan," *Mamm* said. "I can't understand a thing you're saying."

Susan sat down with a sigh. "I'm not sure where to start really. Perhaps I should have told you what's been going on before this, but it didn't seem like it would amount to much. But now..."

"What's happened?" *Mamm* asked, leaning forward.

*Daett* lifted his eyes from *The Budget* and looked at Susan closely.

"James has been making eyes at Teresa for some time," Susan admitted. "I know that's shocking, and I warned Teresa about it. But really, she couldn't do anything about it."

"James?" *Mamm* questioned. "Deacon Ray's James? Surely Teresa isn't returning his attentions. She's promised to Yost."

"She didn't encourage him at all, *Mamm*," Susan said. "I talked to her about it. Then tonight James comes out as bold as he can be and asked to speak with her. I told him no, that Teresa didn't want to speak to him because there would only be trouble. Well, it didn't do any *gut.* James asked Teresa directly, and she said she would speak to him. They went off a ways and talked in private."

"*Daett,*" *Mamm* said, "I think you'd better get involved here."

Susan didn't wait for her *daett* to intervene.

"Can we just sit here and allow this marriage to Yost happen?" Susan asked *Mamm.* "You know in your heart it isn't right."

"*Nee,* I do not know that," *Mamm* said. "But it's not up to me anyway. We are a community, Susan. You of all people should know this. I like Teresa, just like you do. She's a wonderful girl, but she is what she is. And she has done what she has done. Nothing can change that. We certainly can't have her dating one of our young men. Yost was a compromise already, mainly because Deacon Ray felt sorry for him."

Menno cleared his throat. "What did James tell Teresa tonight?"

"I couldn't hear what they said," Susan said. "But Teresa said James wants to see more of her, perhaps even bring her home on Sunday nights. He said she doesn't have to marry Yost if she doesn't want to. That he could work things out for her somehow."

Menno sighed. "The boy is being very reckless. But at least it's his doing and not Teresa's. You're sure she didn't give him any encouragement?"

"I didn't hear them talking, *Daett,*" Susan said. "But Teresa said she didn't."

"Well, I'll have to speak to Deacon Ray about this," *Daett* said. "I'll give him to understand that Teresa didn't try to hide anything and that she didn't encourage the boy. That should place the blame for this matter where it belongs. Hopefully Deacon Ray can talk some sense into his boy's head. Just because he's the deacon's son doesn't give James the right to flaunt the rules. He has to live by the will of the community just like the rest of us."

"That sounds like a good plan," *Mamm* agreed.

Susan cleared her throat.

"While everyone else is making their confessions," she said, "perhaps I'd better make one of my own."

"You haven't been thinking about leaving again?" *Mamm* gasped.

"I'm afraid I was," Susan said. "I'm sorry, but such thoughts still cross my mind."

"I will take care of this problem tomorrow," Menno said. "Perhaps that will help with your temptation to leave."

"Thank you," Susan said, getting to her feet. "I think I'll call it a night."

They both nodded as she closed the stair door behind her.

At the top of the stairs, she knocked gently on Teresa's door.

"Come in," Teresa answered softly.

Teresa was nestled under the covers with baby Samuel beside her fast asleep.

"*Daett* is going to speak with Deacon Ray tomorrow," Susan said. "They know this is not your fault."

Tears formed in Teresa's eyes and she mouthed *thank you* to Susan.

Susan nodded and closed the bedroom door behind her.

# Chapter Twenty-four

The dream was a rush of *Englisha* automobiles, of faces he didn't know, of long, winding blacktop roads in big cities, and of fear. Menno tried to fully awaken. He rubbed his eyes. Breathless, he sat up in bed and pushed back the covers. Beside him Anna slept, her breathing steady and deep. Moving his stocking-clad feet across the bed, he dropped them to the floor and stood and then pulled on his clothing in the darkness. Walking over to the open bedroom window, he looked out across the dark night. He bent over to lean closer to the windowpane, listening.

Faint sounds rose in the night air coming from the barnyard, the noise of horses banging in their stalls, the low sigh of cattle breathing in mass. Why was his heart so troubled again tonight? *Da Hah* had blessed him beyond measure with possessions, with a *frau* who loved him, with children who were *gut* members in the church. His dreams should be happy, not troublesome.

Was it the temptations of the world coming back to draw him again? Surely it wasn't. He had turned his back on his sin those many years ago. And yet, even now his face burned with the shame. He had left behind a girl with a great pain in her heart, simply thankful to have gotten off so easily.

Walking past the bed, Menno paused and listened to Anna's deep breathing. She was still sound asleep, but even if she should awake, she would understand him being up. A man visiting his barnyard even in the night hours was understandable. What she would not understand was what he needed to ponder. But there was no reason she should know of such things, even now after all these years.

The bedroom door squeaked on his way out, but he didn't slow his steady pace toward the washroom. In the darkness he found his shoes and slipped them on and then draped his work coat over his shoulder. Stepping outside, the brisk spring night air felt *gut* on his face.

Walking past the barn door, he leaned over the wooden yard fence, watching the outlines of the cattle in the field. They lay in the grass, their mouths moving shadows in the starlight as they chewed their cud.

Thoughts ran through his mind, his dream a background of noise from another time and place. It had been so many years ago. Why was this coming back now to disturb his peace? Was Carol looking for him? That was not likely and almost impossible. Why would she wish to see him?

The child would be the only reason, but even that made no sense. Carol had said the child had been lost. His eyes traced the horizon which danced with a thousand twinkling stars. The outline of the cattle below blended in with the hue of the darkened grass.

He saw Carol's face again as it had looked on the day she told him about the coming child, the hope written on her face, the longing in her eyes. How quickly those eyes had darkened when he showed no joy at her news. But surely she hadn't expected him to follow her into the world?

One of the cows stood in the field, stretching and staring at him. He pushed the new thought away, but it came back with greater force, presenting itself again. What if the child had not been lost? His fingers dug into the wooden rail of the fence. This was not possible. Carol would not lie. Yet, had he not lied when he spoke to her of love? Had he not lied with his silence upon his return to the community?

So was it also possible Carol had lied to him? Such a lie would have made it easier for both of them. Especially him. Had she loved him enough to have spared him the decision to leave his people for her world?

"*Gott im Himmel*," he whispered to the night air. "Is it possible that I have an *Englisha* child?"

But it could not be true. It simply could not. Even if Carol had lied he would have known. He would have had to know. True, he had left the next month, his term of service over, but surely he would have felt the truth. He was not that stupid. Or perhaps he was, and perhaps that was why Carol never came around again, not even to say good-bye on that last day. The day when all the others had gathered to wish him well on his return home. His heart had burned with the pain of her rejection, thinking she had blamed him for everything, while all the time he was the one who was rejecting. He was the one who was placing the blame on another person's shoulders. And she knew and had made it easy for him. Was it possible?

"Dear *Gott*," he said. "I am a greater sinner than even I knew. Why have You not destroyed me those many years ago? I am a hypocrite. A wolf in sheep clothing. One thing to myself, and another thing to You and the others."

Menno hung his head and began to weep, the sobs shaking his shoulders. A cow moved closer from the shadowy grass, coming over to stand a few feet away. A low *moo* escaped its mouth, a sort of moan full of questions. He glanced back toward the house. What if his *frau* awakened now and came looking for him? He would have time to move inside the barn before her dim light came to the door, but at the moment it hardly seemed worth the effort.

What a relief it would be to tell her everything. To speak the words inside of him, express the fears roiling in his heart, tell her of the nightmares that haunted him. She would understand, would she not? He hesitated, his eyes on the windows of the house, but no flickering light appeared from the deep shadows.

The moon would be up soon, and he would be visible from the house. Well, let Anna see him. Perhaps then the thoughts would come into form more easily. This weight on his chest which smothered his heart might be removed by the questions in her eyes, by the sheer force of her will to know. But she had never doubted him, never asked why, never probed the things he had done during those long-ago years.

What did she think Amish boys did while serving their times in *Englisha* hospitals? Spend their time keeping the *Ordnung*? He hung his head. This was not a time to blame the others for what he had done. Likely few had fallen as low as he had, driven by the intoxicating freedoms of the great city.

Even those who hadn't come home, choosing instead to stay in the world with their *Englisha* girlfriends, had behaved better than he had. Always he had thought of them as making the worse choice, but had they? He studied the stars, seeking an answer, and finding only the pain rising in his own heart. He had made his choice, and they had made theirs. Perhaps the agony pounding in their hearts was worse than his, but it hardly seemed possible.

Should he be making confessions to Bishop Henry? But what confession? *That I think I have fathered an Englisha child?* Bishop Henry would wish to know on what grounds he made such a statement, and he had none. Only his fears driven by desperate dreams in the night.

He had made confessions at his baptismal vows. Confessions, and promises to forsake the world and all its allurements. Bishop Henry would certainly want further confessions now if he knew about the *Englisha* girl, but what *gut* would that do? He had already made his peace with *Da Hah* and with the community. Living one's life in holiness and humility was a penance and confession all of its own. A life lived was more powerful than words spoken. Did not his people believe this?

"But I have sinned greatly," he whispered to the stars, "if I have fathered a child who lived and then I walked away from my responsibility."

The nearby cow lifted its head, mooing again, her nose only inches away now. He jumped back in surprise and moved further down the fence. He placed his weight back on the top rail. The cow looked at him and then moved the other way, settling back on the grass with a solid thump.

A dim light came on in the house, and he watched for a long moment before walking toward the doorway. Anna met him at the front door, holding her robe shut with one hand, a kerosene lamp in the other. Her long hair spilled out from under her night *kapp* and hung over her shoulders.

"What are you up for?" he asked, stepping inside.

"I could ask you the same," she said. "But I assume it's because you're troubled like I am. I just had an awful dream."

"Come," he said, "dreams are not always true. We must not let them bother us. It is *Da Hah* alone who remains ever faithful and true."

"But does He not speak through dreams?" she asked. "I believe He does, and I believe you need to hear this one."

"Come, let us go into the bedroom," he said. "Lest we awaken someone."

Sitting down on the bed he waited while she climbed under the covers.

"It was an awful thing," she said. "It was all rushed together like dreams are, but yet it all seemed so clear. I saw the wedding right after the baptism. Poor Yost Byler standing there in his new suit, his heart full of joy. Teresa took his hand and made her promises. I saw Yost take her home, and she was placing food on the table for him. You should have seen how happy Yost looked.

"Then I saw the children—two, maybe three. They were all *gut*-looking children, and Yost was so happy. And Teresa looked happy from what I could tell. Then I saw Teresa leaving, just like that. Running down the road, leaving the children, leaving Yost, leaving the house they lived in. She left everything. That's so unlike her, Menno. Why would I have such a dream?"

"I don't know," he said. "But dreams are not always to be trusted."

"Is it just my fears talking?" she asked, nestling under the quilt. "Teresa wouldn't do something like that. I don't think so anyway. What do you think?"

"*Yah*, perhaps it is just your fears," he said. "I don't think she would do such a thing either."

They both settled themselves and moments later Anna's even breathing filled the room. But Menno stayed awake, staring at the ceiling until the moon rose, flooding the world outside the bedroom window with white light. Eventually he drifted off, awakening to the loud clanging of the alarm clock. The first light of dawn was already written in the sky.

# Chapter Twenty-five

‖

M enno finished his chores after breakfast, leaving the harness-ing of the horse till the last minute. The day had dawned clear, without a cloud in the sky. He really ought to be out in the fields fin-ishing the spring plowing, but he had promised. The trip to Deacon Ray's place must be undertaken today.

Teresa was hanging out the first load of wash when he led Toby out of the barn. She smiled and waved, nearly losing the wooden pins she held in her mouth. How like an Amish woman the girl was becoming, and so determined to make a go of things. The least he could do was put in a *gut* word for her with Deacon Ray. And there might even be more he could do, but that would have to wait. By now James would surely have spoken with his *daett,* and this visit might well be expected.

With the horse fastened to the buggy shafts, he swung the lines in through the storm window and climbed in.

Teresa gave him another wave as he drove by the wash line. She shouted, "Have a good trip now!"

"Don't work too hard," he hollered back. Once out on the road, he slapped the reins, pushing Toby to a faster pace. Who knew how long this conversation might take, and he needed to get back to his farmwork. In the meantime, he might as well lean back and enjoy the ride. Not often did he get a chance to travel alone. *Mamm* and Susan were usually along on Sunday mornings, and during the week any good farmer stayed close to home. There was so much work on any farm in the community.

Menno sighed. He needed help around the place, but from the

looks of things, Susan didn't plan to patch up her differences with Thomas anytime soon. He might as well look for a hired hand, but those were difficult to find. Young married men with their need to support growing families wanted to run the whole place and move into the main house. Any unmarried farm boys were usually kept busy on their own *daetts'* farms. Perhaps he could mention his need to Deacon Ray this morning. The man visited many Amish communities in his travels with Bishop Henry.

Menno waved as he passed Emery Yoder's wife traveling the other way. She must be going down to Livonia to the Dutch Barn for shopping. A trip into Salem would usually require a much earlier start.

In the open fields to the west, a team of horses plowed the land, the black soil rolling over in a steady stream as one of the Esh boys handled the reins. Menno leaned out of the buggy, ready to wave, but the intent gaze of the driver never came his direction. Now there was a true farmer at heart, intent and eager at his work. Perhaps Ezra would allow his son to take a job away from home? Menno settled into the buggy seat again, pondering the thought. It was unlikely. Ezra needed all three of his sons for the nearly 200 acres the family owned. Besides that, they raised garden produce to sell to *Englisha* customers. There was not a chance Ezra would allow one of his sons to work for another farmer. And soon the boy would have a girlfriend, be ready to marry, and want to move somewhere on his own farm.

Why not ask Ezra if he knows of someone? It could do no harm. And there was Ezra walking out of his barn right now. Menno slowed down and pulled into the driveway.

"*Gut* morning," Ezra greeted, approaching the buggy with a ready smile. "What brings you out on the road this morning?"

Menno pushed open the buggy door and leaned his head out. There was no reason to tell Ezra where he was going and why.

"Saw your boy out plowing," Menno said, motioning toward the field with a tilt of his head. "Mighty fine young boys you have coming up there. Any chance you have a spare one?"

Ezra laughed. "I think you know the answer to that question."

"That's what I thought," Menno said. "Any chance you know of a young man looking for farmwork? I sure could use one come spring. I'm not getting any younger these days."

"No change between Susan and Thomas?" Ezra asked, leaning against the buggy wheel.

Menno shook his head. "And even if there was, they wouldn't get married until the fall."

"I'll ask around," Ezra said. "You never know."

"Good men available to work are hard to find," Menno said. "Thanks. If nothing else, I can perhaps prime the pump. Get a hired hand while the girl makes up her mind."

Ezra stepped back with a wave as Menno pulled out of the driveway. He drove down the road deep in thought, approaching Deacon Ray's farm ten minutes or so later. Menno pushed his hat back on his forehead, scanning the fields. If Deacon Ray was out working, he could save time by tying up along the fence and walking out to him. No team of horses was in the fields though, so Menno kept going to the driveway. Pulling in, he caught sight of Deacon Ray peering out of the barn window.

The deacon waved, and Menno turned his horse in that direction, coming to a stop beside the barn. Climbing down, Menno tied up and pushed open the barn door.

"*Gut* morning," Deacon Ray greeted, leaning on his pitchfork. "I'm afraid you're catching me a little late at my chores. James ran into Salem early this morning to get a part for the disk so I'm still at them without his help."

"At least you have your plowing done." Menno tried to smile, pulling his hat tighter on his head. "I've still got mine to finish, so I'll try not to keep you long."

"I'm not surprised you've come over," Deacon Ray said, taking a seat on a hay bale. "Sit down, Menno, as this might take a while, and we're both old men."

"So did James tell you about Sunday night?" Menno asked. "I thought he might."

"*Yah,* your thinking would be correct," Deacon Ray said. "We had quite a going over on the subject when he arrived home. I don't think we got to bed until after midnight. I've not been up that late since my days of taking Esther home from the hymn singings."

"I know what you mean," Menno said. "I've been quite troubled myself. I promised Anna and the girls I'd come over to speak with you."

"You won't be trying to bend my mind, Menno?" Deacon Ray asked, shifting on the straw bale.

"Not really," Menno said, "as I know it doesn't bend easily, but I wanted first of all to make it clear that this was none of Teresa's doing."

"So you're sticking up for her?" Deacon Ray asked.

"It's the way things are," Menno said. "It's not just sticking up for a person when it's the truth."

"So you're that certain of the matter?" Deacon Ray asked.

"*Yah,*" Menno said. "What does James say about it?"

"Pretty much what the girl said, I suppose," Deacon Ray said. "He had his feelings hurt that she turned him down. I can't imagine what got into the boy to take such a thing upon himself."

"He's your son; maybe he thought he had special privileges," Menno said.

Deacon Ray laughed. "I doubt if Bishop Henry will be taking excommunication up over this matter."

Menno smiled. "Not likely, but you know that others will start thinking the same thing soon. It's bound to happen. What do you think gave James the nerve to challenge you in the first place?"

"The boy's got a hard skull," Deacon Ray said. "And I won't be changing my mind just because the community starts asking questions. Teresa comes from outside. We can't change that fact. We've been supportive of her more than we probably should already. Right now I'm wishing I'd never listened to Yost's wild idea that evening."

"Is James interested in Teresa?" Menno asked. "Or just feeling sorry for her?"

Deacon Ray picked a straw out of the bale, chewing long on the stem. "It's hard to tell with that boy. He's never been able to settle down with any girl. I don't know how many girls he's taken home, and he always has some reason not to ask them home again. Maybe he sees something different in Teresa, something *Englisha,* something forbidden. You know how that can pull on a man's heart."

Menno studied the straw-strewn barn floor. "So what do you plan to do if he continues giving Teresa attention? What am I supposed to tell her to do?"

"I am much troubled about the situation," Deacon Ray admitted. "I am treating James like any other boy, exactly as if he were not my son. But James made some points that's got me to thinking."

"*Yah?*" Menno inquired, waiting patiently as silence settled between them.

Deacon Ray cleared his throat. "James asked if I have never done anything that needed forgiveness. He asked if *Da Hah* now keeps me forever in His debt because of it. He claims the girl is doing all of this to give her son a better life than she had, that she is willing to sacrifice her own happiness by marrying Yost Byler to accomplish this. He said that few of our own people would be willing to submit to such a thing."

"And do you believe this to be true?" Menno asked.

Deacon Ray looked at him. "I should be asking you that question. She lives in your house."

"Teresa is a decent girl," Menno finally said. "And she is learning our ways quickly. From what Susan says, James is speaking the truth."

"I wish to know how you feel, Menno. Please answer me carefully," Deacon Ray said. "You know what will happen if we're wrong on this. Such a girl could cause much sorrow and unhappiness in the community. How many *Englisha* girls have ever joined this community, especially ones with a child and no husband?"

"I see that your mind has gone in much the same directions as mine," Menno said. "And I am quite thankful I don't have the leadership of the community to think about."

"You can thank *Da Hah* each day for such a gift, Menno," Deacon Ray said. "The burden of the church lies heavy on my shoulders. But you have not told me yet what you think about this."

Menno leaned back on the hay bale, watching the sunlight dancing on the barn windows. "I agree with James," he finally said. "And I also agree with him on another point."

"*Yah,* what is that?" Deacon Ray asked. "About her being better than our people by putting aside her own happiness? But how can we judge such a thing, Menno? Our people have their faults, and we are just men after all. But all the years we put into the training and right upbringing of our children cannot be thrown away as nothing. It has to count."

"It does," Menno said. "Though that's not what I meant to agree with. I don't wish to interfere with anything between you and James. Nor am I trying to say James is right in his affection for Teresa. That is, if he has any."

"Then what are you saying?"

"It was the part about not being free of past sins ourselves," Menno said. "You know that neither of us have done as we ought in our younger years."

Deacon Ray spat out his straw stem. "I know," he said. "It's hard to live right in the big cities. That's why I thank *Da Hah* often that our young people no longer have to serve the country in such a manner. We have been blessed that the current government requires no service time at all. Who would have thought that day would ever come? And I dread a time when it might be required of us again. You know how many young men we lost to the world during those years."

"The flesh of man is weak," Menno said. "Mine must have been among the weakest of them all."

"There is no sense in pointing fingers now," Deacon Ray said. "I drove an *Englisha* automobile a few times. And that without a driver's license. But both of us came back to the community, and for that we can thank *Da Hah*'s mercy in preserving us."

"I agree," Menno said. "But it leaves us still guilty."

"*Yah*," Deacon Ray said, "but it has been forgiven."

Menno cleared his throat. "You asked what I think. Truth is, I think we need to allow Teresa's baptism without requiring her to marry Yost. And since they have started a relationship already, she can continue it if they wish, but on her own free will and not because we require it."

Deacon Ray drew in a deep breath. "So now I see where you're going, Menno. Is this why you have come over? Are you asking me to change what has already been decided by the ministry?"

"I'm not trying to do anything, Ray. I'm simply saying what needs to be said. This thing with Teresa is getting out of hand. Would it not be wiser to adjust while we still can?"

"You're still thinking of our time in the world, aren't you?" Deacon Ray asked. "I have made my sins right with the church. No one could ask for more than that."

"I'm only asking that you consider in the light of what we've been through ourselves, if Teresa should not be allowed to join the church without any requirements that she marry Yost. And look at us. We had the benefit of godly parents, the love of the community, and still the world pulled hard on our hearts. What must it have been like for a young *Englisha* girl who had none of that?"

"You know that Bishop Henry will not appreciate this. Even if I would consider it," Deacon Ray said.

"But it is the right thing to do," Menno said, his voice low. "The girl needs to know that she can join the church without being forced into a marriage. It may save much trouble for her and Yost later."

Deacon Ray stroked his beard. After a few silent moments, he spoke. "I will speak with Bishop Henry on Sunday. If the girl does not give us any other cause for trouble, I do not see why she cannot be allowed to marry Yost on her own free will."

"And if she chooses not to?" Menno asked.

"Well, it certainly won't be James who will seek her hand," Deacon Ray said. "I will see to that. But I do agree that if the girl has proven herself sufficiently, we can accept her into the community without the marriage requirement. That was Yost's idea anyway. I want you to know that. And James will forget about the matter once the girl is no longer under pressure. Once he sees she's free from the requirement to marry Yost, that'll be the end of it for him, I'm sure. As for Yost, he will not give up so easily. He will still hold her to her word to marry him. I heard they've already spoken at length at your house."

"Yost did come over," Menno said, getting to his feet. "And perhaps you will be proved right."

"So it is decided," Deacon Ray said, managing a smile. "If Bishop Henry and the other ministers agree, then that is how it will be."

"I have plowing to do," Menno said, opening the barn door. "I had better get back to work."

"Here comes James now," Deacon Ray said. "If all goes well, we'll have the field ready for planting in a few days."

Menno untied Toby and climbed into the buggy. He waved to James, who was riding in on his lathered horse. James looked at him with a curious expression as he waved back. Menno had forgotten to ask Deacon Ray about the hired hand, but that would have to wait. The more important matter had been taken care of. Teresa would be free to make up her own mind about Yost. Deacon Ray might have eventually come to this conclusion on his own, but it hadn't hurt to help him along. And it did feel better now that he was doing something to help Teresa. Menno slapped the reins as the buggy rattled southward on the dirt road.

# Chapter Twenty-six

✦

Susan left the bread dough on the kitchen table and looked out the living room window. There was no sign of *Daett* yet, so he must be having a long talk with Deacon Ray. Was that a *gut* sign? Not likely. James must have told his side of the story, and Deacon Ray no doubt was laying down the law. If things went really badly, Teresa would not be allowed to continue attending instruction classes. That would be a blow she would not easily recover from.

"Stop pacing back and forth," *Mamm* commanded. "*Daett* will be home when he's home."

"Did he say anything more this morning about Teresa?" Susan asked.

"He's troubled like I am," *Mamm* said. "But I suppose Deacon Ray is just as troubled with James involved now. So we have to trust *Da Hah* to work this out for us."

"I'm sorry this whole thing has happened," Susan said.

*Mamm* sighed. "It's not entirely your fault, but perhaps you see now what happens when one goes out gallivanting into the *Englisha* world."

Susan pressed her lips together as she returned to the table and kneaded hard on the bread dough. Telling *Mamm* what she had been thinking would only make things worse, but if Teresa had to leave she planned to go with her to Asbury Park.

"I hope you won't be holding this against the ministers if they decide things differently from what we'd like," *Mamm* said, as if she were reading Susan's thoughts. "Remember, they have the whole weight of the community's well-being on their shoulders."

"I don't think I'll ever understand," Susan said. "But I will try to trust, even when I can't see my way through."

"Listen to me, Susan," *Mamm* said, turning to face her. "I know you like Teresa, and so do I. But it's not easy keeping a holy life in this world of ours. Look at what's out there. You should know better than many. You've been there. And there are our young people to think about. Our ministers can't ignore that."

"There's got to be some way," Susan said. "It's simply not right to make Teresa go back."

*Mamm* sighed again. "I don't know that she's going back, Susan. And you don't either."

Susan stepped back from the bread dough, which now lay fully kneaded on the kitchen table. Little pieces of white flour and dough hung from Susan's hands. She wiped her hands on her apron.

*Mamm* looked up from the kitchen sink as buggy wheels crunched into the graveled driveway. Susan made a move toward the washroom door, but *Mamm* shook her head.

"Let *Daett* come in when he wishes and explain things to us," *Mamm* said. "Sometimes hard things need to be thought about for a long time before they are spoken."

"Please, *Mamm*! I've got to know!" Susan begged.

The outside washroom door slammed before *Mamm* could answer, and Susan stepped forward to pull open the door. Teresa came in, meeting Susan's eyes with her own. She gripped the empty wash hamper in her hand.

"Whew! Three loads of laundry washed and hung out. I thought I would never get it all done," Teresa said. "And did you notice that your dad is back?"

"I know." Susan turned to her *mamm*. "Can she come with me, please?"

"Go, you two! Teresa, go with Susan and hear what *Daett* has to say," *Mamm* said, waving with her hand.

Susan gripped Teresa's arm until they reached the barn. Letting go, Susan pulled the door open, stepped inside, and waited until Teresa entered before closing the door. The odor of horses and hay rushed over her. In the dim light, her *daett*'s figure appeared by the stalls. He was carrying Toby's bridle in his hand. He threw it over a wooden hook on the wall before approaching the girls.

"We thought we would come out to see what news you brought," Susan said.

"I don't have much to say right now," Menno said. "Deacon Ray and I had a *gut* talk."

"Is that all?" Susan asked. "How did he receive your explanation?"

"Please tell me, Mr. Hostetler," Teresa said. "I want to know. Even if it is bad news."

"It's not bad news, Teresa," Menno said, leaning against the planks of the stall. "We had a long talk, and Deacon Ray is as concerned as I am. I'm not sure how everything will turn out, but Deacon Ray is going to speak with Bishop Henry about changing some things."

"Like what?" Teresa asked. "You said it wasn't bad news."

Menno smiled. "*Nee,* Teresa, it's not bad news. Deacon Ray agrees that you should not be forced to marry anyone you don't wish to. Of course, you still can marry Yost if you desire to, but we might have jumped to conclusions too quickly by forcing you to marry as soon as you are baptized. I'm sorry about that, but perhaps it's not too late. The ministry can still change things if they so choose. That is, if you want them to."

"I don't understand," Teresa managed. "What is being changed?"

"You might be able to get baptized without having to marry Yost Byler," Susan said.

"Is that what you mean?" Teresa asked Menno.

"*Yah,*" Menno said. "If you keep the *Ordnung* and listen to the instructions like everyone else, I don't think any of the ministers will object to you joining the church without marrying Yost."

"What if I want to marry Yost?" Teresa asked. "We are promised to each other."

"Then it can be done *after* your baptism, like any other couple considering marriage," Menno said. "And I will give you a place to have the wedding, like I do for my own daughters."

"Oh, Mr. Hostetler!" Teresa said, her voice breaking. "You're so wonderful. But you really don't have to. I can get married any old place."

"*Daett*!" Susan said, her face the picture of relief. "This is such a turn of events. What brought it about? Deacon Ray rarely changes his mind about anything, and I can't imagine he would have given in to James."

Menno shook his head. "We talked things over, and he didn't change his mind about James and Teresa. And I didn't try to change that. I only wanted to make sure Teresa's name stayed pure and to get this unjust marriage requirement removed. No one should have to marry because they want to join the community. And I believe Deacon Ray now understands that Teresa is really trying to be part of us, and that her heart is in the right place."

"I don't know what to say," Teresa said, tears streaming down her face. "You really didn't have to do this for me. I was only concerned about being made to leave. Both Yost and I are fine with the wedding as it is planned."

"But you don't have to marry him now," Susan said. "Isn't that right, *Daett*?"

"Well, the ministry must meet and decide. But if they decide as I think they will, she won't have to," Menno said. "It will be up to her."

"But I can if I want to?" Teresa asked again.

"*Yah*. And Deacon Ray thought that was what your choice might be," Menno said.

Teresa nodded. "That would be the best thing for everyone concerned. And for Samuel. He would have a father then."

"Well, I have to get to my plowing," Menno said. "Deacon Ray already has his disk out in his field."

"Come!" Susan said, pulling on Teresa's arm. Outside Susan turned toward her. "Teresa, you don't have to marry Yost! So please don't be stubborn about it."

"I'm not being stubborn, Susan. I'm being practical."

"Teresa, please," Susan begged. "You know you have feelings for James."

"So tell me what kind of boy is James?" Teresa asked.

"I don't know what you mean."

"Yes, you do," Teresa said. "You may think I don't know your people's ways. But Susan, I'm not stupid. Why does James not have a girlfriend already? Can you tell me that?"

"I wouldn't know," Susan said. "He's dated several Amish girls, but he doesn't last long with any of them. I've never bothered to ask about the matter—or even think about it."

"I have," Teresa said. "And he's that kind of boy. He's flighty like Samuel's father was. He makes flutters in the air as he comes around—and flutters into a girl's heart. He's bold, even brash at times, like when he speaks up for me, even promising to take me home a few times from the hymn singings. But his promises don't seem to go any farther than that, Susan. Do you understand what I'm saying?"

"Yost hopes your cooking is good. That's all he wants. So don't do this to yourself," Susan said. "There might actually be a chance for you with James now. Lay low until after your baptism and see what happens. James might have finally found a girl who is just right for him."

"*Me?*" Teresa laughed. "Me right for James? Ha! Nothing has changed, Susan. I am still an unwed *Englisha* woman with a baby. If I start getting out of my place, how do you think that will be taken by Deacon Ray and the other ministers?"

"But Deacon Ray is agreeing that you can do what you wish about marriage."

"Only if the ministers concur. But even then I don't dare, Susan. It would only mean trouble in the long run. Yost will be fine. I shouldn't expect more."

Susan sighed. "You sure try hard to think like an Amish woman, don't you? I thought you were *Englisha* at heart."

"Maybe I'm afraid I still am," Teresa said. "But I'm not changing anything with Yost, other than maybe the wedding date. That was very sweet of your dad. Do you think he really will give me a wedding like I'm one of his daughters?"

"If *Daett* said he will do it, then he will," Susan said. "But I'd be more concerned about who you're having the wedding with than the wedding itself."

*Mamm* opened the front door. "Will you girls please stop prattling out in the yard and share your news with me! I want to know what the menfolk have going on."

"Teresa has been given a *gut* word," Susan said when they approached the house. "*Daett* thinks the ministers are going to change their terms. Hopefully she can get baptized without marrying Yost Byler. Don't you think she should promptly drop the old man?"

"Susan!" Teresa said. "Don't speak like that."

"That is *gut* news," *Mamm* said. "But aren't you making plans before you know for sure?"

"Oh, it will happen," Susan said.

Teresa cleared her throat. "Thank you for your kindness to me. I don't deserve any of it. Certainly not the wedding Menno is offering me."

"A wedding?" *Mamm* asked.

"*Daett* promised to give Teresa a wedding just like he would for me," Susan said.

"I said it wasn't necessary," Teresa said at once. "The way we have it planned now is fine with me."

"You and Yost," *Mamm* said, ignoring the interruption. "*Daett* promised to give you a wedding here? Why, I think that is a *gut* idea! I would have thought of it soon enough myself. Especially since now it won't have to be on your baptismal day—if all goes well. But come, we have to get busy now, before the day is completely over. Are you done with the washing, Teresa?"

"Yes," Teresa replied. "I only need to bring in some of the clothes from the line. I'll bring in the rest after dinner when they're dry."

"*Daett* could use some help in the fields," Susan said as *Mamm* turned to go inside. "I heard him complaining under his breath."

"Well, I don't think we can get you married quickly enough to change that this spring," *Mamm* teased.

"That's not what I meant," Susan protested. "I'll go help him this afternoon. Don't we have time?"

*Mamm* thought for a moment before answering. "*Yah*, but you have never plowed before. That's what *Daett* is doing."

"I can start on the disking," Susan suggested. "That's what seems to be bothering him. Deacon Ray is already in the fields with his disk."

"And Deacon Ray still has a son at home," *Mamm* said. "But don't be too hard on your *daett*. He's bothered more about getting the crops in the fields than anything Deacon Ray is doing. Late corn will mean a late harvest, and you know what that means. Hard times this winter."

"That's why I'll go help him after lunch," Susan said. "I know how to disk."

"Can I help?" Teresa asked, her eyes shining. "I've never done anything like that in my life."

"That's why you shouldn't now," *Mamm* said. "I don't think Yost is needing a wife who can disk. Cooking will keep him happy enough."

"Please!" Teresa said, her eyes pleading. "I want to experience this for myself. I don't care what Yost has to say about it. And for Samuel's sake, I want to experience a little of what he will go through growing up. It will so comfort me in any troubled times ahead."

"I suppose you can," *Mamm* allowed. "Just don't fall off. I don't want a mangled girl on my hands."

"Oh, I won't!" Teresa squealed. "I'll get the wash off the line right now."

✦

# CHAPTER TWENTY-SEVEN

Susan held the reins to one of the Belgians as her *daett* threw on a harness, fastening the straps securely under the huge animal. Beside her, Teresa clutched the reins on the bridle of the other horse, her eyes still shining as the horse bent its neck down to get at stray pieces of hay on the barn floor.

"Hang on to him!" Susan ordered with a laugh.

"But he must be hungry," Teresa said, struggling to keep from getting knocked over.

"They've had plenty to eat," *Daett* said. "They just can't resist another bite of food. Given a chance they'd eat themselves to death."

"Is that true?" Teresa asked, pulling hard on the halter.

Susan nodded.

Teresa's horse raised its head, blinking its eyes close to her face. Teresa laughed. "I do think he's pleading with me."

"Don't give in to his tugging on your heart," Susan said. "Colic and founder may happen if a horse eats too much oats or rich food. It can kill them."

"Okay, that one's ready," *Daett* hollered out, slapping the horse on the rump. Susan led him forward.

"Don't worry," Susan said as she went past Teresa. "Just hang on to the reins. These horses are well trained. He won't go anywhere."

When she reached the barnyard, Susan waited beside the field disk until Teresa appeared, leading the second horse through the open door. She looked stressed, her arms stretched as she held the reins while the horse tugged, wanting to go faster.

"It's going to run away from me!" Teresa shrieked. "How do I get it to stop?"

"Don't be afraid, that's the first thing," Susan said, dropping her reins on the ground and running over to help. "I thought you wanted to do this on your own," she teased.

"I do!" Teresa gasped. "I just didn't think I should get killed in the process."

Susan took the lines from Teresa and tugged hard, pulling back on the horse's head. "Whoa! There, now. You know it's somebody new leading you, don't you?"

The horse shook its head and then rubbed Susan's arm with its long nose.

Moments later Menno came out with the last horse.

Susan held the lines to two of the horses while they were hitched up to the disk harrow.

Teresa stood back watching.

When Menno finished, he gave the reins to Susan, and she climbed onto the single seat of the harrow.

"How am I going to learn?" Teresa asked. "There's no place for me."

Menno smiled. "Susan will take them around the field a few times to work off their friskiness. Then she'll stand on the back behind the seat like I used to when I taught her how to drive the disk."

"Get-up!" Susan said. The horses lurched forward, the disk machine clattering into the plowed field.

"Well, I'd best get back to my plowing," Menno said, turning to go.

Teresa watched him leave, his broad shoulders stooped. How sweet the man was under all that gruffness the Amish men carried around with them. Who would have thought it at first? She looked toward Susan making the turn at the other end of the field, swinging the horses around without slowing their walk.

What must it be like to know such things, she thought. Being able to handle a team of horses? Knowing how to work soil into a condition that would grow food? Knowing what it felt like having a father stand behind you, guiding your hands while you learned to work a disk?

She knew how to cook some now, and do laundry, and even sew a bit, but farm work was another matter. Teresa glanced over to the long lines of wash still swinging in the warm, spring afternoon breeze. This morning she had done all of that. Everything from checking the oil, adding fuel, and starting the gas motor on the washer to hanging the pieces of wash on the line with wooden clothespins. Even using the wringer no longer raised the hair on her arms with fear. Susan's tales of children getting their hands caught in its spinning rubber rollers had sounded like a horror movie. "If your fingers ever get caught," Susan had said, "hit this white bar like this. It will release the pressure." She demonstrated by hitting the bar, and the wringers immediately separated.

Teresa had tried it for practice, but she had never needed to do it for real. Now the rolling bars barely got her attention. She just made sure she held the garment a few inches from the spinning rubber, letting go before it was too late. It seemed natural, almost like breathing. Teresa brought her attention back to the field. Susan was halfway back, sitting on the seat with both hands on the reins. The disk bounced as it hit something, but Susan seemed undisturbed as she kept her feet on the boards under her.

*I'm actually going to do this!* Teresa thought. The idea had been exhilarating in the house—another thing to learn in this strange community. But now as she watched it looked quite dangerous. Unlike the washing machine wringers, a person could get killed by those wicked-looking rolling blades, to say nothing about horses with long, powerful legs that could easily run away. "Don't be scared!" she told herself. "If Susan can do it, I can."

Susan waved as she turned the horses around again.

"One more round," Susan hollered, "and then I'll give you a chance."

"Okay!" Teresa yelled back, admiring how easy Susan made it look. How graceful her friend was, riding effortlessly on the metal seat. The circus performers she had seen on TV back home couldn't have looked any more graceful.

Teresa laughed at the thought. How long had it been since she had watched television? Months now, yet it seemed like years. All her mother's warnings about missing what she used to have were so off mark. If Mom only knew.

The thought of her mother turned Teresa's smile to worry. What was Mom doing on such a wonderful spring day? Sleeping likely, or getting ready for another afternoon's work at McDonald's. That was if she still worked there. Mom didn't know anything better, didn't believe there was anything better. And yet there surely was. And Teresa was living it.

Why couldn't Mom come here and see for herself what she was experiencing? Teresa sighed. Like that was going to happen. Mom would have freaked out a long time ago. One look at Deacon Ray with his long, stern face and white beard. One whisper of who you had to marry, and Mom would have gone running home before the next sunrise.

"But see, Mom, you're so wrong," Teresa whispered. "These people do know what they're doing."

And now that they knew her better, they had seen fit to remove the restriction that she marry Yost Byler. But Yost Byler would be exactly what she needed in a husband. No more running around after men who caused shivers to run up and down her spine, but left horrible consequences in their wake. Yost Byler gave no shivers, but he was a safe man. And that's what she needed. She would marry him, truly and completely leaving behind all her old life.

"Yes, I will marry Yost Byler," she said to the open fields. "I have finally come home."

Susan approached with the team.

Teresa's heart started to pound.

"Ready?" Susan asked as she brought the team to a stop.

"Yes, I guess so," Teresa said. She moved forward and tripped, sprawling onto the ground, ending up with the huge, round feet of the horses inches from her nose.

"Oh my!" Susan said, getting down and helping Teresa up. "That's not a good way to start your day's adventure."

"I might get killed yet," Teresa worried, taking Susan's hand. "But let the journey begin! I'm ready."

Susan laughed. "You are a hardy soul, indeed. Now sit on the seat, brace your feet on that board," she said pointing. "I'll be standing right behind you."

"What if I make you fall off?" Teresa asked.

"Don't worry about that. If I have to, I'll jump sideways. I won't get hurt."

"And what about me? I'll be alone with the horses!"

"Just holler '*whoa*' really loud and pull back on the lines. They'll be glad to stop," Susan said.

"Oh Lord, have mercy on me," Teresa prayed as she positioned herself on the metal seat and braced her feet.

"Now take the lines with both hands," Susan instructed. "They will help you balance if you lean lightly backward, keeping some tension on them."

"Okay," Teresa said. "But will you take care of Samuel if I die?"

"Come on!" Susan laughed. "It's not that hard."

"That's easy for you to say."

"Okay, here we go!" Susan said. "And this will be bouncy, so let yourself go with the flow. Kind of let your body flop around. Don't fight it and soon you'll get the rhythm."

"I think my brains will go flying out!" Teresa said, hanging on to the lines.

"Get-up," Susan ordered. She clucked. "Come on, boys! Teresa, I'm right here with you. It will be fine!"

The horses moved forward, tightening the traces with a soft snap. Then they lurched forward.

"How do I turn?" Teresa screamed.

"You just pull the reins to the left or right. I'll tell you when," Susan said in Teresa's ear. "I'm watching where we're going."

Teresa hung on and closed her eyes for a few moments.

"A little to the left," Susan said.

Teresa's eyes whipped open and she jerked the lines left. The horses swung wide, their heads arched sideways.

"Not that hard next time," Susan said. "Pull back to the right."

Teresa jerked the lines right, and the horses' heads and bodies swung the other way.

"Here! Give me the lines!" Susan shouted in Teresa's ear. "Hang on to the seat for a minute."

"I'm ruining your dad's plowed field," Teresa moaned as they bounced along.

"It's nothing that can't be fixed," Susan said, bringing the horses back to a straight line and then stopping them. "Now here, try again."

"Oh my! I can't!" Teresa cried, but she grabbed the lines. "This is much harder than it looks."

"Yes, but you can do it. Now, *gently* turn them to the left," Susan instructed. "Gently...gently."

Teresa pulled, her touch lighter this time. The horses adjusted, turning slightly.

"Now turn gently to the right."

The horses moved right as Teresa guided them. She let off the tension on the reins.

"You did it! See, it's easier than driving a car," Susan said.

"I've never driven a car," Teresa retorted. "So I wouldn't know."

"You're doing fine," Susan said. "Now say 'get-up' and cluck to them."

The horses moved forward in a straight line.

"Now we're coming to the end of the field, so take the horses to the left. Gently...not too hard," Susan instructed. She reached around and added her hands to the reins.

They made the half circle with four hands on the lines. Once the horses were going straight, Susan let go.

"What an awful-looking line I'm leaving," Teresa howled, as she looked back. "It looks like wavy lines."

"You're doing fine for your first time. We'll straighten it out on the way back," Susan said, chuckling. "You didn't do any harm."

"Speak for yourself," Teresa said. "I'm getting off when we get back to the barn."

"Are you sure?" Susan asked. "This is just your first round. You'll get the hang of it."

"It's all my heart can handle," Teresa said. "I'm getting dizzier by the minute."

"Do you want to stop now?" Susan asked, a bit alarmed.

"No," Teresa said, "but I'm getting off at the barn."

Minutes later, as they approached the barn, Susan said, "That was quite *gut.*"

Teresa pulled back the lines, bringing the horses to a halt. She handed them to Susan, turned, and then jumped off in one leap, going down to her knees with the momentum.

"Are you okay?" Susan asked.

Teresa brushed off her skirt. "Glad to be alive mostly. I sure hope Yost doesn't plan on me doing much of this."

"I think he has his farming under control," Susan said. "If you can cook for him, he'll be a happy man. But really, Teresa, you did *gut* for your first time. You should try it again."

"I'll see about that tomorrow," Teresa said, moving toward the fence. She stood watching as Susan took the horses down the field. Across the fence she saw Menno wave to her. *He must have been watching. I guess he's okay with my clumsy performance. Yah, he's probably used to girls who don't know how to drive horses the first time they try. After all, he probably taught all of his girls. He's a good-hearted man who tolerates the learning process.* She smiled and waved back to him.

Remembering the laundry on the line, Teresa washed her hands at the spigot in the barn, allowing the wind to dry them as she ran over to the clothesline. She checked several of the garments for dampness and found them dry to the touch. Going into the washroom she retrieved the hamper and headed outdoors again.

"That was *gut* work in the fields," *Mamm* said with a smile when Teresa came in with a heaping load of clean wash. "I was watching. We'll make a farm girl out of you yet."

## Chapter Twenty-eight

The early afternoon sun spilled through the green trees of John Troyer's place. The rays fell onto the newly mown lawn. Church benches were spread out, some running parallel to each other with wide spaces between, others cutting across at right angles. Under the shade of an old oak, several men sat trading stories, leaning forward at times to laugh and sitting back up as they chewed on their toothpicks. Behind them the front door opened, and the second round of young boys from the dinner tables came rushing out, pulling on their hats as they ran across the grass toward the barn.

Deacon Ray's son, James, came up behind Thomas Stoll and tapped him on the shoulder. "I have to speak with you," he whispered.

"About what?" Thomas asked, pausing in the middle of the flow of boys.

"Not here. Out in the barn where it's private," James said, motioning with his head toward the men seated near them.

Thomas laughed but followed James out to the stables. "So what's the big secret, huh? Are you planning some stunt tonight you don't want the men to know about?"

"*Nee*," James said. "I just think you and I need to get on the same page concerning our girls."

"You have a girl?" Thomas asked, looking at him in surprise.

"Not yet," James said. "But I'm moving in that direction."

"You're not planning to move in on Susan, are you?" Thomas wasn't laughing anymore.

"If I wanted to do that," James replied, "I certainly wouldn't tell you, you big oaf. I'd let you find out for yourself *after* I had her safely in my buggy."

"So what have you got in mind?" Thomas asked, still not smiling.

"It's about that crazy scheme of yours to get rid of Teresa," James said. "You know, hitching her up with Yost. Well, it's not working. As *Daett* told me last night, the ministers will no longer be holding her to the engagement. I think *Daett* figures I'll forget about Teresa now, but he's wrong. So, what I want you to do is back off on encouraging Yost."

"*Yah,* I heard about the change," Thomas said, chewing on a toothpick. "But what do I have to do with it? I only went to speak with Yost that once."

"That's why Yost will come whining to you about Teresa not being required to marry him on her baptismal day. And when he does, I don't want you to give him any encouragement regarding Teresa," James said.

Thomas broke into a smile. "Aren't you getting the cart before the horse? Or has Teresa agreed to let you take her home after the hymn singing?"

"*Nee,*" James admitted. "I haven't even spoken to her about that, which brings up another reason I wanted to speak to you. Let's go visit the girls together this afternoon. Invite them out for a nice sunny walk on the lawn."

"You want me to go see Susan and take you along?" Thomas laughed. "Like that will do any good for either of us."

"I don't see you speaking with her now," James pointed out, "let alone taking her home on Sunday nights. Working with me, I'm sure you can improve your standing with Susan. You should have spun your schemes with me a long time ago!"

Thomas stared off into the distance, thinking.

"If you stick with me," James offered again, "you will be talking with Susan this afternoon."

"What makes you think the girls will say yes?" Thomas asked.

"Well, they wouldn't if it were just you or me alone with one of them," James said. "But together, it's more likely they'll agree. It won't mean quite as much, you see. At least they can tell themselves it will be just an enjoyable walk and talk—nothing more. And Susan might enjoy herself with you if she feels the pressure is off a little. We could kind of ease into their good graces."

Thomas considered it for a few minutes. "Okay, I'm with you."

"There's Menno coming now," James whispered. "We'll follow him in our buggies in a few minutes. After he's out of the driveway."

"Shh…" Thomas lifted his finger to his lips, motioning toward the ladder that led to the haymow.

The two young men scurried up just as the first of the men came into the barn to retrieve their horses for the drive home. Peeking out of the cracks in the barn siding, they waited until the men had their horses hitched and lined up at the sidewalk to pick up their womenfolk.

"We forgot something!" James whispered, sitting down in the hay and throwing his hands in the air.

"That would be our sisters," Thomas said as he watched the women coming out of the washroom, their bonnets pulled forward.

"We'd better drive them home first," James said. "It'll take too much fuss explaining why we can't. So how about we meet at the old bridge later? We can go together from there."

"What we don't go through for love," Thomas groused as he climbed down the wooden ladder.

"Love is worth it!" James asserted, looking down at Thomas's black wool hat. Following his friend outside, James grabbed his horse and led him to his buggy. He hitched up, got into the one-seater, and waited until Thomas had pulled forward. At the sidewalk, two of Thomas's sisters were waiting. Behind them Edna and Vera stood, waiting for him. James pulled to a stop and they came toward him as Thomas's sisters climbed into their buggy.

"Howdy," Edna said, pulling herself up the step and moving to the far side of the buggy.

"Why are you two so late?" Vera asked, walking around and getting in on the other side.

"I didn't know I was," James said, holding his horse until Thomas moved out of the way.

"We were waiting forever," Vera said. "The old men are already leaving."

"Maybe I'm an old man," James told her. "I didn't see a lot of boys leaving before we did."

"I think everybody was slow today," Edna said.

"Thomas and I were talking," James finally offered. "I'm going out with him this afternoon."

"Now where would you two be going?" Vera asked. "I can't imagine the two of you having someplace to go together. You don't hunt frogs in the creek anymore."

"None of your business!" James replied good-naturedly.

"I'm sure they have grown-up things to do," Edna said.

"I've been waiting a long time for James to do some grown-up things—like stick with one girl for a while," Vera said. "It's an embarrassment the way he acts."

"Maybe he has his reasons," Edna said.

"I do," James said, getting a word in edgewise. "And someday, Vera, you will have a husband and have to watch that sharp tongue of yours."

"I didn't say anything that isn't true," Vera snapped. "And I'll find a husband who doesn't mind being told the truth. Unlike some people I know. And you *are* an embarrassment, James. I even heard you were out talking behind the buggies the other Sunday night with that *Englisha* girl who is promised to Yost Byler."

"Vera!" Edna exclaimed. "I heard the same thing but didn't believe it was true."

"Well, let James tell us if it's true or not," Vera asked, looking at her brother. "Is it true, James?"

"And what if I did?" James asked, not bothering to confirm or deny. "*Daett* knows about it, so you don't have to even think about tattling."

"I can't imagine you confessing much of anything," Vera said.

"What were you talking to that *Englisha* girl about? I'm sure it wasn't about love. You don't even speak with Amish girls about that."

"Teresa is planning to join the church and community," James said. "So don't be knocking her. She's not *Englisha* anymore."

"I wasn't knocking her," Vera said. "I like her. I just can't imagine what *you* wanted with her."

"Maybe it is none of your business," Edna said, shifting on the buggy seat. "If *Daett* knows about it, then I'm sure it's taken care of."

"You are a hopeless case, always sticking up for James," Vera chided. "It spoils him."

"Well, maybe if you'd be sweet like I am," Edna said, "some young man would be taking you home from the hymn singing tonight. I saw Emery Yoder's boy looking at me today."

"You're a little young for such thoughts," James said. "And leave Vera be. She'll have plenty of chances yet. Some boys like a spitfire version of a woman."

"I'm sixteen and you can mind your own business, thank you very much." Vera glared at James.

James laughed. "I'll be sure to warn Peter about you the next time I see him."

"You'd better not!" Vera said. She looked out and watched the scenery through the open buggy door.

"Don't worry, Vera," Edna said. "James is just teasing. He really likes you deep down."

"Sure I do. That's why I don't want to get rid of her," James teased. "And if I warn Peter, she'll stay around the house forever as an old maid."

"I don't think I'm the one to be worried," Vera snapped. "You are the one who can't keep a girl."

"Woo hoo!" James laughed. "And what would you say if that were about to change?"

"I'd say you are dreaming," Vera said. "You aren't capable of settling down. Ever."

"I don't agree," Edna said. "If James finally finds a girl he likes, then there's no reason he can't settle down."

"Why can't you ever agree with me?" Vera asked her sister.

"Because you're always wrong!" James inserted, laughing as he gave Vera a nudge with his shoulder.

Vera glared at him but said nothing.

"Well, here we are...home at last," James said, turning into the driveway. "And am I ever glad to get rid of this cloud of pestilence and thunder hanging around my buggy."

"I'm just telling you what is true," Vera said, climbing down. She waited for Edna to join her. "Behave yourself this afternoon with Thomas. Whatever you're planning. You aren't little boys anymore."

"I'm going to warn Peter," James hollered after them as they walked to the house. "The poor man needs to be told."

Vera looked over her shoulder, faked a sweet smile, and held the front door for Edna.

James waited until they'd entered the house before turning the buggy around. The horse hesitated, swishing its tail at the end of the driveway.

"Come on, it won't be far," James encouraged, flicking the reins against his horse's back. Turning east at the first fork, he arrived at the bridge to find Thomas already waiting. With a wave of his hand he motioned for Thomas to take off. Thomas grinned, looking happier than he had in a long time.

The afternoon sun warmed the sides of the buggy, so James pushed open the door, allowing the soft breeze to move through. What would Teresa say when they arrived at Menno's place? he wondered. Surprised no doubt, but surely she would agree to speak with him, especially with Thomas along. Even Susan shouldn't object to an hour or so spent on the front lawn. But what if she *did* object and turned Thomas away? Would that not cause Teresa to do the same?

And why hadn't he thought of this sooner? What had come over him to think that the spat between Susan and Thomas wouldn't affect even an innocent talk on the lawn? He ought to turn back now before it was too late. But it was already too late. He would have to tough the thing through. Closing one door of the buggy shut, he stayed close behind Thomas as they rattled down the dirt road.

James shifted on his seat, remembering what Vera had said on the way home from church. The girl had a way of getting under his skin with that sharp tongue, but on this point she was simply wrong. He did not pursue girls until they were willing to have him drive them home, and then dump them. It simply wasn't true. He was interested in much more than the pursuit. A wonderful girl would be well worth the catch.

And Teresa was different than any of the other girls. Whether she was the one he would marry was another matter. But that didn't need to be decided at the moment. For now, the *gut* heart she had was enough reason to know her better.

"*Gut* afternoon," Susan's *mamm* said after she opened the door.

"*Gut* afternoon," Thomas said, his face in a stiff smile. "We would like to speak with the girls, with Susan and Teresa."

Anna didn't move. "They don't want to speak with either of you."

"But it's only for a little while," Thomas encouraged. "James and I thought they might like to walk around the lawn with us."

"I can only tell you what they told me," Anna responded. "You should ask them home on a Sunday evening before you just drop by."

"I guess so," Thomas said, turning to go.

"That wasn't a good idea after all," Thomas hissed as they walked back to their buggies.

"It was an awful, horrible, rotten idea," James agreed, feeling his neck burn. "I'm sorry."

"Well, don't feel too bad," Thomas said, relenting. "It was worth a try. Anything is worth a try to reach Susan."

# CHAPTER TWENTY-NINE

Teresa watched from the upstairs window of Susan's room, hiding behind the dark-blue curtains. Below her Thomas and James were walking toward their buggies, stopping to speak a few words before untying their horses and pulling out of the driveway.

"You shouldn't watch them leaving," Susan said. She was lying on her bed, her nose in a book. "Thomas is good riddance, but I'm having second thoughts about James. Maybe he's not so bad after all."

"His face was bright red," Teresa said. "I could see it from up here, the poor boy."

"I suppose he's not used to having girls tell him to take a walk back to his buggy," Susan said. "At least not without seeing him first."

"Maybe I should have spoken with him. But I don't think so," Teresa said. "It won't make things any easier. Besides, if he's serious, he'll be back again."

"You sound awfully confident of yourself," Susan commented, looking up from her book.

"Not really," Teresa replied, moving away from the window. "But I know his type. The harder the contest, the more interested they are."

"Oh!" Susan laughed. "So now we are reeling in the fish. I didn't think you had it in you, Teresa."

"No, it's not that," Teresa said as she moved to respond to a cry from Samuel across the hall. "Just a moment and I'll be back."

Teresa left the door to Susan's bedroom open, entered her own, and picked up the kicking baby. Bringing Samuel back, she sat on the floor and put him beside her on a blanket. Samuel blinked in the bright light, his eyes drawn to the window. Teresa ran her fingers through his wispy hair.

"My little sweetheart," she whispered. "You're such a darling!"

"So what was this about James?" Susan asked, closing her book.

"He thinks I'm playing hard to get," Teresa said.

"So this afternoon will really help reinforce that," Susan said.

"Yes, it will. And I think he'll be back. But once a girl says yes they lose interest."

"I don't think Thomas is like that," Susan said. "But then maybe he is. Perhaps that's why he lost interest in me. I guess I was too available."

Teresa looked up from the baby. "Susan, you know you might be wrong about Thomas. Don't you think he deserves another chance?"

"You didn't see Thomas acting embarrassed when they were walking back out to the buggies, did you?" Susan asked.

"I wasn't watching him."

"Oh, I see," Susan said with a grin. "So you *do* have an interest in James?"

Teresa blushed. "That's not the point, and you know it."

"I think we should pray long and hard about your situation," Susan said.

"Shh…" Teresa held her finger to her lips. "I think I hear something. A buggy's coming."

"They go past the road all the time," Susan said, picking up her book again.

Teresa stood and walked over to the window. She pushed the drapes aside again; this time Samuel was cradled in her other arm.

"It's him!" Teresa gasped. "He's come back."

"Won't they take no for an answer?" Susan said, rising and moving toward the window.

"No, it's just James. Thomas isn't with him."

Delight flashed across Susan's face. "My, talk about answered prayer! I do think you may be right."

"I can't talk to him." Teresa looked pale. "I have Samuel to take care of. He's not fed yet."

"When *Da Hah* moves, there are always ways to say yes." Susan took Teresa by the arm. "Samuel can wait for such an important thing as you visiting with his future *daett*."

"Susan, please! Don't say such things," Teresa protested. "James doesn't want another man's child. Besides, Yost may come visiting soon. You know it's about time for him to be back."

"Just come!" Susan said, leading Teresa, who was still holding Samuel, out of the bedroom.

At the bottom of the stairs Anna was waiting for them. "I see James has come back. What shall I tell him this time? And don't you think it's about time you girls did your own talking?"

"I agree with that," *Daett* said from his rocking chair.

"But Samuel needs to eat," Teresa protested.

"I'll tend to the baby for a few minutes," *Mamm* said, taking Samuel from Teresa's arms. "You can walk around the corner of the porch if you need a little privacy."

Susan shook her head. "You will sit on the porch swing and have a nice long talk," she ordered. "And I want to hear no more argument out of you."

Teresa slipped on her coat, her cheeks flushed. Without a backward glance, she walked to the front door and opened it before there was even a knock. She might as well face James quickly. Let him think she was eager to see him. It wouldn't matter. One look at her face should clear him of any misconception.

"Oh, it's you!" James said from the bottom of the steps.

"Yes, it's me," she replied. "You've come back."

"I'm sorry about earlier," James said, coming up to stand beside her. "I understand why you refused to see me. That was very clumsy of me bringing Thomas along. May I speak with you for a few minutes?"

Teresa looked over her shoulder at the closed door. "We can sit on the swing to talk. I'm afraid it can't be for long though."

James followed her across the porch. The chains on the old swing groaned as they sat down. Silence settled around them for long moments.

Teresa glanced at James out of the corner of her eye. He was young, his arms bristling with muscles from the farmwork, the side of his face she could see unlined. Right now he was staring straight ahead. Clearly he was different from Yost—with other things on his mind than whether she could wash clothes or bake bread.

"I'm very sorry about how sudden and strange our relationship has been proceeding so far," James finally said, his voice strained. "It must seem very odd to you. First, I talk with you after the Sunday night hymn singing, and then I show up here unexpectedly. That's probably not how things are done in the *Englisha* world."

"I wouldn't worry about my old world," she said. "I've almost forgotten it already. It's strange how such things fade away and so quickly. I thank the Lord every day for the wonderful opportunity I have of living among the people of the community. It's been an answer to my most fervent prayers."

"I suppose you never thought about someone like me," he said, looking sideways at her.

Teresa laughed. "No, but I doubt if you ever thought about some-one like me either. I mean, how could you have? Your people don't do the wrong things that I've done."

James shrugged. "You must not hold us up too high. We are also made of flesh and blood. We have our failings and shortcomings like anyone else."

"I don't see any of your unmarried girls with babies," Teresa said, rising to her feet, her cheeks burning. "James, you're a kind man, but you really need to go now. And you shouldn't come back like this again. I'm okay now. I know I don't have to marry Yost Byler if I don't want to. I really appreciate what you did for me—or tried to do for me. Menno has promised to give Yost and me a nice wedding after I'm baptized, just like the ones his own daughters had. That's more than I ever dreamed of. And James, I have you to thank for that. This way, I can always look back and speak to Samuel of my wedding day.

A wedding day like all the other mothers in the community had. Thank you for that."

"*Nee,*" James said, raising his hand. "I'm not trying to do things for you, Teresa. Well, maybe I was that first night. Maybe it started like that, but it's more than that now. Teresa, I want to know you better. You have such faith in *Da Hah*, such trust in Him, and apparently you'd marry Yost Byler even though you don't love him. All for the good of your child. That shows a wonderfully, deep, *gut* heart, Teresa. I'm attracted to that. Can you see that?"

"I won't change my mind, James," she said, "for a whole bunch of reasons."

"Please, Teresa, sit down," James said. "Let's talk about it. Perhaps I can explain myself better."

"Samuel is hungry," she said. "I can't leave him for Anna or Susan to take care of. They do enough for me already. And Susan will want to leave for the hymn singing soon. You really should go, James."

"Ah…" He jumped to his feet. "I have the perfect idea. I'll wait and drive you and Susan to the hymn singing. Afterward, I'll bring both of you home. You don't have to be embarrassed of me or worry I'm going to pressure you into anything. I'll drop you off after we get home and leave."

"What good would that do?" Teresa asked, regarding him with a tilt of her head.

"I don't know," James said. "Perhaps you could see then that I'm not the awful person you seem to think I am. We could talk at least."

"You're not awful," Teresa said. "I know that. The problem isn't with you; it's with me and my situation."

"Please let me take you," James said, ignoring her words.

Teresa absently bit her lip as she thought for a moment. "I'll have to ask Susan."

"I'll wait," he said.

Teresa walked across the porch, her long dress brushing the floor and railing. At the corner she turned to look back.

James smiled.

Teresa felt an odd sensation in her stomach at the sight of his warm smile.

"Well, what did he say?" Susan asked as soon as Teresa opened the door. She was sitting on the couch with the squirming baby.

"He's still on the porch," *Mamm* said.

"James wants to drive us both to the hymn singing and bring us back," Teresa said. "I told him I'd ask you."

"Is he staying afterward?" *Mamm* asked.

Teresa shook her head.

"And you agreed?" Susan said.

"I said I would ask you."

"It's okay with me," Susan said. "I think it's a good thing, Teresa. Here, take the baby. Go upstairs with him. I'll bring James in, and when you're ready we can leave."

"We never had such *kafüffles* when we were young people," *Mamm* commented.

"That's because you didn't have as much fun," Susan said, waving Teresa upstairs with the back of her hand.

Teresa made her way up the stairs with a prayer on her lips. *Dear God, I can't believe I'm doing this. I said I'd never entertain such thoughts of young men again, and here I am agreeing to go somewhere with one. I do think I'm still the same girl I was. Will You help me do the right thing?* Teresa took Samuel into her room and laid him on the bed. He cried, but she stilled him with a whispered, "I'll be with you in a minute, little one." Finding a match in the dresser drawer, she lit the kerosene lamp, and then fed the baby by its flickering light. He watched her with wide-open eyes, seeming to search the depths of her soul.

"Oh, you poor child!" Tears ran down her face. "How could I have brought you into the world without a proper father? I see now how wicked it was of me. I was thinking only of me and what I needed. I promise you, I won't do that anymore, little one. I'll put your interests first—only yours. I'll find you the best father I possibly can. I don't care what my heart wants. It's what you need that's important. And what you need is someone stable. Someone who will provide for you.

Someone who doesn't run away when rough times come. Someone who will love me regardless of how fat I become or how ugly I get in my old age. I promise you, baby Samuel, that you will have someone like that for a dad. I have the faith in my heart that God has given to me. I know He will not betray you…will not betray *us*."

Samuel blinked and swallowed. His eyes were deep and full with flickering shadows dancing on their mirrored surfaces.

Teresa would not let Samuel down. She would marry Yost as soon as she was baptized.

# Chapter Thirty

W hen she had finished feeding Samuel, Teresa came down the stairs, pausing on the last step before entering the living room. James stood to his feet when she entered and smiled generously.

Teresa hardly knew how to respond. Couldn't he notice the baby in her arms? She was not an unsoiled girl. She was a mother without a father for her child. She was something surely shameful in the Amish world. Her face ought to be burning with shame. Instead, she found herself returning his smile.

"It's high time we get going," Susan said, taking Samuel from Teresa's arms and handing him to *Mamm* seated in her rocking chair.

"He's a good-looking child," James said, nodding toward *Mamm*.

"And well-tempered," *Mamm* agreed. "And I guess I should know with nine children. But they all were girls. Maybe baby boys are naturally better tempered."

"Oh, I think they are!" James said, grinning from ear to ear.

"Now *Mamm*," Susan said. "Why did you go give James a chance like that? You know girl babies are always easier to take care of."

*Daett* laughed. "Babies come from *Da Hah* in all shapes and sizes," he said, "and I was perfectly happy with my nine girls."

"There you go," Susan said. "That's well-spoken, so wipe that grin off your face, James. Now we better go before we miss supper at the hymn singing."

James held his hand out. "Shall we go then?"

Teresa stared at his outstretched hand. Was she supposed to take it? Was he leading her out to the buggy? Surely not. The community had no such practices that she had ever seen. James must simply be inviting her to come.

"Oh," Teresa said. "Yes. I'm ready."

Susan was already at the front door, waiting. Teresa walked past James, keeping her eyes down, not looking at his face. Opening the door, Susan smiled, motioning for Teresa to go first. Walking together in silence toward the buggy, the two girls climbed in while James untied the horse.

"It's awful tight in here," Teresa whispered. Why had she not thought of this before? There was hardly room for two, let alone three people.

Susan smiled. "We do this all the time, and it's okay. All you do is move out to the edge of the seat, and the boy sits in the middle."

Teresa glanced at James, who was coming back with the tie rope in his hand. Sitting in the middle was definitely better than sitting in someone's lap, she supposed. But they wouldn't do such things here. She had to stop thinking such thoughts from the past.

"Well," James said, climbing in, "are you comfortable, Teresa?"

"I'm okay," she replied.

Susan got in. "Just don't run over the dog," Susan said.

"But there is no dog!" James said, making the turn, the buggy squealing its wheels on the metal side rollers.

"That was a joke!" Susan laughed.

"Thomas never mentioned you cracking jokes," James commented as he leaned forward to check for traffic before pulling out on the main road.

"Maybe Thomas doesn't always see things," Susan said. "And next time you come calling, please leave him at home. You'll get a much better welcome."

"Come on now, Susan," James chided. "Thomas is a nice man. And he cares about you."

"Are you his go-between now? Sent to sweet-talk me into something?" Susan asked. "I thought better of you."

James laughed. "I wouldn't even think of trying that. I was just stating the obvious."

"Well, you're not going to change my mind about him," Susan said. "So please don't even try."

"So what is your opinion of our community now, Teresa?" James asked, glancing sideways as he changed the subject.

"I think it's wonderful," Teresa replied. "It's even better than I thought it would be."

"A glowing report then," James said. "That's *gut*. And what do you think of the young people?"

"Well, the girls have been nice to me," Teresa said. "And it's something how well everyone is brought up."

"That's saying it differently," James said. "I guess we *are* 'brought up.'"

"You can be thankful for that," Teresa said. "I expect the rules and the parents watching what the young people do can seem a little overbearing at times, but believe me, the other way is not good. I should know. I longed many times for a mother who cared about what I was doing."

"Was your father ever around?" James asked.

"Not that I remember," Teresa said.

"Your parents were divorced then? And you didn't have visitations with your father?" James asked. "I thought the *Englisha* had laws about such things when the parents aren't together?"

"My mother wasn't married to my father," Teresa admitted reluctantly. "I guess I got used to it. But I don't want that kind of life for Samuel. That's what brought me here."

"You really shouldn't pester Teresa with so many questions, James," Susan warned.

"I'm sorry," James said. "I was just curious. And I think it's *gut* what Teresa's doing. Not many girls would do that for a child."

"Thank you," Teresa replied. "That was a nice thing to say."

"That's because I'm a nice person," James answered with a smile.

"You're also arrogant and full of yourself," Susan retorted.

"That's also true," James admitted, turning into the driveway. Lines of buggies were parked by the barn. He pulled the buggy to a stop at the end of the walk.

"Now, you are taking us home again, right?" Susan asked after stepping down.

"Of course," James said. "I wouldn't leave you stranded."

"Just checking. You never know about boys." Susan walked around the buggy to join Teresa.

James ignored the remark and clucked to his horse. They took off toward the barn.

"The boys are staring at us," Teresa whispered. "What are they thinking?"

"They're wondering why James brought both of us to the hymn singing," Susan said.

"Why *did* he bring us?" Teresa asked.

"Because he likes you," Susan said. "Don't be silly. You know that. What do you think of him?"

"You know the answer to that," Teresa said, "You know I've already made up my mind about my future, so don't entertain any other thoughts."

"James is turning out to be nicer than I thought he was," Susan said, holding open the washroom door. "Maybe you ought to give him a chance."

Stepping inside, Teresa removed her shawl and bonnet and lay them the large pile. Already she knew how to find them again when the time came to leave for home. The feeling was good, like she was already a real Amish woman, even before she was baptized. This morning Bishop Henry had asked her a question in German, and the answer had come a little slow, but it had come. Even Deacon Ray had smiled his approval. But what would he say about his son bringing her to the hymn singing? He wouldn't like it…not at all. She really must convince James on the way home that his attentions were not wise. He needed to find himself a good Amish girl, one who had a father around while growing up and a mother who took care of her.

"Teresa," Susan whispered in her ear, "are you okay? We need to go inside."

"I was just thinking," Teresa said, trying to smile.

Susan shrugged and led the way in. The murmur of the girls in the kitchen dropped when they came in, resuming moments later to the normal level of cheerful chatter as the two young women blended in and greeted everyone.

Teresa stayed close to Susan, nodding at the greetings and smiling her own. All the while, James's face stayed in her mind—the crinkles when he smiled, his approval of her reason for coming to the community, how strong his hands were on the reins as he clucked to his horse. Could a woman want anything more in a man? A man like that who could plow fields, milk cows by hand, and still have a heart that seemed to understand and appreciate a woman's heart and motives...

The world of Asbury Park had certainly produced nothing of that kind. There might be good men in Laura and Robby's world, but not like the men here. The men here were simply better. Here there was the closeness to the earth, this realness which took one's breath away. But did Yost Byler have all those things? Surely he must. No matter, she had to be satisfied with what was good enough and not reach for what was not hers. James's future belonged to an Amish girl, one who would be good enough for such a perfect man.

A male voice from the living room rose above the conversation. "We are so glad to have the young folks here for supper tonight. If everyone is here, Deacon Ray will lead us in prayer."

Teresa listened as James's *daett* prayed, his voice rising and falling with the German words as he led out with "*Unser Vater im himmel...*"

"Our Father in heaven," Teresa translated as she mouthed the words along with him. Joy flooded through her heart. She was standing here with these people, eating supper with their young people, saying with them that God was her Father. There could not be more to ask for. This great God whom they worshipped would surely smite her for reaching beyond what she'd been given. "Help me stay humble, God," she added under her breath. "I am so thankful for what

You have given me already. I really want to be happy with Yost and the love he offers. I'm sure You will help me make this clear to James so that he will understand. I want to do what You want me to do."

Deacon Ray finished the prayer, and conversation in the room resumed.

Teresa waited with the other girls until the boys had gone through the line before moving to fill her plate. There was meatloaf on the table, already half gone, but a young girl appeared with another pan and slid it onto the table. Potato salad sat beside the corn and green beans. Bread and jam finished out the main course. Beyond that sat pies—apple, cherry, and chocolate cream.

"There's so much to eat!" Teresa commented to the girl in front of her. "I'll get fat soon."

"Then you'll look like a real Amish girl!" The girl laughed.

"I didn't mean that! I don't think any of you are overweight," Teresa replied instantly, chagrined.

Even though Eunice was smiling, she hadn't looked happy at Teresa's initial comment.

"Perhaps not," Eunice said, adding, "I saw you came with James tonight. Was he at your place this afternoon?"

"He stopped by for a few minutes," Teresa managed. She felt the heat rising in her face. Her face must be blazing red. Oh why hadn't she looked closer who was in the line in front of her? Of course Eunice would have objections to James even speaking with her, let alone driving her here in his buggy.

"Does Susan have her buggy here?" Eunice asked. "I don't remember seeing it."

"No," Teresa admitted. "James brought both of us, and he's driving us home again."

"Really? Is he seeing Susan and you just came along for the ride? James would be nice enough for such a thing."

"I don't think so," Teresa said, her heart racing.

"Really…" Eunice turned her attention to filling her plate without waiting for any more comments.

Teresa kept distance between them until they reached the end of the table. She moved to sit at the other end of the room. If Eunice was upset with the situation, likely others would be also. This could bring nothing but trouble for her baptismal Sunday, which was coming up soon. Bishop Henry wouldn't smile any longer at her progress if controversy stirred.

"Please, dear God," she prayed, staring at her plate of food, "I'm not trying to cause any trouble for anyone. And remember Samuel. Bless him and help me keep him safe and loved."

Someone sat on the bench beside her, but Teresa didn't look up. Whoever it was likely had more comments to make about James bringing Susan and her to the hymn singing.

"I wouldn't let Eunice bother you," Susan's soft voice said beside her.

Teresa jerked her head up. "Oh, it's you!" she said in relief.

"Eunice was just hoping James was driving me around," Susan said, "so she can make a final move on Thomas."

"Love is so horrible and messy," Teresa moaned. "I don't want problems before my baptismal."

"You aren't making any problems," Susan assured her. "Don't worry about it. And don't look so white. People will think we're starving you at the house or working you half to death."

"I'll try," Teresa said, taking a bite and chewing. It tasted so good it almost melted in her mouth. Tears stung in her eyes, but she refused to release them. God would help her through this. He would remember Samuel.

# Chapter Thirty-one

⊹

Teresa closed the songbook as the last notes of the Sunday night hymn singing hung in the air. The round clock on the living room wall said nine o'clock on the dot. As usual, the young people's time was closing with punctuality. Nothing else was normal though. Teresa's heart was racing at the thought of driving home with James. Sure, Susan would be along, but James would be seated in the middle. She'd have to speak to him again. There were things she would have to tell him, even with Susan along. Words that would be hard to say. Perhaps it would be better to say nothing and just jump out of the buggy and run for the house the moment they got home? James had promised, had he not, that this was only a drive home and nothing more.

"We're ready to go," Susan said, interrupting Teresa's thoughts.

"Okay." Teresa got to her feet. Moving down the center aisle between the boys and girls, Teresa kept her eyes on the floor. Surely her face must be burning—her neck certainly felt on fire. The young people had to know what James was doing and were probably wondering why. And well they should. It made no sense according to their strict traditions. No girl should be riding home with a boy who wasn't her brother unless there was a good reason. And she was an outsider.

In the washroom they found their wraps in the light of the gas lantern. Teresa double-checked to make sure she had her own. With the way her mind was going, she didn't want to accidentally pick up someone else's wraps. Stepping out into the night air, the cool breeze brushed across her warm face.

"James's buggy isn't here yet," Susan said. "We must have come out a little too soon or else James was held up."

"How can you tell the difference between buggies?" Teresa asked, peering into the darkness. The night was broken only by the light coming from the washroom window and the low lights from the approaching buggies.

"You'll learn," Susan said. "Every boy has something a little different on his buggy. Maybe a light that's set wider apart or a piece of reflector tape in a certain spot. And his horse, of course. That's the best way to tell—if it's not too dark to see the horse."

"How will you know James's buggy?" Teresa asked.

"I'm not sure about his buggy," Susan admitted. "I haven't seen it that much, but I'm sure his horse will stand out. James drives one of the best horses around. It holds its head high up in the air. And there will be enough light from the headlights to see that."

"How did you tell Thomas's buggy from the others?" Teresa asked.

"Let's not talk about that," Susan said. "Here comes James! See how the horse holds up its head?"

Teresa followed Susan down the walk. Approaching the buggy, she waited until Susan had gone around and had climbed in before she pulled herself up the step.

"Good to see both of you again," James said, holding himself off the seat with his hands on the dashboard until Teresa and Susan were seated. He sat down between them, letting out the lines and his horse dashed forward.

"It's a good night for driving," Susan said as they moved through the darkness.

Teresa looked outside at the twinkling stars above. They looked so beautiful, so clear, so majestic and pure. Unlike what she was feeling at the moment with James's leg crammed tightly against hers.

"Yes, it is," James agreed, pulling out to pass a buggy. He stayed well away from the ditch.

"Don't try to show off," Susan said. "I know you have a fast horse."

"I'm not trying to show off." James laughed. "I just get tired of holding him back."

"I see the hymn singing hasn't made you any less conceited," Susan said. "I figured singing holy songs would sanctify your soul a little." She smiled.

"Ha!" James said. "Now I see why Thomas doesn't want to drive you home on Sunday nights. Your tongue is sharper than a hay-mowing blade."

"Just think what it will be like when I get older," Susan retorted. "My husband won't need to waste money on a hay cutter."

James roared with laughter. "I'll have to tell Thomas about that," he said.

"And you think this will help you how?" Susan asked.

"Look, Susan," he said, "I'm not trying to help myself. I'm just driving you home and dropping you off. Although I must say I'm enjoying myself more than I figured I would. No wonder Thomas is working so hard to get back into your good graces."

"Believe me," Susan said, "I was nice to Thomas for years, and look where it got me."

"So be nice to him again," James said. "He's sorry, you know. And he would be delighted."

"I don't want to delight him, James." Susan groaned. "Let Eunice do that."

"That's not what Thomas wants, Susan," James said, his voice turning sober. "Poor Thomas is lonely tonight and full of pain. His heart is throbbing in the hopes he can see you again someday. But no, you cruelly send him away and lock the door behind you."

Susan laughed. "Now if Thomas could talk like that," she said, "perhaps I'd listen just to hear the sound of his voice."

"I doubt if he can," James said, slowing his horse to make the next turn. "It's not everyone who can."

"You're both so conceited you're in danger of blowing up," Susan commented. "And come to think of it, if Thomas could talk like that, he'd be singing it in Eunice's ear, so what good would that do me?"

"You shouldn't be so bitter, Susan," James corrected. "We are to forgive you know, and Thomas is very sorry."

"Now how do you know that?" Susan asked.

"Because I'm his friend."

"So tell me something," Susan said. "Did Thomas take Eunice home while I was gone? I've often wondered."

"Thomas behaved himself pretty well while you were gone," James said.

"That's not answering my question, James," Susan noted.

"Maybe it's not my place to answer," James said.

"That's all I need to hear," Susan said.

"Yes, I think he did," James admitted. "But he figured out his mistake pretty quickly."

"Too bad he didn't figure it out before he kissed her," Susan shot back.

"My, my," James said. "I'm glad I'm not on your bad side. That would be an awful place to be."

"Just remember that," Susan said.

Teresa cleared her throat. "I think Susan is a very wonderful person. I wouldn't be here today if it weren't for her."

"Now that's a good point," James agreed. "Susan *is* a very nice girl after all."

"That's a pretty plain thing to see," Susan said smugly.

"Now who's full of herself?" James asked, as he turned into the Hostetler driveway. "Well, here we are, ladies! And it has been a mighty pleasant evening. Perhaps we can do it again sometime?"

"I don't think so," Susan said, climbing out of the buggy. "At least not with me along. Teresa, well, that's another matter. You'll have to speak to her about that."

"*Yah*," James said. "I think I do need to speak with her. Will you stay out here a few minutes, Teresa?"

"I'm not sure," Teresa said, her voice weak. "I thought you said you'd just bring us home and nothing more."

"I won't keep you long," James said.

Perhaps now was the time to tell James what needed to be said. And if Susan wasn't here, that would make it even easier.

"Take your time, Teresa. I'll wait up for you," Susan said, disappearing into the darkness.

"I'm sorry about ignoring you on the way home," James said, as he settled into his side of the buggy. "I really wanted to speak with you, but perhaps it's better with Susan not here."

At least he wasn't as close now. It made talking to him easier.

"That's okay," she said. "It was fun listening to the two of you talk. I never had friends like that while I was growing up."

"I'm sorry about that," James said. "But maybe there's still time to make up for it. The people in the community have really taken you up well."

"You have all been wonderful," she said. "But James, the truth is this can't go on between us. It can't."

"What do you think is going on, Teresa?" he asked. "I just brought you home. There's nothing wrong with that."

"From the looks I got at the hymn singing, there seems to be plenty wrong with it. I know your traditions enough to know that when a boy takes a girl home after hymn singing it implies he's interested in dating her. And that can't be, James," she said. "I've tried and tried to explain this to you, but you don't seem to listen."

"I *am* listening, Teresa," he said. "But I don't want to hear what you're saying because it's not right."

"But it *is* right, James." She looked at his face in the darkness. "Everything I have told you is the way it is."

"Maybe it's only the way you think it has to be," he said, pushing his hat back on his head. "I know that you feel bad about your past, but I also know I really admire you in spite of it. I would like to see more of you, Teresa. Can't you open your heart a little bit for that? If you find that you don't like me, you can always send me away. But give me a chance."

"I don't seem to have much success in sending you away now, James," she said. "So how would I be more successful in the future?"

He smiled, the outline of his face showing in the dim buggy lights.

"I'll know when you're serious about not liking me, Teresa," he said. "Your eyes will agree with your words."

Teresa sighed. "I didn't know it was that obvious."

He laughed. "It's not a bad thing, Teresa. Follow your heart! Can't you do that?"

"Maybe I'm tired of following my heart, James. I'm tired of where it leads me. You believe following my heart can only lead to good things, but I know better. I've gone very far down the wrong road, and I don't want to do it again. And now I have Samuel to think of. Yost is more than willing to be a father to him, to help me bring my baby up the way I want him to live."

"And you don't think I would?"

"I'm not sure. And I can't use Yost as a fallback option. It's not fair to him."

"I wouldn't worry about Yost," he said. "I'll talk to him about this and explain."

"No, you won't, James. You don't have anything to tell him because you're not sure about me and I'm not sure about you. And what of all those other girls you've known, James? The Amish girls? What was wrong with them? And none of them had a baby without a father. Were they not good enough for you? And if so, how can I be when I've already sinned in such a horrible way?"

"Some things can't be explained neatly," he said. "You're different from the other girls."

Teresa laughed bitterly. "You can say that again."

"And why bring up the other girls I've dated?" he asked. "Does it bother you?"

"A little," she said. "Mostly because I'm not sure you'd stay serious if I allowed myself to become serious. You seem to like the chase."

"You don't have to worry about that, Teresa," he said. "I promise."

"That's not good enough for me, James. 'I promise' doesn't carry much weight in my world. And look how lightly you're treating my promise to Yost. I *did* promise to marry him."

He sighed and looked out into the darkness.

"I'm sorry, Teresa," he finally said. "I really am. Isn't there some way you will at least think about this? Take as much time as you wish, but don't shut me out of your life. Yost can be taken care of easily. Believe me, he'll understand."

"I'm going in now, James. We've been alone too long already."

"Will you think about what I've said?"

She took a look into his eyes. "I'll think about it, but don't count on anything." With that she climbed down the buggy steps.

"I'll be thinking about you," he said as she walked toward the house. His words hung in the night air.

Teresa heard the buggy wheels behind her squeal as he turned around in the driveway.

Susan was sitting on the couch when Teresa walked in.

"The baby's asleep upstairs," Susan said. "You didn't send James away for good, did you?"

Teresa shook her head as tears sprang to her eyes.

"You poor thing," Susan said, standing to wrap her arms around Teresa. "It will work out okay in the end. It always does."

"But what if it doesn't?" Teresa wailed. "I promise things, but I can't seem to keep anything I promise."

"You must trust *Da Hah*," Susan said. "He's not led you wrong so far, has He?"

Teresa shook her head, covering her face with her hands. "I can't believe I told James I'd think about what he said!"

## Chapter Thirty-two

Yost tossed the harness onto the horse's back and then reached under to grab the belly straps in the dim light filtering through the cobweb-laced barn window. A quick pull snapped the weakened point where the metal clip had worn a groove across the leather.

*"Acht,"* Yost groaned. "Now, I'll never get back in time for the chores."

Running into the milk house, Yost found a roll of wire and large pliers. Returning to the waiting horse, he patched the broken leather with a wire hook and tightened the rest of the straps with care. Leading his horse outside, Yost blinked in the bright Saturday afternoon sun and pulled his straw hat over his forehead.

The horse stood unmoving as Yost fastened the tugs and threw the lines into the buggy. Climbing in, he hollered, "Get-up there," and the horse plodded out of the driveway. Yost settled into the buggy seat and pushed back his hat, his brow troubled.

Were even half the things true which he kept hearing about Teresa? If they were, they were still hard to believe. Yet, Mose's boy, Amos, was not one to make up stories. If he said Deacon Ray's son, James, was driving the *Englisha* girl to the hymn singings, then it must be true. Why hadn't someone told him sooner? If Amos hadn't needed to borrow the small disk for his *mamm*'s garden, he still wouldn't know.

That's what came from thinking all was well. Teresa had been doing so *gut* with her instruction classes. If this rumor was true, Bishop Henry would be bringing those to a fast stop. Deacon Ray would surely not tolerate his son having anything to do with an *Englisha* girl, let alone one with a child.

Yost urged his horse on, his buggy rattling south. At the road leading to Deacon Ray's place he paused, his horse almost coming to a stop. With a shake of his head, he turned right, slapping the lines.

The best thing would be a talk with Teresa herself. Perhaps this could all be straightened out without either Bishop Henry or Deacon Ray being involved. That would be the best outcome. Because who knew what complications would arise if those two began speaking their minds.

Was this what one went through with getting married to a woman? This trouble, this unexpected turn of events, this news which fell out of the sky on one's head. Yost ran his fingers through his beard. Surely after the vows were said things would not continue so. Surely a woman could only cause so many anxious moments.

But now was not the time to be asking such questions. Now was the time to find out what went wrong and fix the problem. And surely there were plenty of *gut* things to enjoy with a woman in the house to offset any trouble she might bring with her. There was supper on the table for one, and clean clothing for another. Both were worth some unpleasant situations, perhaps even very unpleasant situations.

Menno Hostetler's place appeared in front of him, and Yost pulled back on the reins, slowing his horse to a walk. It would not do to dash into Menno's driveway like some wild unkempt youngster with dust flying off his buggy wheels. He was a grown man.

Someone was on the front porch with a broom and dustpan. Yost squinted in the bright sunlight. Was it Teresa working on a Saturday afternoon? The girl disappeared, and he shook his head. It could have been Susan. But still, even if it wasn't Teresa, Anna would be continuing her education in the community's ways. If Susan was not idle on a Saturday afternoon, neither would Teresa be.

Pulling up to the hitching post, Yost climbed out. Behind him the barn door opened and Menno came out.

"Good afternoon," Menno said, a smile playing on his face. "What brings you out on such a fine day?"

"Ah…" Yost cleared his throat. There was no sense in spilling everything into Menno's ears. He had little control over what Teresa did when it came to love. "I think I had best be speaking with Teresa if she's around."

"The women were working on the Saturday cleaning the last I was in the house," Menno said. "That and baking bread and pies. Do you wish to stay for supper? I'm sure there's plenty of food."

Yost swallowed hard. Now this was a temptation hard to resist, but cows didn't take well to off-schedule milking. "I...I'd like to..." he managed to get out, "but the chores are not done. I should really be getting back, but perhaps some other time?"

"You're always welcome," Menno said. "I'm sure if you go up to the house and knock, Anna will welcome you. She probably saw you arrive."

Yost nodded and tied his horse to the hitching rail as Menno went back to the barn. With hesitant steps, Yost moved toward the front door. When he was still at the bottom landing, the door opened and Teresa stepped out.

"Good afternoon," she said with a smile.

"*Gut* afternoon," Yost said, brushing a piece of straw off his shirt-sleeve. "I hope I'm not keeping you from your work, but I thought we had best speak a few words with each other."

"We're almost done for the afternoon," Teresa said. "Anna said I should come out and see what you want. We can sit over there, if you wish," she continued, nodding toward the porch swing.

"I can't stay long," Yost said, "but I do keep my thoughts better in order if I'm sitting. I hope I will not be saying things that should not be said."

"I suppose there are many things that should have been said some time ago," Teresa said, leading the way to the swing. "But the ways of the community are new and strange to me."

"I can imagine," Yost said. "But it was not your place to say what needs to be said. I should have been here a long time ago—back when I first heard the ministers were no longer requiring you to agree to a marriage before being baptized."

"*Yah*," Teresa said, not looking at him.

"Are you changing your mind…about the wedding?" Yost asked. "I know I should have been making plans with you, but I was waiting for you to come to my place, as we talked about the last time I was here."

When Teresa remained silent, Yost continued. "Do you still plan to say the vows with me at your baptismal?" he asked. "That wouldn't take too much planning and would keep things very simple."

"What if I changed my mind?" Teresa asked. "A woman can always do that, and apparently your ministers agree that I should be able to."

Yost shook his head. "Does this have something to do with a proper wedding day? I can't provide a big wedding which is why we should be married at your baptismal. But I have my place ready after the wedding. I am able to support you and the child well enough. I understand that is important to you."

"It's not the wedding day, Yost," Teresa said. "Menno has offered to give me one here when I get married. Isn't that nice of him? I can't say how much I appreciate that."

"They are nice people," Yost said, staring across Menno's freshly planted cornfield. He might as well get to the point. "So is it Deacon Ray's boy who is holding you back? I was told that James drove you and Susan around on Sunday. Is this placing thoughts into your head? You know that James cannot give you a home for your child right away. And you can't keep on living here with Menno and Anna, even if you are baptized."

"I really don't know what to think, Yost," Teresa admitted. "I can't say I've changed my mind, but I do want to take Menno up on his offer. It would be so sweet to have a real Amish wedding. I know I don't deserve it, but I also haven't deserved much else offered to me by the community. I do want to thank you again for the help you are offering me. It is very kind of you."

"So you have spoken to James about love?" Yost asked.

Teresa sat in silence, her hands clasped in front of her.

"I see that you have," Yost said.

"*He* has spoken to me, Yost," Teresa corrected. "I did not bring up the subject with him."

"None of this is acceptable, Teresa," Yost said, getting to his feet. "I hope you realize that. This cannot go on. James puts girls through his life like bundles of cornstalks thrown into the threshing machine. He has no plans to make a home for your son or for you. All this situation will accomplish is trouble, and then you will have nothing left. I insist we get married on your baptismal day as we planned."

"I need time to think, Yost," Teresa said. "Surely you can understand that."

"You didn't need time before, Teresa. When you first came here, you were small in your own eyes. You thought anything was *gut* enough for you. You were thankful to have a chance at a husband, just as a *frau* should be. Now look what has happened to you. James talks sweet to you, and your head gets so big that your *kapp* hardly fits anymore. If you don't promise me that you'll marry me on your baptism day, I will go to Deacon Ray on my way home and have a talk with him. When he hears that James has spoken to you of love, it will not go well for either of you."

"I'm sorry," Teresa whispered. "I didn't want any of this to happen. I came here only to find peace for my son. I'm not trying to make trouble."

Yost studied her face, but she kept her eyes on the porch floor. "Will you promise me again to marry? And agree there will be no more trouble about the date?"

"You wouldn't consider waiting until Menno can give me a wedding?" Teresa asked.

"I've waited long enough," Yost said, leaning against the porch rail. "I will not have such an uncertain thing hanging over my head. But perhaps I can give you some time to think about this. I know that the words James has spoken to you are still going around in your head. But you must put them away. If you want to continue with the wedding as I have decided, then pay a visit to the house sometime before the baptismal. Susan can come along, and we can talk while she cleans. Is that not fair enough? Otherwise I will stop by Deacon Ray's place on my way home."

Teresa stood and walked over to stand beside him. "Yost, I thank you for wanting to provide a home for me and be a father for Samuel. It's more than I deserve. I don't ask you to love me. I won't even expect that. But if you can wait and let me have the wedding here sometime after my baptismal day…"

"*Nee,* I will not," Yost said. "I've waited long enough. My house has waited long enough. I want this done—finished as soon as possible."

When Teresa said nothing, Yost reached forward and took her by her arms and pulled her toward him. Hesitating only a moment, he then kissed her. When she struggled against his force, he relented and released her.

Teresa looked down as tears formed in her eyes.

Yost watched her for a few moments and then took her by the hand and led her back to the porch swing.

"I do not wish to cause you trouble," he said. "I see I have wounded your heart. I don't know how to be with a woman since I have never been married, but I will try, Teresa. Yet sometimes words must be spoken by a man to his future wife that may be hard to hear. They may even hurt as I see they do now. Still, I am not sorry that I have spoken them. You must understand how our people work. It isn't acceptable that an unwed mother should be living in the community without a husband. If you were Menno's daughter, it still wouldn't be right. It's a shame we should not be asked to bear, Teresa. That shame will be done away with when we say the vows. Do you understand that?"

Teresa nodded, still not looking at him.

"I am glad you understand," Yost said. "I'm sure you realize the need to keep your word to me." With that he stood again. "I really must go back to my chores. I'm already late. I will wait for you to pay a visit. You don't need to let me know in advance when. I'm always working around the farm. Goodbye, Teresa."

"Goodbye," Teresa whispered. She watched as Yost walked across the yard, untied his horse, and climbed into his buggy.

Yost gave a little wave before he drove down the driveway. He settled back into the seat as his horse headed north. Not even Deacon Ray could have handled that better, he figured. He hadn't faltered or given in to the *Englisha* girl's imaginations. He was ready for marriage, ready to have a wife in his house.

# Chapter Thirty-three

✦

Teresa sat on the porch swing as she watched the buggy disappear into the distance. The rustle of the wind through the green leaves of the nearby oak seemed her only solace against the words and actions from the man who would be her husband.

The front door opened slowly and Susan stepped out.

Teresa waved her off with one hand, wiping away her tears with the other. When Susan didn't leave, Teresa relented. "Oh, Susan!" Teresa cried. "That was so hard."

"What did that awful man have to say?" Susan asked, sitting down beside her.

"Nothing I didn't already know," Teresa said. "And he kissed me. He didn't ask or give me time or anything. He just grabbed me and kissed me."

"Start talking!" Susan ordered. "Tell me everything."

Teresa dried her eyes. "He said, basically, that James is blowing a lot of hot air, and that he—Yost—is the only one who will make a decent husband for me and provide for Samuel. He doesn't want the wedding at my baptismal called off or even postponed."

"You don't have to marry him," Susan reminded.

"I know, Susan, but maybe I need to," Teresa said. "I'm different than you are. You forget that. I have a son without being married. And it's not like I haven't been kissed before."

"You're not *that* different," Susan asserted. "And a kiss taken is different than a kiss given."

*Mamm* opened the front door. "Is everything okay, Teresa?"

"Yes." Teresa attempted to smile. "We're just talking."

"Okay, if you're sure," *Mamm* said, waiting a minute before closing the door.

"Continue!" Susan commanded, glancing at Teresa. "But first let me say this. I think it's awful that you're letting Yost mess up your mind about James. You had a good time with him Sunday night. And that's nothing to be ashamed of."

"Yost threatened to speak with Deacon Ray about James if I don't agree to the wedding on my baptismal day," Teresa said.

Susan laughed. "And you're afraid of that? You know the ministers said you could do what you wish about marriage."

"Yost doesn't think Deacon Ray is going to take the news well that James has been driving me around," Teresa said. "Even though you were along, I think he's right. So there's really only one choice—the one that has been present all along. What is best for Samuel? Yost was right about that. James is uncertain. I can't take a chance on him. Not when I think of Samuel. At least with Yost I know what I'm getting. He will be true to me and faithful to Samuel."

A buggy could be heard coming on the road. Susan looked out and said, "I can't believe that man's coming back!"

Teresa followed Susan's gaze. "I don't believe it's his buggy, Susan," she said.

Seconds passed before Susan responded. "Hmm, I don't think so either. How did you know?"

"Because I know what my husband-to-be's buggy looks like," Teresa said.

"It's Deacon Ray's buggy," Susan observed. "I wouldn't worry. This can't be about you. Not twice in a row. I suppose he's out on his normal Saturday afternoon rounds. He might even go on by to Ada's place, although I haven't heard anything about what her boys might have done wrong."

"He's slowing down." Teresa groaned.

"Come inside!" Susan said, grabbing Teresa's arm. "He will speak with *Daett* in the barn."

"What's going on?" *Mamm* asked, coming out of the kitchen as they rushed inside.

"Deacon Ray is calling," Susan said. "I didn't want to be seen on the front porch."

"I'm so sorry for all the trouble, Mrs. Hostetler," Teresa said, her face white. "I'm afraid this will be about me again."

"Come dear," *Mamm* said. "Let's not jump to conclusions. Deacons have work to do in the church that we don't always know about. Menno will speak to him, and he'll tell us if we need to know anything. Did you and Yost get things worked out?"

Teresa sat down before answering. "Yost insists on holding the wedding on my baptismal day," she said. "He doesn't want to wait, and he doesn't want all the fuss. I guess that would make things easier for everyone."

"Remember, you are welcome to hold a wedding here," *Mamm* said. "But it would be good if Yost would agree to it."

"I think she should tell the man to go back to his tumbledown farm and stay there!" Susan said.

"Susan! Don't be disrespectful. And that's Teresa's decision, not yours," *Mamm* said. "At least Teresa has a prospect for a husband. You're not doing so well for yourself in that area, Susan."

"That's not a nice thing to say!" Susan protested.

"Sometimes the truth has to be spoken," *Mamm* said. "Don't discourage Teresa if she wants to marry Yost."

"Thank you, Mrs. Hostetler."

*Mamm* smiled. "You look a little peaked from your time with Yost. Perhaps you should rest for a while. Samuel might need feeding, and Susan and I can finish the afternoon cleaning."

"I'll help first," Teresa said, getting to her feet. She picked up the broom and dustpan. "Samuel isn't crying yet, so I'm sure he's fine."

*Mamm* smiled. "Why not work on your room then? I will take over for you if Samuel starts to fuss."

"Thank you," Teresa whispered, slipping up the stairs. At the landing, she entered her bedroom and began to sweep. Questions swirled through her mind until the broom grew still. Deacon Ray was out-side and what did he want? No doubt it had to do with James's inter-est in her. It had to be. Nothing else made much sense.

Taking the broom with her, Teresa crossed the hall into Susan's room. Stepping up to the side of the window, she peeked around the edge of the drapes. Menno and the deacon were standing by the buggy, deep in conversation. Menno had a foot up on the buggy wheel, and Deacon Ray was gesturing with his arms.

"Oh, dear God," she whispered, turning to kneel beside Susan's bed. Burying her head in her hands, she wept. What trouble she had brought to these good people's lives. Before she came they had been living peacefully, enjoying the blessings God gave to all humble hearts, and now look what was happening. Perhaps she should have listened to Susan and returned to Asbury Park.

"Oh, if it weren't for Samuel, I would," she wept. "But I promised Samuel I wouldn't take him back there. Oh, God, please have mercy on me and my baby."

Standing to her feet, Teresa peeked around the window shades again. The men were still there. Menno was now standing with his arms folded across his chest, his lengthy beard flowing over his hands. Deacon Ray still looked like he was doing most of the talking.

Should she go out and speak with them? The question brought an end to the tears. Perhaps if she humbled herself, explaining to Dea-con Ray that she wasn't trying to cause any trouble, that she was still considering Yost Byler's offer of marriage, he might understand. No doubt Deacon Ray thought she was trying to steal his son.

Teresa went down the stairs. *Mamm* was working in the living room, and looked up with questions in her eyes.

"I'm going out to speak with the men," Teresa said.

"I'm not sure that's wise," *Mamm* said. "It might not be you they are speaking of."

"I think it is," Teresa said, trying to smile down at baby Samuel in her arms. He was watching her with steady eyes. At least he wasn't crying, so he must not be hungry yet.

"You're going outside?" Susan asked from the kitchen doorway.

"Let her go," *Mamm* instructed. "I'll watch Samuel for you."

Teresa handed Samuel to Anna and then walked to the front door, opened it, and stepped outside.

Both men looked up when she appeared on the porch.

"Help me, God," she whispered over and over as she walked toward them.

The men turned to face her directly.

"Teresa," Menno said and nodded.

"I'm sorry to bother you," Teresa said, her voice trembling. "But if this conversation is about me, I would like to be involved."

"It is about you, Teresa, but you should not have come out. I would have told you later. That is our way," Menno said.

"I'm sorry," Teresa said, "but it seemed best that I come out and speak to both of you."

Deacon Ray cleared his throat. "Since you're out here, perhaps this is *gut*. It will give me a chance to ask you questions without Menno passing them between us. Such situations can cause misunderstandings. So let me ask you, why are you trying to catch my son James as your husband? I agreed with Menno that we shouldn't force you to marry Yost on your baptismal day, but I did not think you would pursue my son. This is a serious matter. I believe it calls your instruction and baptism into question. I cannot see how we can baptize you and accept you into our community if you so plainly go after one of our boys."

"I have no such intention," Teresa asserted, raising her eyes to meet the deacon's. "James is the one who came to me, and he is the one who asked to drive Susan and me to and from the hymn singing."

"Are you blaming James for this situation?" Deacon Ray asked.

"No," Teresa said. "I blame myself. My heart is sinful. Please have patience with me. I didn't come to the community to marry anyone. I came because of my son, Samuel. I came so he could have a better life. I have not encouraged James. Has Menno told you Yost was here earlier? That Yost and I spoke at length? I told him I am still willing to marry him, but I would like some time to plan the wedding."

"You are still willing to marry Yost?" Deacon Ray asked. "I'm not asking for your promise to marry him, but will you assure me you are truly willing to marry the man?"

"I am willing," Teresa said. "I'm sorry for the trouble and confusion."

Deacon Ray cleared his throat again. "It's not like our own people make no problems. I guess we should be used to it. Right, Menno?"

"There is always trouble, it seems," Menno agreed.

"But not this kind of trouble," Teresa said.

Deacon Ray shrugged. "Let me be clear, and then I will go. I have strong objections to you and James seeing each other. Do you understand that?"

"I do," Teresa said, tears springing to her eyes. "I have not encouraged James in any way. Please believe me."

"We believe you, Teresa," Menno responded, smiling.

"Then I will expect you to have nothing more to do with him," Deacon Ray said, his eyes staring into hers. "And I will be telling James the same thing."

Teresa nodded. Having said her piece, she turned and walked to the house. At the front door she didn't look back. She opened the door and entered to the howling of a hungry baby. She wiped her hand across her eyes and took Samuel from Anna's arms.

"Thank you," Teresa said. "I'll go upstairs and feed him."

"Did it go well?" *Mamm* asked.

"It went well," Teresa said, smiling tightly through the tears.

"They didn't ask for any promises?" Susan asked, coming out of the kitchen.

"No," Teresa said. "I understand what I need to do."

Teresa took Samuel upstairs. She soon heard the sound of Deacon Ray's buggy wheels moving down the driveway. She wiped away the last of her tears. Minutes later, as she paced with Samuel on her shoulder while gently patting him on the back, she again heard buggy wheels from the driveway.

Teresa crossed the hall to Susan's room and looked out the window. Menno was driving the buggy out of the lane at a fast clip.

*I wonder what that's about?* she thought. *At least it's probably not about me. I've certainly had enough trouble for one day.*

# CHAPTER THIRTY-FOUR

The day was warm and sunny, a gentle breeze moved across the open fields. Teresa was driving the buggy with Susan seated beside her. Cleaning supplies were stashed under the backseat.

"I can't believe I'm going to clean Yost Byler's house!" Susan exclaimed. "I also can't believe you're driving, for that matter!"

"I have to learn sometime," Teresa said with a grin. "I'm going to be a real Amish woman. And you know I can't go to Yost's place by myself. It wouldn't be proper…and I don't know where he lives."

"And I can't believe you're still considering marrying that man," Susan said.

"Someday you'll have to stop complaining and just accept this," Teresa said.

She and Susan waved at two women when their buggy rattled past them on the narrow road.

"I'm sure glad Maud Miller and her daughter Esther don't know where we're going," Susan commented, looking back at the disappearing buggy.

"It's not a shameful thing to visit the man who will soon be my husband," Teresa declared.

"I keep thinking I'll wake up and find it's all been a bad dream," Susan muttered.

"And what else did you expect? You don't see James hanging around, do you? Not after his father expressed his strong disapproval. He ran like a rabbit for the tall grass just like I said he would."

"I'm sure James has good reasons for the way he's acting," Susan said. "I think you should wait and see. He may have something planned."

Teresa laughed. "James is being an obedient member of the church. And if I plan to be a good member of the community, I have to support its ways too. Perhaps you have forgotten that aspect of the community, Susan."

"Perhaps. You do seem to be better at accepting the community's restrictions than I am," Susan said.

"Don't you want to make your mom and dad happy, Susan?" Teresa asked. "Your mom looks at you some days with a sad look in her eyes. She worries that you don't plan to stay here. And I'm beginning to think she's right. Susan, are you planning to leave after my wedding?"

"Sometimes you're too smart for your own good, Teresa."

"I know your heart, Susan. And you do have a tender one," Teresa said. "Few people would have sacrificed like you did so that I could come here."

"I did have my own reasons, you know," Susan said. "Some of which weren't all that noble."

They rode in silence, listening to the creak of the buggy, the crunch of the wheels on gravel, and the clip-clop of Toby's hooves hitting the road. Teresa held the reins taut as they halted at a stop sign. She clucked, urging Toby forward.

Susan smiled her approval.

With the wheels rattling forward again, Teresa looked over at Susan. "I'll be sad to see you go. You've become like a sister to me. I'd love to have you around. Don't you want to see Samuel grow up? And Yost and I will probably have children. They'll surely be cute like Samuel."

Susan laughed. "And what will I be? The Amish old maid?"

"There's always Thomas," Teresa said. "Maybe you shouldn't give up on him."

"I do declare! *Mamm* has surely set you up to say these things to me," Susan asserted with a glare.

Teresa shook her head. "No, she hasn't said a word to me about you and Thomas."

"Okay, I believe you. It's just that the way the community has treated you isn't garnering my goodwill. And that certainly isn't helping my feelings for Thomas. The ministers shouldn't have pushed you to marry Yost in the first place. And they should have looked at your heart instead of focusing on your past."

Teresa shrugged. "Maybe that was a little pushy, but I might have come to the same conclusion myself. It was an awkward and difficult situation. And if they hadn't done what they did, how would Yost and I have gotten together? He might never have considered me without the prompting of some people in the church."

"I still can't believe you're marrying an old codger like Yost Byler. He doesn't even keep his house clean."

Teresa kept her eyes on the road ahead. "Can you think of a better way for Samuel to be accepted fully? I can't."

"Sometimes we have to be true to our hearts and dreams, Teresa," Susan said. "Keep after them until *Da Hah* helps us."

"Don't lecture me about dreams, Susan. Living here in the community is where my best dreams have come true."

"And that includes an old bachelor with a dirty house?" Susan questioned.

Teresa looked out the side of the buggy before answering.

"I can clean his house, Susan," she finally said. "And I can wash his clothes. I can bake his food. In return, he will be a good father to Samuel. Yost will even give Samuel his good name. Those are my dreams, Susan. They might not be yours, but they are mine."

"I'm not trying to make you feel bad," Susan said, giving Teresa a sideways hug. "I will try to keep my mouth shut from now on. If you're happy, that's *gut* enough for me."

"Thank you, Susan." Teresa wiped her eyes on her sleeve. "I'm trying to drive, and soon we'll end up in a ditch if I don't concentrate."

"I'll grab the lines at the last minute, so don't worry," Susan said. "And we're almost there. That's Yost Byler's place up ahead."

"That one?" Teresa asked, staring. "That's where Samuel and I will live?"

"I'm afraid so," Susan said. "I tried to tell you."

"It will take an awful lot of cleaning up," Teresa admitted. "But the Lord will help me. We'll soon have it in good shape."

"You haven't seen the inside yet," Susan warned. "I haven't either—not for years, anyway. There's probably mold growing on the walls by now."

Teresa turned into the driveway. "Surely it can't be that bad, Susan. Straw, I may believe, but not mold. Yost doesn't look moldy."

"That's because you've always seen him when he's talking to you about the food you're going to make for him," Susan said teasingly. "And he probably cleaned up to call on you."

"Oh no! Did you think to bring food? I didn't! How could I forget such an important thing? What kind of wife am I showing him I'll be?" she wailed.

"Don't worry," Susan interrupted. "I threw in a loaf of the fresh bread you baked yesterday. That ought to get Yost's mouth watering until the wedding at least."

"You are such a dear, Susan," Teresa said, coming to a halt in front of the barn.

Faint strips of weathered white paint hung to the siding. Cracks split the wood, leaving long spaces with hay hanging out. Thin strands of the dried grass blew in the breeze.

"The barn needs painting," Teresa commented, not moving from the buggy.

"Let's get out and get busy before I start running my mouth again," Susan said as she climbed out to unhitch Toby.

Teresa climbed down and looked around. She took small steps toward the back of the buggy where she pulled out a mop bucket, a broom, and a bag of rags. "Where do we go from here?" she asked Susan.

"I think we find the man who owns this dump and sweep him away with our brooms," Susan said, loading her own arms with supplies.

Yost had watched the approaching buggy through the barn window, wiping a few cobwebs aside so he could see better. *Yah*, it was Teresa. And Susan was with her. What was he supposed to do? He'd been tossing and turning in bed the last few nights, expecting that soon the girls would come.

His mind went back over his last meeting with Menno. Yost had never seen Menno so worked up as he'd been that night a few weeks ago. Not in all the years he had known him. Menno had nearly banged the door down, getting him out of bed. He'd been awakened from a sweet dream about Teresa, probably because he'd just visited her that day. In his nightclothes and carrying a kerosene lamp in one hand, Yost had opened the front door.

"I'm here to tell you something, Yost!" Menno had announced, not even bothering with a pleasant greeting.

"*Yah?*" Yost rubbed the sleep from his eyes. "I was just over there today. Why didn't you speak with me then?"

"You're not going to marry Teresa!" Menno continued, ignoring the comment.

"*Yah*, I am," Yost asserted, blinking his eyes in the dim light of the kerosene lamp. "There's nothing you can do to stop me."

"I saw you with Teresa today. I saw everything. I saw you force your affections on the girl. Teresa may not be my daughter by birth, but I'm not standing for that kind of conduct, even in a suitor. You're not the kind of man to make Teresa a good husband. She has no one else to speak up for her. At first, I wasn't willing, but when I saw you with her today, I knew I couldn't let it pass."

"I didn't do anything!" Yost protested. "I was only talking to her. *Yah*, perhaps a little roughly, but what's wrong with that?"

"I saw you forcing a kiss on her. You may think that's a little thing, but I saw the look on young Teresa's face. You're not marrying her. She should have sent you packing right then and there. Or I should have."

"She knows her place," Yost defended. "And there's nothing you can do about this. Teresa didn't complain to me or anyone else that

I know of. And if she did, well, it was just a misunderstanding. You can ask her yourself. I apologized afterward, telling her I wasn't used to being around women. I'm sure Deacon Ray will be very understanding of my side of the story. That is, if it comes to that. Menno, stay out of this."

Menno's face hardened. "Then perhaps we can talk a language you do understand, Yost. If you don't call off this wedding personally—face-to-face with Teresa and without telling anyone you and I talked, including Teresa—then I will let Deacon Ray know you've been breaking the *Ordnung*. I know about the tractor you use in your fields. You know the *Ordnung* strictly forbids tractors being used to pull wagons and any other piece of farm equipment. You may have thought you lived so far north that no one would notice, but I know this for a fact, Yost."

Yost blinked in the flickering lamplight. Was Menno serious? Was he threatening him?

"And if you think you can ride that out with a little confession and repentance, think again. I'll raise objections about any man marrying a girl living under my roof who has deliberately and consistently broken the *Ordnung*. I'll insist on at least a six-months proving. And after that I'll find something else you're doing that goes against the community. And I'll find something, Yost. Trust me, I'll look hard enough to keep you on proving restrictions for as long as it takes. What little reputation you have will be in shambles. No Amish woman will marry a man who has been on proving for months and months. No one, Yost."

Yost swallowed hard. Menno was serious. And who would believe his word against Menno's? He'd be even more of a laughingstock in the community. His mind flashed to the square baler hidden in the barn. No, he didn't want someone watching him closely. His ruse that his *Englisha* neighbors had helped him with a few bales out of the kindness of their hearts wouldn't be accepted.

"I'll consider your words, Menno."

Menno seemed satisfied—at least for the moment because he then turned, got into his buggy, and drove away.

Yost had considered the issue carefully. There would be no backing down on the threat—not with that blaze in Menno's eyes. Menno had taken Teresa on as his daughter. And everyone knew Menno chose only the best men as mates for his daughters. Yost decided he stood no chance at all in riding this out. Ach, *how stupid to let go and grab Teresa that way.*

And now here was Teresa with Susan in his own yard. He might as well face her and get this over with. But there was no way he was telling the truth about the matter. There were other reasons which could be used to explain this.

"Here he comes!" Teresa whispered.

"Like I said," Susan muttered, "he could use a good sweeping."

"Shh!"

"*Gut* afternoon," Yost said, approaching them with a broad smile. "I was wondering when you two would be appearing. I thought you might have forgotten about your promise, Teresa."

"No, I didn't," Teresa said. "And Susan has come along so we can get lots of work done."

"That's *gut*," Yost said, his smile disappearing. "I have been looking forward greatly to this day. I cannot tell you how much, but I need to speak with you first, before you start with the work."

"Yes?" Teresa stared at him.

"Let's go inside the house instead of standing out here," Yost said.

"What am I supposed to do while you speak with Teresa?" Susan asked. "Am I supposed to stand out here until you're done?"

"Oh no," Yost said, smiling again. "You can come in and start cleaning. I have nothing to say to Teresa that you cannot hear."

"I see," Susan said, following Teresa up the walk.

They entered the house. Teresa and Susan laid their supplies down by the front door and removed their bonnets. Spider webs hung on the corners of the ceilings, and dust covered the hardwood floor. Susan didn't look at Teresa as she waved a paper bag around before placing her bonnet on the floor.

Yost didn't seem to notice.

"The kitchen would be a good place to start cleaning," Yost said. "Teresa can begin in the living room after I've said what I need to say."

"Okay," Susan said, marching past him.

Teresa stayed beside the dusty couch even though Yost motioned for her to be seated. He sat down in a broken rocker, the handrails on both sides split in the middle.

"I hope you won't take this too hard, Teresa," he said, looking up at her, "but I have decided it's best that we not be wed on your baptismal day."

"That's nice of you, Yost. Menno will be glad to give us a real Amish wedding sometime afterward."

Yost cleared his throat. "No, that's not what I meant. This is hard for me to say, but I must make myself clear. I do not wish to hurt your feelings. You have already had many things in life go wrong for you—like your son being born without a father to give him a good name. Yet I must tell you, Teresa, that I've decided I will not wed you."

"What!" Susan poked her head through the kitchen doorway and stared at Yost.

"You've decided you won't marry me?" Teresa asked, her face white. "Is it because I have sinned in bearing a child without a father?"

Yost hung his head. "I would not put it in such words because *Da Hah* forgives us all for our sins. But, *yah,* your past bothers all of us, I'm sure, but this concerns another matter."

"Now this I've got to hear," Susan said, coming into the living room.

Yost looked at her. "I'm talking with Teresa, but I suppose you might as well stay and hear what I have to say. You are, after all, seeing Thomas, so you will surely understand this matter."

"I am *not* seeing Thomas!" Susan sputtered.

Yost ignored her and turned to Teresa. "It is like this. I am older now, going on in the years *Da Hah* has given me on this earth. True, there are still some years left, and I had hoped to have a wife to spend the remaining years with me. These are the thoughts I had the first day I visited you, and I pushed them away, believing they were not from *Da Hah*. Now, though, I must face them. If I wed you, we may have children—many children in the years to come. Even when I am an old man children may come. I am not poor, as you can see. I have cattle and a farm that is paid for. But I do not want to have children in my old age. Especially long after I am too old to work in the fields. The expense would be great. So I must tell you, Teresa, that we will not be wed. I know you want a father for your son, but it cannot be me."

"Cast me over the barn roof!" Susan said. "Now I've heard everything."

Yost ignored her again. "I will tell the community I have chosen to not honor our promise to each other. I will take on that burden if you will allow me one request," Yost offered, holding up his hand.

"Yes?" Teresa asked, her eyes intently looking at his bearded face.

"I ask that you clean the house like you planned," he said. "And that you cook a meal."

"We brought along a fresh loaf of bread," Teresa said. "Will that work for the food?"

Yost smiled. "That is a *gut* start, but I am hoping for a full supper—with mashed potatoes, gravy, and maybe even pie."

"We'll do what we can," Susan interrupted. "We have to get back before dark, so we need to get to work."

Yost jumped to his feet. "I will get to work in the barn then."

As soon as Yost was out the door, Susan put her hands on her hips and faced Teresa. "Well, now doesn't that beat everything! There's got to be more to this than what Yost told us. The old fellow wouldn't change his mind that easily. There has to be something else."

Teresa burst into sobs. "I wonder if Deacon Ray knows about this? Will I still be baptized and accepted into the community? And what about Samuel? What will happen to him?"

"Now, now," Susan soothed. "You haven't been listening to a word I said. Teresa, be thankful Yost turned you down! He has more sense than you do. I must say, this is the best news I've heard in weeks. Now let's get busy and then get out of here before he changes his mind."

"How can you be sure I won't be thrown out of the instruction class?" Teresa wailed.

"We'll take that when it comes," Susan assured her. "I don't think we should ask many questions right now. I think we should get to work, leave, and when we get back home not say a word about anything until Bishop Henry pours the holy water over your head."

Teresa nodded and grabbed the broom. She attacked the cobwebs on the ceiling.

# Chapter Thirty-five

O n the Saturday night before baptismal Sunday, James came in late from the barn. He took a seat on the couch across from where his father was reading *The Budget*.

When his father kept reading, James cleared his throat.

"Is there something you want?" his *daett* asked, still not moving the paper or looking up.

"I need to tell you something," James said. "Something about Teresa."

The paper came down and Deacon Ray glared at his son. "I hope you're not having wild thoughts about that girl. Because I will hear none of that nonsense. I already told you that."

James sighed. "*Daett,* we can make this easy or we can make it hard. It's up to you. I'm asking Teresa if I can take her home after she's baptized. You know that Yost broke their engagement."

"Yes, I know that. And that means nothing to you." The paper went up again. "Why are you bringing this up on the night before the baptismal? Are you trying to get me to object to Teresa's baptism?"

"Of course not! Let me put it clearly, *Daett.* Do you want there to be a stink over this or not?"

His *daett* lowered the paper again. "Of course I don't want a problem."

"I'm telling you this because I don't want there to be hard feelings between us when this is over. The truth is that I am hoping Teresa will become your daughter-in-law."

Deacon Ray stared at his son for a long moment. "You've spoken with Teresa on this matter? She has agreed and is promised to you?"

"No, but she will agree."

"You are always sure of yourself, son. But this situation with Teresa is going too far."

"I know the woman, *Daett*," James said. "She has a heart of gold. And she will consent to marry me."

"And you think she's *gut* enough for you? Even with her little boy born out of wedlock? You realize he comes with the package, don't you?"

"It's not a question of who's *gut* enough for whom. We can all become better persons, *Daett*. Didn't you and *Mamm* grow after your marriage?"

Deacon Ray grunted.

"Now that I've told you this, I hope you won't object to the baptism tomorrow."

"Are you ordering me around, James?"

"No, *Daett*. I'm asking as your son. Will you please not make trouble? I love Teresa, *Daett*."

"And if the girl eventually leaves you after you're married? What am I to say then? That I told you so? That would be small comfort for everyone."

"Teresa will not leave me," James said. "With all you've put her through, she would have left long ago if she were the type to give up."

Deacon Ray grunted again and raised the paper. "I'll have to think about this."

"Thanks, *Daett*," James said, getting to his feet. "You will learn to love her someday."

"I'm not promising anything about tomorrow."

"I know," James said, a soft smile on his face. "You have a *gut* night now."

The next morning, a blaze of bright sunlight spread across the hardwood floor, bouncing upward to illuminate even the darkest corners of the Millers' living-room ceiling. Ezra Miller's wife had done her Saturday cleaning well, Teresa thought, watching the line of boys follow the ministers up the stairs as the congregation sang. Not a cobweb in sight. But then, this wasn't Yost Byler's house.

Yost looked happy enough this morning. He was sitting over in the men's section. *He must still be thinking about the big supper we left him.* Teresa thought, holding back a smile. *Likely he lived on the leftovers for days.* This was her baptismal Sunday, and not the time to be smiling on such a somber occasion. The other girls getting to their feet were keeping their eyes on the floor, as properly befitted the day. Teresa fought against the wild happiness springing up inside her. Any minute now she was going to laugh out loud if she wasn't careful. Surely it must come from the fact that she'd been raised in the *Englisha* world so she'd always be a little different.

Teresa waited until the last girl was on her feet before handing baby Samuel to Anna. He wrinkled up his face to cry, but Teresa looked away. Samuel would just have to fuss. Anna would take care of him. Slipping down the aisle, Teresa fell into the end of the line. That she was last hadn't mattered all summer, and it didn't matter now. The only thing that was important at the moment was making it through the last instruction class and having Bishop Henry baptize her.

Susan had pressed the point on the day they'd driven home after cleaning Yost Byler's place. "First of all, don't even tell *Mamm* how happy you are that Yost backed out."

"I'm not that happy," she had protested, her hands tight on the reins.

"Yes, you are," Susan said. "You just don't know it yet. Keep your voice down on Sundays when you speak with the other women. Try not to draw attention to yourself. Ask *Mamm* or me any question you might have about the *Ordnungs* brief. You don't want to break any rule—spoken or unspoken. And above all else, don't speak with James no matter how much he tries to speak with you. He's up to something, but trust me, it will only make trouble for you if it happens too soon. Time is your best friend now."

Well…Susan had been wrong about one thing. James hadn't made any attempts to speak with her. Which shouldn't have troubled Teresa, but somehow it did. Her whole future was troubled now. At night she lay awake, looking at Samuel's crib and crying. Samuel had no father to look forward to now. She had failed her son miserably. And Deacon Ray had forbidden James to speak with her—which was clearly the reason he hadn't tried.

Really, she ought to be crying this morning too instead of feeling this joy bubbling up from her heart. Perhaps the Lord—*Da Hah*—was looking out for her in some way she couldn't understand. That must be what it was, and this was His sign. He would help her raise Samuel as a Father Himself. Were those not the words Menno read the other morning from the Scriptures? Something about God being a father to the fatherless?

Ahead of her, the long line of boys and girls moved toward the bedroom door where a round circle of chairs would be set out. Thomas had been in the lead, and he was already inside. He wore what must be a brand-new black suit this morning. Some of the other boys also looked like they had on new suits or freshly brushed ones. Sunlight flittered past the hall window's blue drapes, revealing hardly a speck of dust on the boys' black pants.

Susan had spent part of yesterday working on the last touches for Teresa's new black dress. Teresa looked down at the fabric still crisp and unwrinkled after the ironing this morning. She pressed her eyes together. It would not do to wipe tears with her handkerchief. The crying could come, but later, when it made sense, not during instruction class. She really must stop thinking of Anna and Susan's kindness or the tears would be flying all over the place.

Teresa entered the bedroom and pulled the door shut behind her. The old latch clicked and she jumped. Bishop Henry smiled in her direction as she sat down. Her face must look on fire from how it was burning. Deacon Ray was looking at the floor, paying her no mind.

Bishop Henry cleared his throat and spoke. "We are glad as a ministry that all of you have come to this day. Your lives have now been observed during the time we have been giving you instructions on the basics of our faith. Today is your baptismal day, when you will make holy vows to God and to the church."

Teresa watched his face as Bishop Henry stroked his beard. He seemed lost in thought now, and Deacon Ray looked up, waiting. Was something wrong? Susan had assured her last night that if no one had come to speak with her by then, there would be no problem today.

Bishop Henry's gaze moved down the people sitting in the long line of chairs.

Teresa looked away shyly.

"All of the community stands in agreement today that you are prepared for baptism," Bishop Henry continued. "I have heard no complaints against any of you from the ministers here in this room or from any of our members. If Deacon Ray will read the last of the instructions, we can continue with this day. Hopefully the hour will not go too late with as many of you as there are."

Deacon Ray read in his now familiar voice. Teresa listened carefully to each word. Now that the day had arrived and there were apparently no objections to be raised against her, it might not be necessary to listen as closely. But they were still good words, and she wanted to remember them later. Samuel would soon be saying his first words, and he would need to be taught the truths of the faith, especially as he had no father.

Would Menno allow her to continue living at the farm? They couldn't do that forever, but maybe she could find employment cleaning houses for the *Englisha* people, like some of the young Amish girls did until she could save up enough money to rent a place.

The tears finally ran down her cheeks, and Teresa let them flow.

"You'll be one of us," Susan had told her last night.

Teresa blinked away her tears and looked at Thomas sitting on his chair. He was so strong, so handsome…and so sad. Susan should have been here today, sitting beside him, being baptized the same day as he was. *Oh, dear God*, she prayed, *let me somehow help Susan like she has helped me*. But how could she? Susan was so stubborn, and still so upset that James hadn't come around to speak to Teresa. How strange that was. One day James wasn't supposed to come around according to Susan, and yet on the next he was supposed to. Teresa bowed her head. It was high time to stop thinking such thoughts about James. She needed to listen to Deacon Ray and the instructions he was reading. The moments passed as Teresa wiped her eyes and concentrated.

When there was silence, Teresa looked up to see Deacon Ray closing his little booklet. They would soon go downstairs to sit in the front row. Susan had been clear on that last night. "Don't go back to your seat. Follow the others to the front row. Don't worry if everyone stares at you. That's what people do when you sit in the front row."

"I wish now to give you final instructions," Bishop Henry said. "As church members, you will be expected to keep obeying the rules of the church and to uphold them for the future generations. Our children and our grandchildren cannot be expected to believe like we do if we do not believe our faith with our whole hearts.

"As church members you will be expected to admonish others who do not obey as they ought. This is the way Scripture instructs us to act. If a member fails to listen to you, then you must go to Deacon Ray and explain the matter to him. He will take care of it from there. If there are no questions, instruction is concluded."

He waited a minute or two. "All right. Please file downstairs and sit on the front benches. The ministers will be down soon."

The boys went first, with Thomas leading the way. Teresa brought up the end of the line again, closing the door behind her, the loud click of the latch was muffled by their footsteps on the hardwood floor. Keeping her eyes down, Teresa followed the others down the steps to the benches set up between the living room and the kitchen. Across from them the ministers' bench was empty.

Teresa clasped her hands together to try to still her beating heart. They sat down and joined in the singing, which continued until the ministers filed down the stairs and took their places on their bench. Deacon Ray's black pant legs and shoes were right in front of Teresa, right in her line of sight as she looked at the floor. Behind her she heard Samuel crying, but Teresa kept her eyes on Deacon Ray's shoestring holes. It helped her breathe normally, or close to it.

After the first prayer, Deacon Ray read from Scripture, and then Bishop Henry stood for the main sermon, his voice rising and falling as it bounced off the living room walls.

Time seemed to stand still as Teresa tried not to move. *Quit worrying that people are looking at you,* she told herself. *Relax. Everything is going well.* Moments of embarrassment continued to come and go as the clock on the wall crept forward. Finally Teresa heard Bishop Henry say, "If it is still the desire of these young people to be baptized, then please kneel."

Teresa knelt, going down simultaneously with the girl beside her. There was soon movement at the head of the line as words were murmured and water poured. The sounds came closer until the bishop and Deacon Ray were in front of Teresa.

"And now do you believe in the Lord Jesus Christ?" Bishop Henry asked, his black shoes planted on the floor in front of her. "Do you believe that God has raised Him from the dead, and do you reject this day the world, the devil, and all his evil works? Do you commit to obeying the voice of God and of His church until your death?"

"*Yah,*" Teresa whispered as hands came down on her *kapp*.

"Now I baptize you in the name of the Father, the Son, and the Holy Spirit," Bishop Henry said.

Water poured down Teresa's cheeks from the pitcher Deacon Ray tipped. Long moments passed as the footsteps retreated to the front of the line. Each one stood to their feet, helped by Bishop Henry. Teresa saw his offered hand and allowed herself to be helped to her feet. Then a woman's hand found hers and Teresa felt a kiss on the cheek as she was pulled into an embrace by the bishop's wife. Now would be the moment when the tears should come bursting out, Teresa thought. Instead an awesome joy flooded her heart. Bishop

Henry's wife gave her a welcoming look and the couple returned to their places as Teresa smiled and sat down.

Moments later the singing of the last song began, and when it stopped the young boys filed outside. Teresa stayed seated until the others on the bench got up to walk to the kitchen. Susan found her and gave her a tight hug. "Come with me!" Susan whispered in her ear. She led her friend out to the washroom.

"What's going on?" Teresa asked when Susan closed the door.

"You can't imagine!" Susan said. "James just spoke to me. He had a talk with his *daett* last night. Everything is going to be okay between the two of you. He wants to take you home tonight. You better not say no!"

"Really?" Teresa gasped. "But that will cause so much trouble! He shouldn't do that."

"It's too late. He already did!" Susan said. "Now, we have to get back inside before someone wonders what we're talking about. So what shall I tell James?"

Teresa could only hold tight to Susan's hand and nod. "Tell him yes," she finally said.

## Chapter Thirty-six

🕂

That night after the hymn singing Teresa pulled on her bonnet and shawl as the girls around her gave her strange looks. Susan was nowhere to be seen and it was plain the girls were wondering what Teresa was doing out here with the girls who were leaving in their boyfriends' buggies. Joy rose inside as Teresa tried to keep from smiling. Let them look and wonder, because she didn't understand herself. Why in the world *was* James taking her home from the hymn singing?

"Hold the door a minute," one of the girls whispered to someone ready to leave, as she struggled with her bonnet. Teresa waited until they were out the door, then followed them into the darkness. She was now one of them, and no one could turn her away. It felt so *gut* and so *wunderbar* she could feel the joy all the way down to her feet.

Now the trick was to pick out James's buggy when it drove up. He had slipped out of the hymn singing only moments ago, not even looking at her before he rose to his feet. But that was okay. He didn't need to draw attention to her. She would be sitting beside him in his buggy soon enough.

What was it Susan had said this morning on the way to church? His buggy had two extra strips of reflector tape on the top, but the most important thing to look for was his horse.

"By the front buggy lights, you can see it plainly," Susan had said. "Because no one else has a horse like James's; its head is held high in the air."

Teresa stepped off the walks, straining her eyes toward the line of approaching buggies. None of the horses held his head up high, and how did one see extra strips of reflector tape in this light? Perhaps her heart would feel his approach.

Teresa smiled at the thought, waiting as the other girls moved past her to climb into the buggies. More buggies were getting in line, and there at last was James. It was true—his horse was holding his head higher than any of the others. Joy was rising in Teresa's heart again. Yes, she *could* feel his approach.

Going around two waiting girls, Teresa pushed open the buggy door, hesitating only a moment.

"Teresa!" James said quietly from inside the buggy.

"Yes," she said, relieved by the reassurance. "I doubted myself there for a moment. I'm not used to picking out just the right black buggy by the light of the moon."

His laugh filled the buggy as she climbed in and pushed the door shut. He pulled around the other buggies, and they dashed off into the night. Teresa hung on, her heart racing.

"It's such nice weather tonight," James said when they had cleared the crowd and he'd slowed his horse down some.

"Yes," Teresa managed. "And still so warm."

"Is Susan all right about getting home on her own?" James asked. "I'm guessing the two of you drove to the hymn singing together."

"Yes, she's driving herself," Teresa answered as she smiled in the darkness.

"Maybe I should have helped get her horse out," James said. "I'm still hoping Thomas will take her home someday."

"Thomas can help Susan with her horse," Teresa said, nestling up against him. "At least they're talking to each other. That's a start."

James said nothing, satisfied with her answer.

She looked at the outline of his face in the moonlight.

He glanced down and smiled.

"What do you think Yost is doing tonight?" she finally asked.

"Let's not talk about Yost," he said with a wry smile.

"He was the man I deserved," she said. "I know that."

"Well, I don't know that," James said. "I've *never* known that."

"Are we going to argue on our first time out alone together?" she asked. "Because I'd rather not. I want to soak this in. And please drive me home really slow. I want it to take a long time."

"But Samuel's waiting at home," he said. "Don't you want to see him again?"

She looked at his face.

As if he read her thoughts, he squeezed her hand. "Don't worry. I like the little fellow. And we can freely make plans now."

"I'm tired of plans," she said, moving to sit tightly against him. "So many plans made in the last year. So many thoughts. So much searching for the right thing to do. I just want to enjoy this feeling tonight of being alive with you by my side."

He laughed. "I do feel quite alive tonight," he agreed. "I'm taking you home for the first time—just you and me."

"And we have cherry pie waiting," she said. "Susan and I baked it yesterday. Is that good enough for you?"

"I could use some homemade ice cream, I guess," he said. "Vanilla, perhaps. It goes good with cherry pie."

"Next time I'll make sure we have ice cream too."

"So there will be a next time?" he said with a grin.

"James, I don't think I can take too much teasing right now. It's up to you whether or not there's a next time. Will there be?"

He pulled her even closer. "Of course there's going to be a next time. And then a next time after that. As long as you'll have me."

"What about your dad? Did you really argue about bringing me home tonight?"

"Not really," he said. "*Daett* didn't object when I brought it up in just the right way."

"You persuaded him just like that?" she asked.

"I don't think I needed to," he said. "I think he likes you deep down. How can anyone help but like you? Even old Yost liked you."

Teresa sighed and leaned against him. "I don't want to talk about him anymore! It's enough to be here with you." His hand found her face, and she didn't pull away. She knew he was going to kiss her, and it was hard to keep breathing. And he did kiss her. Gently. Tenderly. Not the way Yost had kissed her.

Had they just broken the *Ordnung*? *No,* she decided. *This was what two people in love do.*

James took her hand and held it, only pulling away when he needed to guide his horse into a turn.

Slowing down, he turned into the Hostetler driveway and stopped by the barn.

Teresa stepped out of the buggy and waited while James tied the horse. Then he took her hand, and they walked to the house.

"When do you want your cherry pie?" she asked when they got inside. "Now or later?" She motioned for him to be seated on the couch.

"I think I'll take it now," he said. "I'm starving!"

"You didn't sing that hard," she teased.

"I think it's my nerves," he said, making a funny face.

She laughed. "I'll be right back."

In the kitchen, she cut a piece of pie and put it on a plate. She filled a glass with milk.

"Aren't you having a piece?" he asked when she entered the living room and handed him the plate and glass.

"Of course!" she said, heading back into the kitchen.

After she returned and sat next to him, they relaxed and ate their pie.

Susan came in. "Well, well," she said. "If it isn't Teresa and James. Bless my heart. This is so *gut* to finally see."

Teresa blushed. "Did Thomas help you with your horse?"

"*Yah,* he helped me hitch up," Susan admitted.

"That's *gut* to hear," James said. "There's hope for you two."

"You can mind your own business," Susan responded with a chuckle. "I think I'll pass on the pie tonight and go straight to bed."

"Did I make her mad?" James asked when Susan was gone.

"With Susan, who knows," Teresa replied. "She might be irritated because she still likes him. Then again, she might not be upset at all."

"This pie is good. Did you say you baked it?"

"Yes. I mean, *yah,* but Susan helped and we used *Mamm's* recipe."

"Well, memorize it…for future use."

Teresa considered the word "future." It was wonderful to imagine. A future with James…Did she dare hope for such a thing? A future with James by her side forever? And James would be the perfect father to Samuel?

James glanced up at the clock, and Teresa followed his gaze.

What time do you have to leave?" she asked.

"Whenever I want to, I suppose," he said.

"I know that's not true," she said. "You're teasing again."

"Yes, I am," he admitted, getting to his feet. "The truth is, I have a full day of field work tomorrow, so I'd better get going."

"You don't have to go until midnight," she said.

He laughed. "I see *someone* has been studying the *Ordnungs* brief."

"I had to." She grinned.

"I've got too much to do tomorrow to stay that late," he said. "But I would like to come back next Sunday night. Do you think you can handle that? And perhaps you can have some vanilla ice cream stirred up?"

"You're an awful rascal," she teased. "So demanding already. Yes, I'll have your ice cream ready."

He moved closer, taking her hands in his. "Teresa, I don't want to embarrass you, but there is something I'd like to make clear."

She didn't move and realized she was holding her breath. She exhaled, trying to do it quietly.

"I know this is a little early in our relationship, but it feels like we've known each other for a long time. Still, you don't have to answer right now if you don't want to. In fact, you can wait as long as you want. But I want to make sure you know that I plan to marry you. Do you realize that?"

She gasped before stealing a quick look at his face.

"I'm serious, Teresa. That is, if you will have me."

"Oh, James!" she whispered. "You know my answer!"

"Tell me," he teased.

She looked up at him.

He stepped closer, his hands reaching out to touch her face. When she didn't pull away, he drew her close to kiss her.

When he let her go, she whispered, "Is that answer enough?"

"I didn't quite make out the answer. Let's try again," he said, kissing her again.

"And now?" she asked.

"I think I got it that time," James said. He let out a long breath. "And now I had better go."

"Is that what Amish boys do after they've kissed their girlfriends?" she asked.

"I wouldn't know," he said. "I've never kissed a girl before."

"James!" she said in disbelief as she followed him to the door.

He laughed and placed his fingers on her lips. "I'll be seeing you next Sunday night, okay? And I may have to ask for your answer again. I may forget what it was between now and then."

"You can ask every night," she assured. "And the answer will always be the same."

"*Wunderbar!* I'll see you then!" He ran down the front steps while she stood in the doorway. Soon his buggy drove by, and its lights faded into the darkness.

She closed the door and leaned against it, the thoughts rushing through her mind. So it *was* better to follow your heart, even when everything seemed so impossible. James was coming back, and he would keep coming back again and again, until the day they would say their marriage vows. Then she would be a real Amish wife and Samuel would have a real Amish father.

"Thank you, dear God," she whispered. "I truly don't deserve any of this."

Then she thought of her mother back in Asbury Park and how she doubted there was a God. Teresa wanted to shout from the rooftops, *Oh yes, there is a God. There is a God indeed. A God who delights in giving those He loves the desires of their heart.*

## The Fields of Home series, Book 1
### *Missing Your Smile*

Betrayed by her boyfriend Thomas, Susan Hostetler leaves her community and moves to the city. Keeping to Amish ways proves difficult as she struggles with adapting to *Englisha* ways. Should she learn to drive? Get her GED? And what to do about the handsome Duane Moran...

When Susan meets Teresa, the pregnant young woman asks her to find an Amish couple to adopt her baby. Should Susan write to her parents to see if that's possible? Will the community believe the baby is hers? Faced with returning home for the baby's sake, Susan must decide if she's willing to give up her newfound freedom and confront the man who broke her heart.

# COMING SOON!
## *Where Love Grows*
## Book 3 in The Fields of Home Series

In Jerry Eicher's conclusion to his popu-
lar Fields of Home trilogy, readers will
be delighted to attend the wedding of
Teresa, the young *Englisha* girl who has
come home with Susan Hostetler to learn
the ways of the Amish—and in fact to
become Amish herself.

But Teresa is not the only young
woman to find romance in these pages.
Susan, long estranged from Thomas Stoll,
the young man she had intended to marry
from her childhood, reunites with him....
just as another man appears on the scene
with designs on her heart. Which man is
the one *Da Hah* has chosen for her?

Amidst the happiness, there is also turmoil as Menno Hostetler, Susan's father,
must face church discipline for a past sinful transgression he's hidden for many
years. At his age, can he endure the humil-
iation and the path to restitution?

With more than 400,000 books sold,
Jerry Eicher's many fans eagerly anticipate each new novel that offers a peek into
the simple and interesting world of the
Amish—a world Jerry knows firsthand.

## From Jerry and Tina Eicher,
### *My Dearest Naomi...*

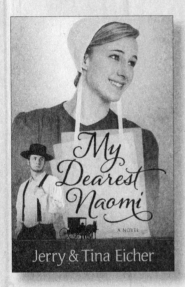

Jerry Eicher's many devoted fans will be enthralled by this endearing novel in letters based on Jerry's letters to and from his future wife, Tina, and their discovery that, indeed, absence does make the heart grow fonder.

When Eugene Mast leaves his Amish community in Worthington, Indiana, to teach in faraway Trenton, Iowa, he also must leave the love of his life, Naomi Miller.

For the next nine months of the school term, Eugene and Naomi keep their romance alive through love letters from his heart to hers, and from hers back to his.

Eugene writes of his concern that in his absence Naomi may find the attractions of another suitor to her liking. Naomi worries that Eugene may fall prey to the "liberal" Mennonite beliefs in the community where he now lives. Both can hardly wait until the school year is up and they're finally reunited.

A poignant and tender love story that will warm the hearts of readers everywhere.

## *About Jerry Eicher...*

JERRY EICHER's bestselling Amish fiction (more than 400,000 in combined sales) includes The Adams County Trilogy, the Hannah's Heart books, and the Little Valley Series. After a traditional Amish childhood, Jerry taught for two terms in Amish and Mennonite schools in Ohio and Illinois. Since then he's been involved in church renewal, preaching, and teaching Bible studies. Jerry lives with his wife, Tina, and their four children in Virginia.

Visit Jerry's website!
**www.eicherjerry.com**

## More Great Books by Jerry Eicher

**The Adams County Trilogy**
*Rebecca's Promise*
*Rebecca's Return*
*Rebecca's Choice*

**Hannah's Heart**
*A Dream for Hannah*
*A Hope for Hannah*
*A Baby for Hannah*

**Little Valley Series**
*A Wedding Quilt for Ella*
*Ella's Wish*
*Ella Finds Love Again*

**Fields of Home Series**
*Missing Your Smile*
*Following Your Heart*
*Where Love Grows*
*(coming soon!)*

**Novels**
*My Dearest Naomi*
*(coming soon!)*

*Longing for a taste of Amish cooking?*

# THE HOMESTYLE AMISH KITCHEN COOKBOOK:

*Plainly Delicious Recipes from the Simple Life*
*by Georgia Varozza*

### Let a Little Plain Cooking Warm Up Your Life

Who doesn't want simplicity in the kitchen? Most of these delicious, easy-to-make dishes are simplicity itself. The Amish are a productive and busy people. They work hard in the home and on their farms, and they need good, filling food that doesn't require a lot of preparation and time. A few basic ingredients, some savory and sweet spices, and a little love make many of these meals a cook's delight. And if you want something a bit more complex and impressive, those recipes are here for you too.

Along with fascinating tidbits about the Amish way of life, you will find directions for lovely, old-fashioned food such as

- Scrapple
- Honey Oatmeal Bread
- Coffee Beef Stew
- Potato Rivvel Soup
- Snitz and Knepp
- Shoo-Fly Pie

Everything from breakfast to dessert is covered in this celebration of comfort food and family. Hundreds of irresistible options will help you bring the simple life to your own home and kitchen.